A KITTEN AND A KISS

When Arabella wrinkled her nose at the dark little mound of caviar Konstantin had spread on a toast point and held temptingly before her lips, he fed it to an ecstatic Raphael instead.

"Enjoy it while you can, Raphael," Arabella's aunt said with a laugh. "Fond as I am of you, I draw the line at feeding caviar to a cat."

Konstantin noticed that all of them—including himself—had begun talking to Raphael as if he might talk back. And, in a way, he did. The Archangel kitten had the most extensive repertoire of cat expressions Konstantin had ever seen. He reflected that the time he had spent with Arabella, her aunt and, yes, Raphael the kitten, were the happiest he had spent since he was home at his father's place in the Volga River Valley.

Konstantin envied Raphael now as the kitten began a slow, crouching ascent up Arabella's exquisite, half-reclining body. She was wearing a simple, high-waisted blue dress with small puffed sleeves. The kitten pounced suddenly and landed on Arabella's breastbone. Arabella leaned on her elbows, laughing, and tossed her head back so her tantalizing riot of curling, flame red hair pooled on the polished hardwood floor. Because she was dressed for an afternoon at home, her hair was tied loosely with a ribbon so the mass of it was allowed to flow down her back instead of being all gathered up in its usual elegant chignon. Konstantin remembered how the fragrant curls had clung to his fingers when he kissed her and he wished he could kiss her again . . .

—from "The Royal Kitten" by Kate Huntington

SPRING KITTENS

ALANA CLAYTON
KATE HUNTINGTON
DEBBIE RALEIGH

ZEBRA BOOKS
Kensington Publishing Corp.
http://www.pinnaclebooks.com

ZEBRA BOOKS are published by

Kensington Publishing Corp.
850 Third Avenue
New York, NY 10022

First Printing: March, 2000
10 9 8 7 6 5 4 3 2 1

Printed in the United States of America

CONTENTS

THE LAST KITTEN

by

Alana Clayton

ONE

"Cats!" said Elliot, Lord Gage, flinging the word into the air with an excess of hostility. "I should be in Town enjoying the Season. Instead, I'm forced to travel into the country to settle a catfight." What sounded like a muffled laugh reached him and he directed his affronted gaze sideways at his traveling companion, Andrew, Lord Stanford.

"I see nothing amusing in the situation," Elliot grumbled. "I can't understand why Aunt Jane would leave her estate in such a coil."

"To protect her loved ones," suggested Drew.

"Good Lord! They're cats; not people. She could have ordered that they be given good homes, but to leave an entire estate to a passel of cats . . ." Elliot failed to find words to complete his thought. "Then to have a complete stranger oversee the animals is more than I can understand." If he were not wearing a hat, Elliot was certain his hair would be standing on end, bristling with indignation.

"A friend, perhaps," suggested Drew.

"Bernice says she has never seen or heard of the woman before. I never thought I'd be grateful to Bernice for anything," said Elliot, speaking of his cousin. "But if she hadn't written, the situation could

have gone on for some time before it came to my
attention. She told me all about this Anne Webster
who somehow convinced Aunt Jane to leave the estate to the cats and appoint her to administer the
funds."

"Perhaps she has a fondness for felines," suggested
Drew.

"Ha! I would imagine it's Aunt Jane's fortune she
has a fondness for rather than the cats."

They turned into the drive leading to Wakefield
House. Lady Wakefield had been Elliot's favorite
aunt. After the death of his parents, he had spent
much of his time with her. It had been a shock when
he had returned from a trip to the Continent to find
that Aunt Jane had taken ill and died suddenly while
he was away. Then to hear the estate was being milked
dry by a scheming opportunist was too much to be
borne. He would set Miss Webster straight in short
order.

Elliot dismounted in front of Wakefield House and
turned to see Drew still astride his horse, peering
around at the house and grounds. "What the duce
are you looking for?"

"Cats. Expect to be attacked by a herd of them at
any minute. Want to be able to run."

"Clever," Elliot remarked wryly, not at all entertained by his friend's wit under the circumstances.

"Elliot," came a cry from the top of the shallow
steps leading to the entrance of the house. "What
has taken you so long? I've been waiting forever,"
complained his cousin Bernice as she rushed down
the steps to his side. "I was certain the estate would
be stolen out from under us before you arrived."

Bernice was younger than Elliot and had always looked up to him. It was a burden for him to bear, for Bernice was overly emotional and usually made much more of an event than was warranted. However, he attempted to cater to her whims when possible, since everyone else had long since learned to ignore her hysterics.

"There's no need to be in such a taking, Bernice. Surely even Miss Webster could not do away with Wakefield so quickly."

"I am convinced the woman would do exactly that if it were possible. She is so mean-spirited, she would not even pay for a few paltry gowns I ordered." Bernice sniffed and raised a lace-edged handkerchief to her nose.

It took an effort for Elliot to refrain from admiring Miss Webster sight unseen. Everyone in the family was well aware of Bernice's habit of ordering far more gowns than she could ever hope to wear. Her father often complained that she was going to bankrupt him, and they would be out on the street with only her gowns piled up around them. However, Elliot reminded himself that he was not here to praise Miss Webster, but to prevent her from misusing his late aunt's estate.

"As you can see, Drew has accompanied me. You should at least greet him before we air our problems before him."

"How do you do, Viscount Stanford?" said Bernice. "I'm sorry you received such a poor welcome, but I'm certain you understand."

"I do, Lady Bernice. Hope our presence will alleviate some of your anxiety."

"If Elliot can save our inheritance from this Webster woman, it will be all I ask."

"The estate comes to me and Bernice receives a healthy bequest," explained Elliot. "But that only occurs after the cats have all passed away."

"It needn't have been that way," complained Bernice. "Aunt Jane could have left our inheritance to us outright. She could have trusted us to have taken care of the cats."

Could she? wondered Elliot. He had never known Bernice to have been overly fond of any living creature other than herself.

"Come now, Bernice," he said soothingly as they entered Wakefield House. "Allow me to rid myself of this dust, then I will confront the harridan who has made your life miserable. We will meet in the drawing room before dinner. And stop frowning or else you'll get wrinkles," he warned, smiling when her brow immediately smoothed beneath his gaze.

They met at the top of the stairs. Elliot was held speechless for a moment. He had last seen her in a London ballroom, her blond hair gleaming beneath the chandeliers, as she danced with Fitzhugh, Lord Berkley. In his late-night musings after her disappearance, he had convinced himself that if they ever met again he would not find the incomparable he first thought her to be, but simply another attractive woman he had once briefly known and admired.

It wasn't anything specific about her he could point out that appealed to him. Perhaps it was a combination of the varied hues of her blond hair; her hazel eyes, which changed from gold to green, and her graceful manner as she made her way through society. But there was one thing of which he was certain—

his attraction to her had not abated during the months since he had last seen her.

The silence had stretched as long as was politely acceptable. Then, Elliot, Lord Gage, did something he hadn't done since his first Season in Town. He stammered.

"L . . . Lady Catherine, what are you doing here?"

The woman paused and observed him dispassionately. She seemed not at all surprised to meet him in the upper hall of his late aunt's home. "At present, I am going down to dinner," she answered in the pleasantly modulated voice he vividly recalled.

The shock of her unexpected appearance began wearing off and Elliot's mental faculties began to function normally once again. "Bernice said nothing about you visiting. Indeed, I wasn't aware the two of you were even acquainted."

"If you would ask Bernice, I'm certain she would agree we know one another better than she would like. In fact, I assume I'm the reason she sent for you. She has threatened me with it often enough."

"What are you saying?" he asked, unable to believe her inference.

"She believes I am stealing your aunt's fortune."

"How could that be?" he asked, surprised again by the turn of events.

"Because Lady Jane left me in charge."

"You're Anne Webster?" he asked, expecting her to laugh and tell him it was all a hum. But when she spoke it was not at all what he expected.

"I am," she replied shortly, meeting his gaze with a defiant look in her golden eyes.

"I don't understand," he said, astonished at her revelation.

"I wouldn't expect you to. But then, I never thought

the need would arise, since I never thought to see you here."

Her answers had been abrupt almost to the point of rudeness, and he could not understand what he had done to deserve such treatment. Perhaps she was as shocked at seeing him as he was her.

Elliot breathed deeply, attempting to order his thoughts. "How do you come to be here?" he asked. "You disappeared from society overnight and weren't heard of after that. All manner of rumors circulated and speculation continues until this day as to what happened to you. Now I find you are living in my aunt's home under an assumed name."

"I have no obligation to explain myself to the *ton,*" she said, making no effort to hide her disgust for the on-dits that kept London gossip alive. "As for the other, I'm living here at your aunt's invitation. The details were handled by Lady Wakefield's solicitor, Charles Quinton. I assure you I've done nothing improper."

"Then why the false name?" he insisted.

"What I call myself is my business," she asserted, lifting her chin in a stubborn manner.

"Not when it concerns my aunt," he shot back, her unyielding manner testing his determination to remain calm.

She did not flinch from his tone. "Your aunt is dead," she brutally reminded him.

"But her wishes live on. And you, for some yet unknown reason, were chosen to carry them out."

"And I am doing so," she spat. "Despite your cousin's attempts to interfere."

"Bernice is concerned about Wakefield House," he countered, attempting to bring some reason back to their conversation.

She gave a bitter laugh. "Lady Bernice's only concern is her inheritance. She has attempted all manner of trickery to gain money from the estate. She even ordered gowns and other personal items, expecting me to pay for them with your aunt's funds."

Elliot allowed his gaze to travel over her from head to toe. She wore a topaz gown ruffled at the sleeves and hem. A delicate teardrop necklace of topaz and diamonds enhanced the neckline of her gown. All in all, she was dressed as exquisitely as he had always seen her. Even though he knew she did not deserve it, he could not keep his tongue between his teeth.

"*Your* wardrobe seems to be more than adequate for country living."

"It is not my expenses we are discussing."

"It depends upon the source."

"And that, too, should be of no interest to you."

In the normal course of events she would be right, thought Elliot, but she had control of a large amount of funds and it was up to him to see she was using them fairly.

"This is getting us nowhere," Arabella replied, her shoulders drooping ever so slightly.

Elliot sensed she was weakening. He remembered their first meeting in London, the jolt that struck him at the first touch of her hand, causing him to wonder whether she was the woman for whom he had been waiting. His resolve weakened at his thoughts, and his voice was softer than he meant it to be when he spoke. "If you would only answer my questions, perhaps we could straighten out this misunderstanding."

But before Elliot could take full advantage of the interval of calm they were experiencing, a mewing sound drew his attention to a small white bundle of fur that was rubbing against his highly polished Hessians.

Lady Catherine bent quickly and picked up the kitten, holding it close to her body. Eyes blinked—one brown, one blue—and focused on Elliot. This was his first glimpse of the source of his problem. No, he thought, the kitten was second. The woman was first.

The kitten stretched a tiny paw out toward Elliot, mewing plaintively.

"He's hungry and so, I imagine, is the rest of the household," judged Lady Catherine. "We'll require more than the few minutes before dinner is served to discuss the situation."

"After dinner then?" he suggested.

"After dinner," she agreed. "And I would prefer to remain Miss Webster for the time being."

Elliot nodded in agreement and stepped aside as she moved past him down the stairs.

Dinner was excellent, but none of the people gathered around the mahogany table seemed to fully appreciate the fare. Conversation was sporadic and, by unspoken agreement, held to impersonal topics. The kitten was fed a saucer of milk, then placed in a basket next to Catherine's chair, where it promptly curled up and fell asleep.

Catherine liked Andrew, Lord Stanford, upon introduction. His unruly sandy hair verged on red, and light freckles were scattered across a slightly crooked nose that had been broken more than once. His face wore a good-natured smile, which undoubtedly had caused many people to underestimate the intelligence that Catherine quickly discovered hidden beneath it.

After dinner, Drew took his port in the drawing

room with Bernice as company. Elliot hoped the excellence of Aunt Jane's port would offset Bernice's chatter, which could drive the uninitiated slightly mad.

Meanwhile, Lady Catherine, carrying the kitten's basket, led the way to the library. A small fire took the chill off the cool spring evening. Placing the basket near the fireplace, she took a seat nearby.

She watched as Lord Gage crossed the room and pulled aside the window hangings in order to look out at the early evening twilight. His appearance had not changed at all since she had last seen him. He was dressed in the first stare of fashion even though he was in the country. His dark hair touched the collar of his blue coat, which spread across broad shoulders. She remembered how confidently he had moved over the floor when they had danced, how courteously he treated her, as if he wanted more from their relationship; something she would have welcomed at the time. She wished they could be on that amiable standing now. But circumstances had changed, he was suspicious of her, and it was only her obstinate streak that kept her from admitting it might seem he had reason. She fought to control the anger she felt at being caught in such a bumble broth.

"Where do you wish to start?" she asked without preamble.

Elliot was once again surprised at her straightforward question. He didn't recall her being quite so blunt when he had met her last Season. "Why don't we begin with your name?"

"You have no right to ask personal questions, my lord. However, I will answer what I can to demonstrate that my wish is also to end this conflict." She smoothed her skirt and looked down at the basket before answering. "Anne Webster was my mother's name. I chose to use it after I left London for personal reasons."

"I don't question your right to it," replied Elliot, "only why you elected to use it with my aunt."

"Your aunt knew very well who I was. In fact, it was she who suggested the name change. There was no deception between us. I had a need to make myself scarce for a time, but it has no bearing on anyone other than myself, and it certainly has nothing to do with Lady Wakefield's estate."

"I have only your word for that."

Her lips curled in a barely discernible smile. "And that is what you must make do with, my lord. As I told you before, my name is my own business. Now, what else do you wish to know?"

Devil take it! She was too stubborn for her own good. Why couldn't she tell him what he wanted? "How did you come to be in charge of my aunt's estate?" he asked, matching her bluntness.

"I imagine Bernice has been filling your head with all manner of tales. Perhaps that I drugged Lady Wakefield and forced her to sign the papers?" She waited a moment, studying him quizzically. When he didn't answer, she continued.

"It's a very simple story. My coach broke down not far from Wakefield House, and we were forced to stop here for repairs. Your aunt and I became fast friends, and she asked me to stay for a while."

"Without even knowing you?"

"Sometimes it isn't necessary. It was as if we had known one another forever. At all events, your aunt did know my mother when they were young. However, when my mother married, they lost touch with one another. Lady Wakefield said she had often wondered what had happened to Anne. She was pleased to learn she had a happy life."

"And where is your mother now?"

"She and my father died in a boating accident."

"I'm sorry," he said.

"There's no need," she replied. "I have been out of black gloves for some time now."

"And after my aunt asked you to extend your visit?"

"We spent many happy hours together. I think she was lonely here in this huge house. She had very little family, and not too many neighbors."

Elliot felt a twinge of guilt. He wished he could have visited Aunt Jane more often, but he had gotten involved in the war effort and time had quickly slipped by.

"Your aunt took ill very suddenly," Catherine continued. "We did everything we could, but it wasn't enough. I think she knew she wasn't going to recover, for she asked to see her solicitor. Before he came, she had a request. I told her I would do anything I could, but I was surprised at what she asked. She wanted to ensure that her cats would continue living as they were accustomed. I suppose she knew, in the normal course of events, they would be relegated to the stables, or perhaps to the home farm at her passing."

Elliot felt the guilt more sharply. That was most probably exactly what would have happened had he inherited the estate direct. "And you agreed to become caretaker for the cats?" he asked.

"What else could I do? The woman was dying. Would you rather I had refused and let her die worrying about her animals?"

"Of course not. I cared a great deal about my aunt,

and I wouldn't have wanted her to suffer in any way. I merely cannot credit that she would put a stranger completely in charge of her estate."

"I told you, she knew my mother. She trusted me. She saw I cared for her cats as much as she did. She knew I would treat them well. That was all that was on her mind at the time. She knew you had no need for Wakefield. You already have several estates and a town house; what more could one person need? And Bernice is well taken care of by her parents. Lady Wakefield often told me that she knew Bernice would squander her part of the inheritance on gowns, but that didn't bother her. She wanted both you and Bernice to enjoy your inheritance, but only after her cats had lived out their lives."

"And what do you get from such an excess of caring?"

The silence lengthened between them as Catherine studied the man seated across from her. Lord Gage's reputation was one of an honorable gentleman who took his responsibilities seriously. She could not blame him for his suspicions; her story sounded weak even to herself. However, that did little to eliminate the irritation his questions brought on.

She had tolerated Bernice with all her temper tantrums, accusations, and sulky disposition longer than anyone should be forced to. She would wager Bernice's parents had welcomed this diversion, which had taken their daughter away for a time and given them an interim of peace.

"It is late, my lord. I'm certain you're weary from your travels, and I have an early meeting with the steward in the morning. From the amount of luggage you and Lord Stanford brought, it's obvious you'll be staying for several days."

"That was my plan," he answered.

"Then, I suggest we continue this conversation to-morrow, when we're both rested and in a better frame of mind."

Lady Catherine picked up the basket and swept out of the room before he could raise an objection. She was right, thought Elliot. It wasn't necessary to settle everything in one evening. Perhaps a few days of ob-servation would tell him more than she would ever reveal.

Elliot slowly made his way down the hall toward the drawing room, hoping to find that some of Aunt Jane's excellent port had survived Drew's thirst. A glass or two would go a long way toward helping him with a good night's rest.

"What happened?" demanded Bernice when he entered the room. "Where is she?"

"Gone," he answered, still distracted by his recent conversation with Lady Catherine—or Miss Webster, as she wished to be called.

"I knew you could do it," Bernice cried out joyfully. "But I never thought you would dispatch her so quickly," she chattered, without giving him time to answer. "When is she leaving? In the morning, I hope. Then we can see the solicitor tomorrow after-noon and get this whole thing straightened out."

"What? Wait a moment, Bernice. I never meant to imply that Miss Webster was leaving Wakefield. She has simply retired for the evening."

Bernice's expression crumpled and she collapsed into the chair behind her. "Oh, no. Don't tell me she has won you over. I couldn't bear that."

"She's done nothing of the sort. Now compose yourself," he ordered sternly. "It's late. Drew and I have traveled all day long. Miss Webster has an early appointment in the morning. We agreed to talk at greater length tomorrow. This problem didn't occur overnight, and it will take more than a few hours to solve. In the meantime, we will all attempt to reside under one roof without the additional burden of histrionics," he said, pointedly staring at Bernice.

"You mean she didn't explain at all?" asked Bernice, not giving up easily.

"As we already know, she claims she is here at Aunt Jane's invitation, and I've learned nothing yet to refute her allegation. It will take a few days to go over the books and see the solicitor, then I may be able to tell you more."

"Oh, botheration!" exclaimed Bernice, slumping back in her chair and crossing her arms over her chest.

Elliot crossed to the table and poured himself a generous glass of port. "Be patient, cousin. I haven't even begun to investigate Miss Webster; I assure you, she will have no secrets when I am finished."

As the door closed behind Betsy, Catherine released a sigh of relief. Her maid was one of the few people she felt she could trust; however, she longed to be by herself, and even Betsy's quiet presence was too much for her at the moment.

The day had taken its toll on her composure, she thought, locking the door and setting a chair in front of it. Putting up with Bernice's constant whining was more than enough for any person to bear, but her astonishment at Lord Gage's unexpected arrival at Wakefield House had shaken her considerably and forced her to exert a great deal of effort in order to conceal her confusion.

The man had always had an unsettling effect on her. Their first meeting in London had left her flushed and near to acting the green girl rather than an accomplished young lady. At first, she had hopes that something more might develop between them and, indeed, she had no objection to becoming better acquainted with Lord Gage. He sought her out at entertainments, brought her punch, and danced the waltz with her. Then, suddenly, his warmth vanished, to be replaced by a politely correct gentleman who seemed to have no real interest in furthering their relationship beyond the public one.

Catherine had relived their moments together numerous times and could think of nothing she had said or done to discourage Lord Gage. Perhaps he thought they would not suit. If so, she could do nothing to change his mind. She still dreamed of him on occasion—when the days had been particularly solitary—but usually attempted to keep him out of her mind since he was no longer available to her.

Now, once again, he was interfering in her life. The reason for Lord Gage's presence was even more alarming than his wraithlike appearance at the top of the stairs. He had been called to Wakefield to check into her management of his aunt's estate. Catherine was humiliated beyond all bearing that he should think her a thief, but even more so that he would be poking and prodding into the privacy of her life.

It was all Bernice's doing. The woman was a selfish creature who thought only of herself. It was her fault that Lord Gage was here; her fault he suspected Catherine of dishonesty. It would be difficult to treat Bernice with the barest courtesy, but Catherine would do her best for Lady Jane's sake.

Ofttimes Catherine thought how much better it would have been had her carriage not broken down outside the gates of Wakefield. True, she would never have met Lady Jane, but then she would also be far away by now, and she would certainly not be forced into such an embarrassing position of having her honesty questioned.

Weariness weighed Catherine down, and she knew she must get some rest in order to face the morning. She climbed into bed and settled herself under the soothing weight of the covers. The white kitten curled up close to her, and soon the comforting sound of his purring lulled her to sleep.

"Sorry to have left you with Bernice last night," said Elliot the next morning as he and Drew approached the stables.

"Bernice will be better when she has someone other than herself to think about," responded Drew in his succinct fashion.

"I doubt whether that will ever happen."

"Children, a home of her own will do wonders for her," judged Drew.

Elliot glanced at Drew in surprise. "What makes you think that?"

"Common sense. She needs something to fill her time. Has nothing now."

"Maybe you're right," said Elliot as they mounted their horses. "Let's take a gallop over the estate," he suggested, turning toward the north fields. "Miss Webster claims she is overseeing the steward as well as the cats. I want to see what kind of a job she's doing."

"Seems to be a competent woman," commented

Drew. "Was surprised. Not at all what I expected from your description."

Elliot felt a pang of guilt at not revealing to his friend that he had previously known Anne Webster as Lady Catherine. But he had made a promise not to reveal her true identity for the time being, and he always kept his word. He was confident Drew would understand once the secret was out.

"I only had Bernice's word for what she was like," said Elliot. "I should have known not to have put a great deal of stock in her opinion. I find Miss Webster much more formidable than I anticipated. Although we spent only a short time together, I found no wrongdoing. But it's early days yet, and I may still find she is not at all what she claims. For now, I'll settle for beating you to the next fence." Elliot leaned over his mount's neck, urging him to his fastest pace, allowing the wind to blow away his troubles for a short time.

Perhaps he should have made his presence known, but he didn't. The woman he currently called Anne Webster was dragging a piece of yarn across the carpet, watching as the white kitten scrambled to catch it with its small paws. Her laughter reached him when the kitten took a tumble, leaped up, and arched his back in an absurd imitation of a full-grown cat.

"You're quite a terror," she said, picking up the kitten and cuddling it beneath her chin. "And it's a good thing. It seems you're my only protector now."

"Do you need one, Miss Webster?" Elliot asked, stepping into the drawing room.

"Need you ask?" she answered quickly, seemingly unperturbed at his sudden appearance.

"I suppose it is uncomfortable to be questioned as to your every deed, but surely you can understand my concern?"

"You did not seem at all concerned until Bernice wrote. Doubtless she accused me of robbing the estate. She's declared that often enough to my face."

"Does she have reason?"

"I'm certain she feels she does. However, I am merely carrying out your aunt's wishes."

Elliot was beginning to regret his remark. It put them at daggers drawn once again, and he found he did not like the feeling at all.

"That is also my objective," he replied as pleasantly as possible.

"And to that end you have spent the morning going over the estate's books. Did you find everything in order?" she asked, lifting her gaze to his.

While he might not fully trust her, he could not help but admire Lady Catherine as he had often done in London. Her hazel eyes appeared golden in the afternoon light, while her hair was pulled back to reveal the delicate lines of her face. Her complexion was smooth and creamy, and her lips looked as if she had just eaten fresh berries. It was apparent why she was considered a diamond of the first water when she graced London's society.

"I haven't completely finished, but I've found nothing amiss yet," he admitted.

"Perhaps you shouldn't relate that information to Bernice. She will be sorely disappointed."

Elliot smiled at her riposte and moved farther into the room. "May I?" he asked, indicating the chair across from hers. She nodded, and he sat, a bit surprised at her cordiality.

"Lady . . . Miss Webster, I hope we may cry peace

until we reach an understanding about Aunt Jane's wishes."

"Peace?" she asked. "I have never gone to war. I was living here quite tranquilly until your cousin came to visit. I have not had a peaceful day since then. If you consider this war, then it was forced upon me. I did not choose it, and I would end it immediately if only I was left alone to continue my promise to Lady Wakefield."

"I will talk to Bernice and ask her not to be so . . . so vocal with her protests."

"I would appreciate anything you could do," she said. "I do not enjoy being at sixes and sevens every moment of my waking hours."

"Consider it done, then," replied Elliot, pleased they had come to some sort of agreement, however small.

"Oh, my, you horrid creature!" exclaimed Lady Catherine.

Elliot wondered what the devil he had done for her to speak to him so before he realized she was not addressing him at all. He followed her gaze to the floor, where the white kitten had discovered his boots. The kitten was reaching up to swat at the tassel decorating the front of the highly polished Hessians. His tiny claws would catch in the tassel, then he would slide down, clawing at the leather as he went.

"I'm so sorry," said Catherine, leaning down to catch the kitten before it could make another leap at the tassel. "Your boots are ruined."

Staring down at the scratched leather, Elliot silently agreed. "Not at all. My valet has a polish that will take care of the damage." He would need to tell George of his prevarication, just in case Lady Catherine asked.

"I hope so. He's probably hungry. I'll feed him, then put him in his basket for a nap. He's really a very good kitten," she insisted. "But he's still a baby and has no one to play with, so he does get into trouble sometimes."

"Quite all right."

"I'll see you at dinner then," she said, gathering up the kitten and setting off down the hall toward the kitchen.

Drew found him there a few minutes later. "Looking downcast," he remarked, seeing Elliot sitting and staring at the floor.

"It's my boots," replied Elliot.

Drew took the chair that Lady Catherine had recently vacated. Resting his elbows on his knees, he leaned forward and studied Elliot's boots.

"Been in a briar patch?" he asked.

"A small white one," replied Elliot with a grimace.

"Ah, the kitten."

"The kitten," Elliot agreed. "And Miss Webster," he added after a moment.

"Miss Webster scratched your boots?"

"No, her attitude is as annoying as the kitten's. No matter how long our conversations, I never seem to learn anything more."

"No progress at all?" asked Drew.

"I haven't finished with the books," said Elliot. "But I have found nothing improper yet."

"Don't look happy over it," remarked Drew.

"Something about Miss Webster is bothering me," admitted Elliot. "I don't know what she's hiding, but there's a mystery to her."

"She's a woman, that's mystery enough," commented Drew with a smile.

"It's more than that, and more than Aunt Jane's will. If I asked her, I'm certain she would tell me it was none of my affair."

Drew remained silent.

"And you agree, don't you?" said Elliot. "In fact, I also agree. I would be just as annoyed if someone meddled in my personal business."

"By the way, been wondering. Where are they?" asked Drew.

"Where are who?" said Elliot, bewildered at the sudden change of subject.

"The cats," said Drew. "Where are all the cats?"

TWO

"Drew asked me a question today that I couldn't answer," remarked Elliot. He was sitting in the drawing room with Catherine, watching her straighten embroidery thread that the kitten had, no doubt, tangled.

He waited for her to inquire about Drew's question. However, she continued with her thread sorting, lips pressed firmly together.

"Aren't you curious?" he finally asked.

"No, only surprised by your concession that there is something you don't know," she remarked.

"That's unfair," he objected, more amused than irritated by her comment.

She glanced up from the thread and studied him carefully. "Yes, I suppose you're right, and I apologize for my rudeness. I'm a bit out of curl about being suspected of cheating your aunt's estate. Now, what was it Lord Stanford wished to know?"

"He asked where the rest of the cats were."

Catherine returned to silently sorting the embroidery thread in her lap.

Elliot waited until it was apparent an answer was not forthcoming. "It does seem to be a legitimate question," he commented.

Catherine breathed deeply, then allowed her hands to fall idle. "I'm certain it is, but the subject is not a welcome one, and is extremely oversetting."

"I thought you enjoyed the cats as much as Aunt Jane. Why should inquiring about them be upsetting?"

"Because I don't know where they are!" she burst out. Her hazel eyes were brimming with unshed tears. She twisted the thread in her lap, undoing all she had done.

"You mean they are lost?"

"Lost, stolen, killed. I don't know which. All I know for certain is that they are all gone except for this little one." She gestured toward the basket by her chair, which held the white kitten. "This is the last kitten. That is why I guard him so assiduously."

Elliot stood staring at the kitten, while the implication of her words reached him. "You can't mean that someone is deliberately doing away with Aunt Jane's cats, can you?"

"I'll leave you to answer that question. But ask yourself, how often do you find cats, or any other pets, leaving a good home to fend for themselves? Particularly so many at one time. I think you'll agree it's enough to make a person suspicious."

"Just how many cats were there before they began disappearing?"

"Seventeen."

Elliot flinched.

"Of course, five were this little one's siblings," she said, motioning to the basket. "At first I thought they would return. Cats sometimes disappear, then return a few days later, perhaps looking a little worse for wear. Lady Jane always said they were like certain gentlemen she knew when she was younger. But the cats never returned. I enlisted the aid of the servants and searched the house from top to bottom, and all the outbuildings, but not a trace of them could be found."

"The neighbors?" he inquired.

She nodded in agreement. "All within a practical distance."

Elliot paced the floor. "Surely there is some reasonable explanation. I cannot believe sixteen cats have disappeared without a hint of where they can be found."

Catherine put her hands to her temples to rub away the pain that was beginning just behind her eyes, then quickly removed them, thinking the gesture might denote weakness. She pulled herself straighter in the chair and squared her shoulders. "If there is an explanation, then I leave it to you to discover, for I cannot."

"I shall enlist Drew's aid and we'll search for the animals. Perhaps they've returned and are just lurking in the stables."

"They are house cats, my lord. They would not take kindly to living in the stables when they have the comfort of Wakefield House at their disposal."

Elliot silently agreed but felt he must do something.

"However look all you want, and I wish you well. There is nothing I would like more than for you to discover them alive and healthy." Unable to go on, she remained silent for a moment, blinking away unshed tears. "I believe I shall rest until dinner. I find myself unaccountably weary."

Elliot remained silent. She would not believe any words of condolence from him since he was there to investigate her management of the estate. Admitting that the cats had disappeared while under her supervision had been difficult, to be sure. He could only watch while she gathered up her thread and the kitten and left the room.

Elliot found Drew returning from the stables.

"Just coming to find you," said the viscount. "Offered to ride with Lady Bernice, but she refused."

Elliot stared at him in mild surprise. "I can't believe it. Catching a gentleman's eye is the only reason she rides."

Drew smiled. "Perhaps it isn't my eye she's eager to catch."

"Nonsense. Some young lady is always attempting to claim your attention. I wonder what Bernice is up to now," muttered Elliot, then dismissed it with a shrug. He had enough on his plate as it was without worrying about his troublesome cousin. "I'll consider it later, but now I need your help." He quickly filled Drew in on what he had found out about the cats.

"Strange goings-on," agreed Drew. "Suppose you want to search for the animals yourself."

"It's the only way I'll be satisfied. I also want to question the servants. Perhaps they've seen something."

"Let's get started," said Drew.

By the end of the day both Elliot and Drew were less than their usual impeccable selves from searching through the stables, outbuildings, and attics of Wakefield House. They had also questioned the servants, none of whom had seen anything out of the ordinary.

Elliot lowered himself into a leather chair in the library, thinking his dust would not harm its surface. "I am at a loss," he admitted to Drew, who took a seat near him.

"Does seem they're nowhere to be found," agreed Drew, taking out his handkerchief and wiping his face.

"What are you looking for?" asked Bernice, entering the room just as Drew uttered his remark.

Elliot saw no reason to keep their activity secret from Bernice. After all, she was the one who had asked him to come and investigate.

"I learned from Miss Webster that all the cats are missing except the one kitten she keeps with her."

Bernice's nose wrinkled. "Yes, isn't it disgusting the way she carries that animal about wherever she goes? It's difficult for me to tolerate, but I do so because I know it was Aunt Jane's wish," she said, looking as pious as possible. "As far as the missing cats, she's making far too much of it. They'll return as soon as they become hungry enough."

Elliot studied the sulky expression on his cousin's face. "Miss Webster makes the point—and a good one, I might add—that these are house cats. Other than a short foray outdoors, they are unlikely to take an extended stay away from their home. Life is too comfortable for them here."

Bernice gave a very unladylike snort of disgust. "Stuff and nonsense! Don't tell me she's reading the cats' minds. They are animals, and nothing more. Animals invariably wander about. It's to be expected of them."

"You know nothing about the disappearances, then?" Elliot asked.

"What?" shrilled Bernice. "You think I had something to do with those animals going missing? I thought you knew me better than that, Elliot. Your suggestion is too lowering by half." Her face crumpled as she buried it in her hands.

"Cut line, Bernice," he said bluntly. "You're no more crying than I am. And I would expect you have rejoiced each time a cat has disappeared."

Bernice raised her head. As Elliot had predicted, not one tear trickled down her cheek. "That doesn't mean I have done away with them," she replied sullenly.

"And I'm not calling you to book on it. I only want to know whether you know anything about their disappearance. Have you seen a stranger about during the past weeks? Anything suspicious occurring?"

"No, nothing of the sort," she replied shortly, still pouting over his treatment.

"Quite a mystery," said Drew.

A silence fell over the group as they each followed their thoughts.

"What about Miss Webster?" asked Bernice, breaking the silence. "She could have done away with them herself."

"Now why would she want to do that?" asked Elliot.

"You don't know, do you?" replied Bernice, with a slight smirk of superiority.

A frown marred Elliot's brow. He was growing weary of his cousin's games. "If there is something I need to know, then tell me," said Elliot

"There is no need to bite my head off," complained Bernice. "Evidently you did not see Aunt Jane's will."

"The first thing I saw when I returned home was your stack of letters. You sounded so desperate, I came straight here, deciding my other business could wait. I'm assuming a letter from Aunt Jane's solicitor is on my desk requesting a meeting. So, no, I have not seen the actual will."

"When you do, you'll find Miss Webster has as great an interest in having the cats disappear as either you or I."

"And that would be . . . ?" Elliot asked.

"Money," replied Bernice, with a satisfied air. "Aunt Jane has left her a great deal of money once all the cats have met their end."

"Are you certain of this?" he asked.

"Absolutely. I was there when the solicitor read the entire will. Miss Webster will not be destitute when she is no longer able to live here at Wakefield House. Of course, by then she could have stolen it all."

"Don't be ridiculous, Bernice. She doesn't have control of the estate without supervision," he scoffed.

"I am certain she is capable of anything," argued Bernice. "Disposing of cats or people. What would be the difference for a person of her ilk?"

"You know nothing about Miss Webster. And if you're indicating that she could have had a hand in Aunt Jane's demise, you must remember there were witnesses, including a physician, present during her illness."

"She could have wrapped it in clean linen and gotten around it," muttered Bernice, loathe to give up her suspicions.

Elliot was more affected by the news of Lady Catherine's inheritance than he allowed Bernice to see. If it was true—and he had no reason to believe Bernice was lying about something that could be so easily confirmed—then why hadn't Catherine told him about it? That was one question he meant to have answered before this night was over.

"I'm going to clean this dust from me," he said. "I'll see you both at dinner." He left the room, for once not concerned about leaving Drew alone with Bernice.

Catherine sat in front of the mirror staring at her reflection while Betsy finished arranging the curls at the back of her head. She had received a note from Lord Gage requesting that she come down early before dinner, and she wondered what was on his mind this time. She was certain it would not be a pleasant interview.

If she had known the trouble it would be to grant Lady Jane's last wish, she would not have been so hasty to agree to the plan. First, there was Lady Bernice's reaction and subsequent dabbling in her aunt's affairs. Now she had Lord Gage to contend with in addition to his cousin. Catherine heaved a great sigh and looked into the mirror one last time to assure herself that she looked her best before rising to make her way downstairs to the drawing room.

"Betsy, remember, you mustn't unlock the door or leave the room until I return."

"Oh, yes, miss. I'll do just as you say. I have my book to keep me company."

"Are you reading the Austen book?"

"I am, miss, and it's as good as you said. Some of the words are still hard for me, but I think I get most of them."

"Mark the ones you have problems with and we'll go over them later," she said, smiling at Betsy's eagerness to learn to read. "I probably won't be late tonight, but take care until I return."

Betsy nodded, followed Catherine to the door, and locked it behind her.

Catherine wasn't surprised to find Lord Gage had arrived before her. He stood staring out of the French doors, hands clasped behind him. There was no advantage to waiting any longer to announce herself.

"My lord, you wished to see me?" she said, stepping into the room.

He swung around at her words, and stood a moment without speaking. "I did," he finally replied. "Would you like to sit?"

She moved farther into the room and took a seat. He remained standing but moved closer to her. Catherine did not like his towering over her but remained where she was.

"This is the first time I've seen you without the kitten," he remarked.

"He's locked in my rooms with Betsy, who has orders not to open the door to anyone but me."

"It will mean a dull evening for her."

"I'm teaching her to read. She's very bright and has made remarkable progress. She's reading Jane Austen tonight."

Elliot was impressed. There weren't many who would spend time teaching their maid to read.

"I take it you didn't find the cats," she said to break the silence.

"Not a trace," he replied.

"Is that what you wished to discuss?"

"That's part of it," he answered, his tone as cold as his gaze. "It seems there is something you neglected to tell me, Miss Webster."

Catherine did not at all like his manner. She had attempted to be civilized, but he seemed to want no part of it. Well, enough was enough; she could be just as distant as he.

"I have not told you many things, my lord. Mainly because it is no concern of yours."

"Some might say the fact that you will receive an inheritance from my aunt when the cats are gone would be a concern of mine."

He had surprised her, and for a moment she merely returned his gaze. "Some might," she agreed. "Others might say it was between myself and your aunt."

"Perhaps it was, but it becomes mine since that could be a motive to do away with the animals. It's true I'm not a cat fancier, but it was my aunt's wish that her pets live out their natural lives. If you are doing anything to shorten them, then I intend to find out."

Catherine felt her face flush with anger. She fought for control before answering. It would serve no purpose to be involved in a row with him at this point. "I can assure you, I have done nothing more to the cats but care for them as best I can."

"But that hasn't been good enough, since all but one have disappeared," he snapped.

"I own you could have done no better by them," she challenged, her voice louder than she intended.

"Why didn't you tell me about the bequest?" he demanded.

She could no longer have him standing over her. Rising to her feet, she stood as tall as she could, which was still a great deal less than his height. "This is the outside of enough! I have had other things to worry about. Your cousin, for one. She has done nothing but cause a disruption since her arrival. Then the cats began disappearing, and I've been distressed about that. I have had more to be concerned about than what your aunt left me in her will. Concerns you and your cousin do not seem to share."

"Why do you think I'm asking you these questions? I'm attempting to find out who would profit by the cats being gone."

"If you're pointing a finger, don't stop at me. Turn to Lady Bernice; she's the one who has been most vocal. Then look in the mirror, because you have a great deal to gain also. I will not be singled out as the villain when there are two much stronger suspects involved."

Elliot's eyebrows rose in amazement. "Me? I have just arrived. The cats have been disappearing for weeks, according to you."

"Oh, I don't think for one minute you would dirty your hands—or boots—with kidnapping cats. But there are many men who would think being paid to do away with the animals was child's play. And you certainly have the resources to do that."

"You're speaking nonsense!"

"No more than you are to me," she retorted. "And I will not listen to it any longer." She was at the door before he knew what was happening.

"Running away only makes you appear guilty," he said.

"I am not running away," she declared, turning to face him. "I am merely leaving so I won't break one of Lady Jane's statues against your head." Her color high, she marched from the room without a backward glance.

"Almost ran me down," said Drew, strolling into the drawing room. "Strange effect you have on the ladies. No wonder you're still looking for a wife."

Elliot managed a strained smile. "Miss Webster

didn't take kindly to my suggestion that she did away with the cats for money."

"Not something that would appeal to a lady," agreed Drew, pouring a glass of sherry for each of them.

"Dash it, Drew! I don't like it anymore than she does, but I can't overlook anyone at this point."

"Perhaps I should have dinner in my room," said Drew.

"You are not going to leave me to dine with Bernice and Miss Webster. I doubt I would survive the ordeal. You are the only one here with nothing to win or lose, so I leave it to you to carry on a civilized conversation at dinner."

Drew gave an exaggerated sigh. "This visit will cause me to be a toss-pot before it's done," he said, pouring another glass of sherry.

Dinner had again been a silent affair, with all manner of emotions boiling below the thin surface of civility, which barely kept it in check. When the men made their way to the drawing room, they found Bernice alone. Lady Catherine had retired to her room immediately after dinner without making any excuse for her absence. Elliot had not needed to hear a reason, for he knew exactly why; she could not bear to be in the same room with him.

It was early afternoon of the next day—a particularly bright, warm spring afternoon. Drew was visiting a friend who lived nearby, and Elliot had decided a ride would clear the cobwebs from his mind. He

reached the stables as Bernice was waiting for her
mount to be brought out.

"Good. I'm in time for us to ride together," said
Elliot.

"What? Oh, no. I mean, I'd rather be by myself
today, it will give me time to think."

Elliot watched as she was tossed into the saddle and
rode out of the stable yard and down the drive. In
her entire life, he had never known Bernice to either
want to be alone or have anything to do with thinking. He wondered what she was up to.

The desire for a ride had left him, and he had
decided to continue work on the estate books when
he saw Lady Catherine leave the house. He had not
seen her since dinner the previous evening. She had
been absent from both breakfast and luncheon, nor
had she seen fit to send any excuses to the company.

Elliot grimaced. Could he blame her? Why should
she be concerned about people who were attempting
to prove her a thief and to drive her out of Wakefield
House? But he could not allow himself to feel guilty.
He had a responsibility to his aunt to see that her
will was carried out to its specifications. He would
not apologize for that.

Elliot found Lady Catherine in a small walled garden, well warmed by the afternoon sun. The kitten
scampered around her feet as she sat on a stone
bench. She gave him a brief glance as he approached,
then returned her attention to the kitten.

"Why haven't you named him?" Elliot asked, nodding toward the kitten.

"I thought if he had a name his loss would be more
difficult to bear," she answered solemnly.

"Are you so certain he will go missing?"

"Despite my caution all the others have," she replied despondently.

"Lady . . . Miss Webster, may I at least call you by your proper name when we are in private?"

"I am in hopes that this will be the last time we will be in private," she replied sharply. "At all events, I would rather you continue calling me by my mother's name. If you use another, you could slip at an inopportune time."

"Surely it would not matter whether Bernice and Drew knew your true identity?"

"If Lady Bernice knew, it would be all over the neighborhood by tonight and in London by tomorrow."

"You exaggerate," he cajoled.

"Not by much," she replied.

"But what would be the harm?"

"I thought we agreed that what I choose to call myself is a private matter."

"It is not merely idle curiosity," he explained. "If you are in some sort of trouble, I am offering to help."

"Thank you, my lord, but I am accustomed to directing my own life."

Elliot reluctantly put the matter aside for the moment but was determined to unveil the reason before he left Wakefield.

"May I sit?" he asked, taking a seat beside her when she nodded in the affirmative.

Elliot took a few moments, wondering how to begin to heal the breach between them. "I want to apologize for yesterday," he began. "I still need questions answered, but I will admit I could have been a bit more diplomatic when we spoke."

Catherine looked at him for a long moment, seeming to gauge his sincerity, then stared out over the garden.

"Do you remember how it was in London?" he asked, deciding to try another tack with her.

"Gossip, crushes, concerned mamas searching for husbands for their daughters, and men doing their best to avoid them. Almack's and its horrible refreshments, balls, hostesses vying with one another for the most impressive guests, caterers, and floral displays, and then even more gossip."

"I meant, do you remember how it was between the two of us?"

"There was nothing between us—a few dances, a little conversation—nothing much at all."

"I greatly admired you when we met," he said, without meaning to confess as much.

"You certainly never allowed it to show."

"I thought to at first, then you became involved with Fitzhugh."

She turned to him, eyes blazing, color burning in her cheeks. "We were not involved. Lord Berkley meant little to me. He escorted me on a few occasions, and he was usually around when we were at the same events, but that was all."

"But . . . I thought . . ."

"That is exactly what is wrong. It is always what you think. You never take the time to find out the truth of the matter before you rush to judgment. Just as you did yesterday," she accused.

"I've apologized for yesterday," he said. "As for London, Fitz told me that you and he were all but ready to announce your betrothal."

"That was never true," she replied firmly.

"I wish I had known," murmured Elliot. "Perhaps

if I had, the past few days would never have happened."

She rose and shook out her skirts. "It most probably would have changed nothing," she said, as Elliot stood. Reaching down, she lifted the kitten, smoothing its soft fur. "If you'll excuse us, we have our daily walk to complete." Without another word, she turned and left the walled garden.

Elliot reclaimed his seat. He had nothing better to do, and the garden was a pleasant spot in which to think. He watched Lady Catherine stroll down the path that led to a bridge spanning the sizable stream that meandered through the estate.

Lady Catherine had been wrong about one thing: If he had known she was not seriously involved with Fitz, he would not have hesitated to woo her himself. There might be women more beautiful than Lady Catherine, but none so in his eyes. And their meetings in London had been completely enjoyable. They had gotten along well, and had found much in common to discuss. There had been no awkward pauses in their conversations. All in all, he had felt she could very well be the woman for him. That is, until Fitz had seen his interest and discouraged it.

To hear Fitz tell it, they had already promised themselves to one another; all that was left to do was to set the date. When Lady Catherine had disappeared suddenly, Fitz had said it was merely to visit an ailing relative, but as time wore on he remained stubbornly silent on the subject. On-dits made the rounds that there had been a death in the family, that she had eloped with an unknown suitor, that she had been kidnapped. There was not a scrap of confirmation to the stories that were circulated, nor was there any information on the true whereabouts of the missing woman.

Elliot was determined to find out how she had turned up in his aunt's household before he returned to London. Perhaps if the situation at Wakefield House was resolved . . . A scream cut through his thoughts. He looked up just in time to see a part of the bridge give way, with Catherine teetering above the fast-flowing stream. He was up and running while her scream still hung in the air.

"Catherine, are you injured?" he asked, forgetting to call her "Miss Webster" in his rush to see whether she was harmed. She was kneeling on the planking of the bridge, holding tight to the railing with one hand and grasping the kitten close with the other. As if sensing danger, the small white bundle of fur clung tightly to the fabric of her gown.

"I am fine," came the shaky reply.

Elliot breathed a sigh of relief as he bent over her. "Come, let me help you up." He pried her fingers off the railing, then took her by the shoulders and stood her on her feet. Her free hand gripped his arm and, no matter how much she professed otherwise, he could still see the fear in her eyes.

"You are perfectly safe," he assured her. "Do you know what happened?"

"I was walking across the bridge—the same as I do everyday—and all of a sudden I felt the boards give way beneath my feet. I jumped back as quickly as possible, and grabbed the railing, hoping it would hold."

"You did exactly the right thing."

"If I hadn't, I would have been . . ." Her voice trailed off as she stared down into the rushing water, icy cold in the early spring weather.

"Don't think about it," he advised. "You're in no danger now. Even your friend seems to be reviving."

They looked down at the kitten held between them. He blinked and gave a soft mew, as if to draw their attention to him.

"Can you stand here just a moment while I take a look as the bridge?" asked Elliot.

"Of course," she replied, withdrawing her hand from his arm.

Elliot trod carefully to the edge of the collapsed bridge. Leaning over, he observed the planks that had given way, then inched back to safety.

"Come along, Lady Cath . . . I mean Miss Webster," he corrected at her sharp glance. "Allow me to escort you back to the house."

Catherine made no objection as he took her arm, guiding her off the shaky bridge toward Wakefield House.

"Bring tea to the drawing room immediately," he ordered as soon as they entered the door, sending servants scurrying to do his bidding.

When they arrived at the drawing room, Elliot turned to her once more. "Are you certain you're unharmed?"

"I'm just shaken a bit."

"As well you should be." He put his hand on her waist and drew her closer. He was surprised when she yielded to the pressure and stepped into his loose embrace.

Catherine was more frightened than she appeared. At this time, the comfort of his solid figure was more inviting than carrying on the dissension that had surrounded them since his arrival.

"What a heartwarming scene."

Elliot looked over Catherine's shoulder to see Bernice standing in the doorway, a bitter expression on her face. Catherine stepped away from Elliot and walked across the room to a chair by the fireplace.

"I assume you've finished your investigation and Miss Webster is completely exonerated of all wrongdoing," Bernice continued.

"Someday, my dear cousin, you will learn to determine the situation before you speak," replied Elliot, joining Catherine on the far side of the room. "Miss Webster has just escaped what could have been a fatal fall from the bridge."

"And you were comforting her. How charming. Did you also play the knight errant and save the damsel in distress?"

"There was no need," said Catherine. "I was able to save myself. Although I do appreciate Lord Gage's helpfulness." She looked up at Elliot and favored him with a smile of gratitude.

"I did nothing out of the way," he replied, just as Drew came through the doorway, followed by the butler and a footman carrying a tea tray.

"Hope you are well, Miss Webster. Heard you barely missed a nasty fall."

"From the servants, I suppose," she said.

"Story probably reached the house before you did," Drew replied.

"Miss Webster was fortunate enough to catch herself before she fell," explained Elliot.

There was a disturbance at the door, and the steward entered without being announced. "Miss Webster, I'm sorry to intrude, but I heard about the accident. I had to see for myself that you were uninjured," he exclaimed, breathing heavily from his race to her side.

"Everything's all right, John. I was able to step back before the planking fell away. No harm was done."

"I don't know what happened," he said, his face turning red with anger. "But I intend to find out. I had my men look at that bridge no more than a fortnight ago, and now this."

"Don't be too hasty," suggested Elliot. "I don't believe your men were negligent."

"What do you mean?" said the steward.

Elliot had not wanted to discuss this in front of Catherine so soon after the incident, but she had to know eventually, and perhaps this was as good a time as any.

"I examined the bridge before we returned to the house, and the planks that gave way did not do so because of neglect. They were cut, and by the looks of the wood, it was done recently."

Catherine's face turned pale, but she remained silent.

"But that's impossible!" blustered the steward. "That would mean it was intentional, and who would want to harm Miss Webster?"

"Perhaps a prank by one of the neighborhood lads?" suggested Drew.

"It would take more than the strength of a lad to do what was done to the bridge," said Elliot. "You see, it had to be cut almost through, but leaving just enough to hold it in place until weight was put on that section. It was not an easy task, and would have taken a man to accomplish it."

"I'm going to see what I can find out," said the steward. "And if I find the culprit, I won't be held responsible for what I do to him."

"Let me know what you discover," Elliot said, as the man turned to leave the room, his cap crushed in one large hand.

The group was strangely quiet after the steward left.

"Bernice, do you know anything about this?" asked Elliot.

"Never say you are accusing me of tearing down a bridge!"

"I'm doing nothing of the sort. But you've been here for some time now. You go riding every day. Have you seen anyone around the estate who doesn't belong?"

"I've seen no one," she denied vehemently, a flush rising on her face. "I own, I don't know why you ask me first thing when something untoward occurs. I am not responsible for what almost happened to that woman."

"Let us take tea," suggested Catherine, hoping to put a semblance of normalcy back into the day. "I could certainly use a cup," she said, beginning to pour the brew with a nearly steady hand.

"Any ideas as to what's going on around here?" asked Elliot, after Catherine and Bernice had left the room.

Drew took a sip of sherry before answering. "Haven't been here long. Hard to guess. Bad feelings between Bernice and Miss Webster, that's for certain. But your cousin isn't strong enough to have damaged the bridge to that extent."

"I agree, and I would dislike having to consider that Bernice would do such a thing. But it didn't just happen by itself. John is fairly well convinced that it wasn't any of the estate's men."

"If the money's enough, they might have yielded to temptation."

"You're right," agreed Elliot. "I suppose there's simply no way to eliminate them entirely."

"What's your next step?" asked Drew.

"I'll tell you as soon as I work it out. In the meantime, any suggestions would be appreciated."

Elliot had spent a restless night mulling over the events that had occurred since he had reached Wakefield House. Discovering that Miss Webster was Lady Catherine Duncan had been a shock to him. It was almost beyond belief that the woman who had touched his heart in London, then disappeared, had all along been living in his aunt's home. From that time on it had been difficult to see her as a threat to Aunt Jane's estate, despite what Bernice had told him.

However, the disappearance of the cats, and finding that Lady Catherine would benefit greatly if they never returned, raised suspicion again in his protesting mind. Just as he thought he could examine her conduct without prejudice, he found her trembling on the bridge and wanted nothing more than to take her in his arms and never let go.

At the end of the night, he was back to where he had started. He could prove nothing against Lady Catherine, or Anne Webster, as she stubbornly insisted upon being called. Nor could he yet judge her innocent of the charges Bernice had brought. The bridge collapse was a confusing factor that could not be attributed to anyone at the moment.

Elliot rose to meet the dawn determined to set matters straight and get on with his life. He could not

dispense with the niggling hope tugging at the back
of his mind, that Lady Catherine might be a part of
his future.

THREE

It was afternoon before Elliot took himself away from the estate books he had been perusing in the library. His mind was dull from reading endless rows of cramped writing and scribbled figures, and he decided to take a ride to clear his head. He would visit the home farm and see how it fared.

He again met Bernice just as she was ready to leave the stable yard, mounted on a lovely sorrel mare.

"Cousin, wait a moment and I'll join you."

Bernice was unsettled by his appearance and her face mirrored confusion. "I'd rather ride alone today, Elliot. Perhaps tomorrow," she quickly suggested. Turning her mount, she guided it toward the long drive that led to the main road. Without looking back, she urged the mare to a canter and soon disappeared from sight.

Elliot puzzled over her reaction while he was waiting for his horse to be brought out. First, Bernice had refused Drew's company for a ride, and now for the second time had avoided his company. He had learned that she rode nearly every day here at Wakefield. Riding was not a sport she enjoyed, even though she was a competent horsewoman. Her fundamental reason for riding—the same as many young ladies—was to meet eligible gentlemen.

Elliot rode slowly down the drive, staring at the hoofmarks the sorrel mare had cut into the moist surface. He wondered where Bernice had been off to in such a hurry.

Elliot's solitary ride led him through the village on his way back to Wakefield. It was a warm afternoon and he stopped at the small inn to quench his thirst with a cool tankard of ale. He wasn't eager to return to the house where he was caught between Bernice's demands and Catherine's silence.

Much to Elliot's surprise, he saw a familiar face when he entered the building. Fitzhugh, Lord Berkley, was sitting at one of the tables, a drink already in front of him. Elliot and Fitz were much the same age and station. They shared mutual friends and attended many of the same events in London; however, they had never formed a strong friendship. When Lady Catherine came on the scene the gap widened between them. They were cordial, but Elliot had avoided Fitz when he was in the company of Lady Catherine. There was no sense in casting sheep's eyes at a lady who was nearly betrothed.

"Fitz, what a place to find you," exclaimed Elliot, as he took a seat across from the man. "I never thought to see you outside of London during the Season."

It was clear that Elliot's unexpected appearance had startled Fitz. "I . . . uh . . . was just on my way to Town. Thought I'd break my journey here."

"Been here long?" asked Elliot, motioning to the innkeeper for a tankard of ale.

"Uh . . . no."

As the two men sipped their ale and exchanged

news, an idea occurred to Elliot. Even though she denied anything serious between them, Fitz had been a particular friend of Catherine's. Perhaps seeing him would make her more amiable. In any event, it was only hospitable to invite Fitz to Wakefield.

"Since you're in no hurry, why not stay on a few days at my late aunt's estate? It's not far from here and has all the comforts of home, including good company. Drew is here with me. We could do some hunting and fishing, a little relaxation before joining the Season. What do you say?"

"I wouldn't want to impose," said Fitz.

"No imposition at all," replied Elliot jocularly. "I insist. Can't have it said I let you stay at an inn when we're so close."

"Why don't I come round tomorrow, then. Give your housekeeper time to prepare."

"No need. I'll wait while you gather your belongings. You'll be dining in style tonight. We have an excellent cook."

Fitz became quieter the nearer the men drew to Wakefield House. Elliot pretended to notice nothing out of the ordinary, and continued a constant flow of conversation, but he still had to wonder what was causing Fitz's unusual mien. As they entered the hall and handed their hats and gloves to the butler, the sound of voices coming from the drawing room was clearly audible.

"I will appeal to Elliott," came Bernice's onerous voice from the open door. "He will not be so mean as to let me waste away here in the country."

"No one is keeping you here," Catherine replied calmly. "At all events, all you need do is go to London and enjoy the Season. You will find no end of entertainment to delight you."

"You know I cannot go and leave you here to steal my inheritance. No! I will beg Elliot to hold a house party here at Wakefield. He will not refuse me company."

"And who would leave London during the Season to come here to Wakefield even should I allow it?"

"Should you allow it?" screeched Bernice. "And just who are you to stop me? I remind you that this estate belonged to my Aunt Jane, and you will have nothing to say in whomever I invite."

"Your aunt left the estate in my hands for as long as the cats are here. If you invite a party, it will be against my wishes and you must bear the expense."

"But, you can't . . ." began Bernice.

"Don't fret so," said Elliot, entering the room. "I have brought you company, Bernice, and although it isn't a party, perhaps he shall do." He stepped aside, allowing the two women a view of the man following close behind. Catherine turned pale and stiff at the sight of Fitz, while Bernice became flushed and agitated.

"I believe you are both acquainted with Lord Berkley," said Elliot, drawing closer.

"Who could forget two such lovely ladies," said Fitz. "Lady Bernice it is always good to see you again. Lady Catherine, it has been too long since we last met."

Bernice's eyes widened and her mouth opened without emitting a sound.

Elliot grimaced. In his rush to get Fitz to Wakefield, he had forgotten his promise to Lady Catherine regarding her true identity. He would apologize at the first opportunity. Even though he was investigating her handling of the estate, he normally would not betray a promise.

"Lady Catherine?" said Bernice, regaining her speech. "You must be mistaken. This is Anne Webster."

"It must be a little hoax on Lady Catherine's part. She is known for her wit in London. I can attest to that, for we became well acquainted during her stay. You were greatly missed when you left Town," Fitz said, his eyes fastened on her.

"I'm certain the Season continued unabated," said Lady Catherine, in a stilted voice.

"But not nearly so pleasantly. Your absence left a hole that no one else could fill," he said, taking her hand and raising it toward his lips.

Lady Catherine pulled her hand away, an expression of distaste flitting across her face and disappearing almost before it appeared.

Bernice did not miss Fitz's expression as he stared at Catherine. Her face flushed with anger and her hands closed into tight fists by her side. She turned her venomous gaze on Catherine. "Why didn't you tell me?" she demanded.

Catherine chose to ignore Fitz in favor of Bernice. "You gave me no time to explain," she replied, outwardly calm. "You entered the house complaining and accusing and you haven't ceased yet. It was far easier to allow you to continue your course rather than thwart it. Besides, it was a private decision, and was of no import to anyone but me."

"If I had known your true identity, then perhaps we could have dealt together," replied Bernice between gritted teeth.

"I doubt, Lady Bernice, whether we could have done so. Your opinion would have been the same if

I had announced I was the Princess of Wales. However, I see no need for your embarrassment, for I was the one who withheld my true name."

"And you still have not told us why," shot back Bernice.

"Now, cousin, get off your high ropes and allow Lady Catherine to retain her privacy," interrupted Elliot before Bernice's anger could escalate.

"And I suppose you were also in on the game," said Bernice.

"I met Lady Catherine last year," admitted Elliot.

"So everyone knew except for me. And you say I should not feel the fool. I insist you tell us what you're up to," she commanded, turning to Catherine.

Feeling guilty about exposing Catherine's true identity, Elliot felt compelled to protect her as much as possible. "Bernice, I have told you, it is Lady Catherine's prerogative what she cares to share with us."

"But . . ." she began to protest.

"No, that is all the conversation we shall have on the subject." He glanced at Catherine, wondering whether she appreciated his efforts, but she did not meet his gaze. She had bent to grasp the kitten, then straightened.

"I must see the housekeeper to arrange Lord Berkley's rooms," she said to the room at large.

"Perhaps I should remain at the inn," he began.

"No," replied Bernice quickly. "Please excuse our brangling. It's a private matter. I would welcome your company."

"My valet should arrive with my luggage shortly," said Fitz.

Lady Catherine gave a nod of acknowledgment before turning toward the door.

Elliot watched her retreat, shoulders straight, back

stiff, and wondered what had gone on between Fitz and Catherine that his mere presence should upset her so.

"Why am I always the last to know anything around here?" demanded Bernice, claiming his attention. "And who is this woman?"

"Miss Webster's real name is Lady Catherine Duncan. Her mother was a friend of Aunt Jane's. She found it necessary to take her mother's name for a time due to circumstances she has chosen not to confide."

"Then I think you should inquire further, for if she cannot use her own name something is amiss."

"I'm certain she has a very good reason, Bernice. But it is not my business to poke into her personal affairs. My interest is limited to the estate, as yours should be."

"Er, perhaps I should leave the two of you to discuss this in private," said Fitz.

"No need; we're finished," said Elliot. "Stay and entertain Bernice. She's been complaining about the lack of company, even though Drew and I do our best to amuse her."

"And where is Drew?" asked Fitz.

"Off to visit a friend who lives not far away. He'll be back for dinner, though. Unfortunately, I have a meeting with the solicitor, but I leave you in capable hands." Elliot gave a smile and a wave and left the two gazing blankly at one another. He hoped Bernice and Fitz had something in common, for he did not plan to return to their company this afternoon.

Elliot did have a meeting with the solicitor, but not until later in the day. He had wanted to catch up with

Lady Catherine before she had time enough to lock herself away with her precious kitten. He found her in the back hall in conference with the housekeeper. As soon as the two women had finished, and the housekeeper had hurried away to make rooms ready for their most recent houseguest, Elliot approached.

"What do you want?" she hissed, before he had a chance to say a word. "Haven't you done as much as you can? Or have you come to gloat?"

Elliot found himself taking a step back. "I had no intention of upsetting you. I came in search of you to apologize. When I invited Fitz to stay at Wakefield House, I never gave a thought to revealing your true name. I was merely offering hospitality to an acquaintance. I hope you'll forgive my mistake. I usually keep my promises."

"Am I to believe that it's merely my poor fortune you chose to break your word at this moment? I think not," she ground out. "And it would have been common courtesy to have advised me of a houseguest *before* you thrust him upon me."

Elliot was taken back by her ferocity. He could not understand her upset. "I cannot see how Bernice knowing your name can cause you any problems. If it will, tell me how and I will attempt to correct it."

"It is not Bernice; it is . . ." Suddenly Catherine's glare dimmed, and she waved a weary hand. "It is past mattering. Nothing signifies now except my responsibility to Lady Wakefield. I would shout my name from the rooftop if it would bring back Jane's cats."

She looked tired to the bone, and Elliot felt the urge to pull her to him and let her rest in the curve of his arms. But he dared not. There was too much secrecy between them. He must prove that she had done nothing untoward, then he would somehow find out why she was hiding at Wakefield House. For no matter what she said, he knew it to be so.

"Why don't you rest before dinner?" he suggested. "I'm certain the housekeeper can manage to settle Fitz and his valet into his rooms."

"I believe I will," she said, surprising him by her immediate agreement.

He watched as she disappeared down the hall. He was no closer to understanding her than when they had met at the top of the stairs. He did not know how to break through the wall of secrecy she had erected around herself.

Elliot released a small sigh of relief as Lady Catherine appeared in the hall outside the drawing room. He had feared she would not come down to dinner that evening. She hesitated slightly in the doorway, as if undecided whether to join the company, then stepped into the room. He went to meet her, hoping to repair some of the damage he had done.

He had visited the solicitor that afternoon, and his findings had relieved his mind. It seemed that Lady Catherine had been handling the estate as well as anyone could expect. In the solicitor's opinion, she was running it far better than most, including the late Lady Wakefield. There was no record of any personal items being billed to the estate by Lady Catherine, but there had been numerous attempts by Bernice to use her inheritance prematurely. That was the basis of Bernice's dislike of Lady Catherine, he judged, for she had rejected every charge that had been made.

Elliot had completed looking over the estate books

the day before and had found nothing untoward. He knew nowhere else to look for wrongdoing on Lady Catherine's part. If she was stealing from the estate, then she was adept at hiding it.

The only question remaining was the whereabouts of Aunt Jane's cats. Lady Catherine took such good care of the last kitten, he could not believe she was responsible for the other cats' disappearances. However, that could just be superb acting on her part. Perhaps it was the inheritance she wanted. He had learned from the solicitor that it was a generous amount.

"Lady Catherine, you look most fetching this evening."

"There is no need for flattery, my lord. I have put your broken promise behind me. I do not have the desire to be continually up in the boughs with you."

Elliot felt a brief shaft of hope that they might pass the evening pleasantly. "Nor do I aspire to remain at daggers drawn, my lady. I hope you believe I meant you no harm this afternoon."

His eyes were focused intently on her, and Catherine tended to believe him. He thought she was angry because he had revealed her true identity, but that had not been the cause for her temper. Unless it became necessary, she would keep the real reason to herself.

Across the room, Fitz turned away from Bernice and Drew. Before he could take but two steps, Catherine looked up at Elliot. "Would you take me into dinner?" she asked, giving him a smile he had not seen since London.

"I would be honored," he replied, offering her his arm.

Catherine did not miss the angry expression that

darkened Fitz's face as she turned away from him. He had better become accustomed to it, thought Catherine, gripping Elliot's arm more tightly than she realized.

"Could we speak privately after dinner?" murmured Elliot as they led the way into the dining room.

"Should I prepare myself for battle?" quipped Catherine, a derisive smile curling the corners of her lips.

"Not at all. I think you'll be pleased with what I have to say."

"All right, then," she agreed. Their conversation would delay any contact she might be forced to endure with Lord Berkley that evening.

Elliot was anxious to talk to Lady Catherine. He wanted to remove the animosity that had sprung up between them since his arrival at Wakefield House. He longed to experience the ease with which they had conversed when they had first met in London. He had discovered a keen mind beneath the golden hair and yearned to explore it further.

He had been surprised that Catherine had not greeted Fitz with greater warmth. During dinner, she had been civil to him, but exhibited no interest in engaging their newest houseguest in conversation. While she had vehemently denied any serious affiliation with him, that did not preclude a friendly acquaintance.

However, she seemed greatly relieved when Elliot suggested the two men have port with Bernice in the drawing room, while he and Lady Catherine attended to a few minor business matters.

* * *

"My lady," began Elliot as soon as the library door closed behind them, "I want to apologize again for disclosing your name to Bernice. It's true, I don't understand why you're keeping your presence secret, but that is no reason for me to ignore your wishes. I didn't consider the repercussions when I invited Fitz to spend a few days here at Wakefield."

"Think no more of it, Lord Gage. It is over and done with. I will make do with the situation. Now, you said there was something you wished to discuss."

Elliot had hoped there might be some thawing in her manner but could see none. Perhaps after she heard what he had to say she would be more kindly disposed toward him.

"Shall we sit?" he asked. After they had settled themselves in chairs facing one another he continued. "I met with the solicitor today. We discussed how the estate has been running since Aunt Jane's passing."

Lady Catherine did not show any anxiety. Evidently, she was not worried about the results.

"He was extremely complimentary toward you. Said the estate was doing better than it ever had. In fact, he was affronted by the suggestion that you might be taking advantage of your position to remove funds from the estate."

"Does this mean Bernice's endless accusations will come to an end?"

Elliot grinned. "I won't promise, but I'll do my best to restrain her. You know, I had to do what I did," he continued in a more sober mood. "I would not have been serving Aunt Jane if I had not."

Catherine rose from her chair and moved to the window. "I can accept your reasoning, but it doesn't make me feel in fine feathers. I've never been accused of chicanery in my entire life."

Elliot followed her to the window. He stood close enough to detect the faint scent of her perfume. Nothing stood between them any longer. Even Fitz's arrival had not seemed to raise any fond memories, for she had shown no preference for his company.

"Catherine," he murmured, allowing his hands to come to rest on her upper arms. "Can you ever forgive me?"

The warmth of his grasp gave Catherine a feeling of security that had long been missing. Could she feel his breath stir her hair, or was it just wishful thinking? She longed to lean back and rest against his broad chest; however, she would not allow herself to give in so easily. This was the man who just this afternoon was questioning her honesty. She was ashamed of herself for being such a fool, for giving into the flattery that rose so easily to his lips. It would take more than a few words from Lord Gage to turn her up sweet.

Catherine took a step forward and turned toward Elliot, effectively removing herself from his hold. "Of course, I forgive you," she said brightly. "I understand completely, and I'll even do my best to forgive Bernice. Although I doubt whether she will ever ask for it."

Elliot laughed. "That would be a miracle, and I wouldn't count on it."

"We should get back to the rest of the company," said Catherine. "I haven't been a very good hostess thus far. Perhaps I can do better now."

"You've had a great deal on your mind," said Elliot. "I know you're still worried about the rest of Aunt Jane's cats, and I haven't given up on finding them.

Drew and I will continue searching. Someone must have seen something."

"I wish you luck. I would ask for nothing more than that they return safely," she replied, her face solemn. "Now, I think we've stayed away long enough."

Elliot did not want to let her go so easily. He yearned to keep their closeness, treasure it, deepen it. But he would not force himself on her, as she had accused Fitz of doing in London. Not wanting to earn her disgust, he moved aside, allowing her enough room to pass, then followed her from the room.

Fitz came to Catherine's side as soon as she entered the drawing room.

"My lady, we have not had time to utter two words to one another all evening."

Elliot did not like what was happening but could do nothing to stop it. Lady Catherine was a grown woman and would make her own choices. No matter how she protested, she and Fitz had spent a great deal of time together in London; he had seen it with his own eyes. Perhaps she was ready to pardon him. He stepped away from the couple and joined Drew and Bernice.

"I will never forgive you for this," hissed Bernice.

"I had given my word that I wouldn't reveal Lady Catherine's identity," said Elliot, weary of his cousin's irrational reactions. "And while you are already up in the boughs, you may as well hear the rest of it. Lady Catherine has done nothing improper with Aunt Jane's estate. I have looked at the books and all is in order. I spoke with the solicitor this afternoon and he said we should count ourselves lucky to have such an efficient person in charge."

Bernice remained silent for a moment, staring at her cousin. "I can't believe she has wound you around her finger so quickly. First Aunt Jane, then the servants and the solicitor. Now you. Is everyone against me?" she asked, turning pleading eyes toward Drew.

"Don't drag Drew into this," warned Elliot. "He's a guest and should not be put upon to take sides."

"Excellent port," said Drew, draining his glass. Excusing himself, he rose and walked across the room to a small table that held decanters and glasses.

"You hate me," accused Bernice, tears filling her eyes.

"Bernice, I don't hate you," Elliot said patiently. "I merely feel you're mistaken about Lady Catherine. Everything points to her being innocent of your charges. Unless you can tell me something specific, and prove it, you must accept my findings."

"Never! That woman is up to something. Why has she been hiding behind another name all these months? Don't tell me that isn't suspicious."

"What she calls herself is no concern of ours. She must have had good reason, but it is not up to us to question why."

"And where are all the cats?" questioned Bernice. "It's odd they began disappearing after she took over the estate. Don't tell me that is not our business."

"I'm looking into that, but I don't think she had anything to do with it. She's too upset over their disappearance, and she guards the last kitten too well."

"She's a good actress, that's all. You forget she'll come into a nice inheritance once all the cats are gone."

It had momentarily slipped Elliot's mind. Was he wrong? Did Lady Catherine want her inheritance as much as Bernice? Elliot allowed his glance to stray to the couple at the other end of the room.

Bernice still simmered with anger over Elliot's defection. However, she followed his gaze, noticing how it lingered on Fitz and Lady Catherine, and smiled. Perhaps he was not as certain of Lady Catherine as he professed.

"You have been avoiding me," said Fitz, having placed himself so that Catherine could not easily escape.

"I've been busy," replied Catherine. "And Lady Bernice has kept you occupied."

"As Gage has you," said Fitz in an irritated tone.

"Lord Gage and I have business matters to discuss. That is why he made this trip to the country. I'm certain he wants to finish and rejoin the Season as soon as possible."

"And you? Will you be journeying to London also?"

"No, I have obligations here yet to fulfill. And as soon as they are finished, I intend to spend some time traveling."

"You should not be traveling alone, my lady. It is unseemly."

"I shall make do," Catherine replied, wishing someone would rescue her.

"If we were wed, I would take you wherever you wanted to go," said Fitz, moving closer.

Catherine stepped to the side, putting a little more distance between them. "I told you in London we would not suit, my lord. I have not changed my mind."

"Give me time to convince you," he murmured, reaching out to her.

"Lady Catherine," said Elliot, breaking their privacy, "would you play something on the pianoforte for us?"

"I'm sorry, my lord, but I must excuse myself. I haven't fed the kitten yet. You must ask Lady Bernice; she plays much better than I."

Bernice appeared surprised at Catherine's compliment, but wasted no time in acting the modest maiden. She hurried across the room and took Fitz's arm.

"Come turn the pages for me," she said, smiling up at him.

"Thank you," said Catherine, as Bernice pulled Fitz toward the end of the room where the pianoforte stood.

"You looked a trifle disconcerted," Elliot replied.

"Lord Berkley is a difficult man to convince that his attention is unwanted," remarked Catherine, immediately wishing she had said nothing.

"If you are having trouble, let me help."

"It's nothing," said Catherine quickly. "I must feed the kitten." She picked up the bundle of white fur, which had been playing around her feet, and left the room with a tepid smile of good-bye.

Elliot rejoined Drew, a worried frown on his face.

"Problems?" asked Drew, pouring a glass of port for Elliot and handing it to him.

"I don't know. I thought once Bernice's accusations against Lady Catherine were cleared away, we might have a few days of peace. But Fitz's appearance only seems to have stirred the waters more."

"Understand they knew one another in London."

"Yes, they did," mused Elliot. "Devil take me! I meant to explain about Anne Webster being Lady Catherine. I had given my word not to reveal her true identity. I didn't feel right keeping it from you, but I had no choice."

"No need for apologies," said Drew. "Knew you had a good reason."

"Thank you, my friend," said Elliot, raising his glass toward Drew. "I don't know what happened between Lady Catherine and Fitz, but she no longer seems to welcome his company," he continued after emptying his glass.

"Lovers' quarrel?"

Elliot shrugged. "I don't know. I'm not that close to Fitz. He allowed everyone to think they were all but betrothed; however, Lady Catherine indicates they were merely friends—and not close ones at that. He was at her side quite a bit during the Season, but so were many others. He attempted to hide it, but he was just as surprised as everyone else when she disappeared without a word."

"How did she turn up here?"

"She said her carriage broke down nearby, and she stayed on at Aunt Jane's request. Then Aunt Jane died and she found herself responsible for the cats."

"Seen any more yet?" asked Drew, abruptly changing the subject.

"Cats? No, not a hair except white ones," remarked Elliot, brushing at his coat. "And that is another cloud hanging over Lady Catherine's head."

"Don't believe she's guilty of doing away with the felines, do you?"

"I'm probably mad not to. She'll gain as well as Bernice and I will once the cats are all gone. But I just can't see her harming them. Don't tell Bernice I said that," said Elliot with a grin.

"My lips are sealed," replied Drew. "If it isn't Lady

Catherine and it isn't you, that only leaves one person with a motive."

"I don't want to think about it," replied Elliot.

They were silent a moment, then Elliot spoke again. "Will you help me keep a discreet eye on Bernice?" he asked. "Only one small kitten stands between her and a multitude of gowns and trinkets. I don't need to tell you to what lengths she would go for that."

"Do the best I can," said Drew.

"Catherine, my dear, at last I have found you."

Fitz had finally been successful at catching her unawares. Catherine turned to face him, studying the man who had driven her from London. He was nearly as tall as Lord Gage, but his build was slighter. He had red hair, icy blue eyes, and pale skin that remained colorless no matter how much he stayed outdoors. His manners were impeccable, but seemed only a thin veneer for a more violent nature that lurked just beneath the surface. He was tenacious, she would give him that. He had pursued her in London until she had fled. Now, he had finally run her to ground again.

"I am merely going about my business," replied Catherine firmly. "I have a great deal to oversee."

"If it were up to me, you would have nothing to do but wear lovely gowns to enhance your beauty."

Catherine uttered a huge sigh. "Lord Berkley, it would be much more comfortable for both of us if you would accept that we do not suit."

"We have been apart too long," said Fitz, smiling at her. "Once we become reacquainted, you'll see we suit perfectly."

Catherine was rescued from answering by Elliot and Drew, coming out of the breakfast room and inviting Fitz to ride with them. She was greatly relieved when the men strolled to the back of the house and out the door to the stables.

However, before she could begin to enjoy her solitude, Bernice bounded down the stairs. "Have you seen Lord Berkley?" she asked, peering into the breakfast room.

"The gentlemen have gone for a ride," said Catherine, hoping to escape any unpleasantness with Bernice.

"Oh, piffle!" exclaimed Bernice. "You probably urged them to leave early so I would miss them."

"Lady Bernice, this may come as a surprise to you, but I have other things to think about than how to foil your romance."

"It isn't a romance," objected Bernice, a flush burning her cheeks. "Lord Berkley is merely a diversion."

"Whatever it is, I wish you success," said Catherine, thinking if a *tendre* developed between the two, it might rid her of both her tormentors.

"You were head over heels for him in London, weren't you?"

Catherine stared at Bernice, dumbfounded by her comment.

"And he paid you no heed, did he? You see, he told me all about it, but asked me to be kind and not let you know." The smirk on her face widened.

"When he knows you better he'll realize there is no kindness in you," remarked Catherine.

"Is that all you have to say? Surely you aren't agreeing with what he says so easily."

"There would be no need for me to deny Lord

Berkley's remarks, for I'm certain you would not believe me. I'll leave it to you to discover the truth on your own."

"The truth? After your deception, you would not recognize the truth if it rose up and bit you. I am still not convinced Aunt Jane knew your true identity, nor that she willingly gave you control of her estate."

"Lady Bernice," replied Catherine patiently "what happened to your aunt occurred just as you were told. You are welcome to question the servants, the doctor, and her solicitor."

"I have done that and they are no more helpful than you. They have probably been offered a handsome amount to substantiate your story."

"Then there is nothing more I can say to convince you," replied Catherine.

"Nothing at all," agreed Bernice, turning on her heel and walking away with her head high.

"It's a wonder she doesn't trip with her nose up in the air so," muttered Catherine, before getting on with the business of the day.

FOUR

The coolness Lady Catherine exhibited toward Fitz had not escaped Elliot's notice. She had declared Fitz nothing more than an acquaintance—and an unwelcome one at that—but many a lady claimed the same when a romance went wrong. It was better than admitting to society that they had been jilted.

Elliot shrugged into the jacket his valet held for him, and stood silently while George continued with his brushing and adjusting; a ritual he had learned to endure for such excellent service.

If there were something between Lady Catherine and Fitz, they couldn't hide it long in as close company as they were. Elliot was certain Bernice was smitten by Fitz, and if she followed her usual course, she would soon know everything about him. If it included an attachment for Lady Catherine, she would keep the news to herself only as long as it took to gather a crowd of one for an audience.

As soon as George was finished, Elliot went downstairs to the drawing room, where they gathered before going into dinner. The scene he stepped into merely justified his belief in Bernice.

She was more or less being held captive by Drew while Lady Catherine and Fitz conversed at the far end of the room. Their voices were low and only a murmur could be heard, but Bernice was straining her ears in an attempt to listen. She merely nodded now and then to Drew's conversation. Anger or jealousy—Elliot did not know which one—twisted her face into a dark mask. He hoped she would be able to control her temper at least through dinner.

"We must join the others, Lord Berkley," said Catherine, hoping to dissolve their tête-à-tête without making a scene.

"They will understand," said Fitz.

"I hope they do, for I don't," replied Catherine.

"It's obvious when two people are drawn together. Others expect them to react unconventionally."

"If you are referring to the two of us, my lord, then you have it all wrong. I am not drawn to you. Neither am I your betrothed, nor do I intend to be in the future. You must get over this idea that we will be wed."

"Your modesty does you justice," Fitz replied. "I realize now that I rushed you in London, that you needed time to adjust your sentiments. You have evidently never encountered such a passion as I hold for you."

He reached for her hand and lifted it to his lips before she could react. Jerking away from his touch, Catherine felt a sense of helplessness. She had done all she could to discourage this man from pursuing her, yet all had failed.

"May I fetch you a sherry?" asked Elliot.

Catherine had not heard him approach. Her attention had been focused on Lord Berkley and finding a way to convince him to look elsewhere for a bride.

"I would like that above all things and, if you do

not object, I will accompany you," she replied, turning and taking his arm.

"Fitz, I believe Bernice had a question for you. Something about fashion, I'm sure," remarked Elliot, leading Catherine away from the glowering man.

"What have you done to Fitz? Usually he's the most affable person I know, but he looks like a thundercloud."

"He's beginning to frighten me all over again," she said without thinking.

"And what is it that frightens you?" he asked, suddenly serious.

"I've said too much," replied Catherine. "Besides, you would no more believe me about Lord Berkley than you would about robbing the estate."

Elliot stopped at the small table and poured a glass of sherry. Catherine's hand shook as she accepted the glass.

"You are upset, aren't you?" he asked, surprised.

"Of course I am," she answered crossly. "Why should I make up such a Banbury story?"

"Catherine, tell me what there is between you and Fitz. I promise I shall take it seriously."

"It would do no good, my lord. Even if you believed me, there is nothing to be done."

"Allow me to be the judge of that," said Elliot. "It's too late now, but after dinner the two of us are going to have a private discussion. I suggest you take time during dinner to make up your mind whether to tell me the truth about Fitz. If not, I shall ask him direct."

Elliot's threat had hung over Catherine during dinner. The excellent repast had tasted like sawdust. She had still not decided what to do when they rose from the table.

"Lady Catherine, would you care to take a walk in the garden? I believe there is enough daylight yet, and the evening is pleasant," said Elliot.

Catherine met his dark gaze and knew if she didn't accept, he would probably question her here in front of everyone. She laid her hand on his arm. "That is a delightful suggestion, my lord."

"Let us all take some air," suggested Fitz.

"Oh, no, I have a new tune I want you to hear," countered Bernice, taking his arm and tugging him toward the pianoforte.

"Drew?" said Elliot, knowing he had more sense than to intrude but unwilling to have him think he was forgotten.

"Don't worry. Shall drink more of this excellent port and listen to the music."

They silently walked into the garden and away from the house. Finding a bench where they would be aware if anyone approached them, Elliot and Catherine took a seat, admiring the varied hues in the western sky.

"Lady Catherine, I wish you would trust me enough to tell me what you are holding back. You want me to believe you, but you must admit you've done nothing to encourage me to do so."

"You cannot accept what I say and be done with it?"

"I would if there was no harm to be done, but something is amiss. Particularly in your alliance with Fitz."

"I have told you. We have no alliance," said Catherine, an edge of hysteria in her voice that he had never heard before.

"Then what is it?" he asked gently, taking her hand in his. "Tell me," he murmured. "It will go no further."

Catherine was susceptible to his encouragement. She had been alone far too long and yearned to confide to a sympathetic ear. For the moment, she forgot he had been her antagonist since his arrival. To share her problem was an overpowering urge she could not refuse.

"You've asked many times why I left London so mysteriously. I did so because of Lord Berkley," she blurted out.

"Fitz?" he asked, a note of bewilderment in his voice.

"Yes," she replied in a firm voice. "At first he was just another pleasant gentleman. I met many in London. They all sent flowers and flattered me outrageously in nearly the same words. It's a game we all play extremely well, as you know."

Elliot nodded. "I've passed nearly every Season in such a manner," he replied, hoping it would encourage her to continue.

"I was enjoying myself until Lord Berkley became overly possessive. He called at my home every day, showed up at every event I attended, and stayed by my side the whole time. I believe he warned some of the gentlemen away from me, for my acquaintances became fewer. Then he began insisting we were to be wed. No matter how many times I refused, he simply acted as if he hadn't heard. He declared we would be married in July at St. George's, and I couldn't persuade him to the contrary. I even heard him telling other people that we were to be betrothed and wed before the Season was over."

Elliot had heard the same thing from Fitz, so he knew that much was true.

"Then one evening he became extremely angry when I once again refused his offer. He threatened to take me to Gretna Green and marry me even if it was against my will. It was too much. I was not at home to Lord Berkley any longer. I began staying at home in order to avoid him until I was a virtual prisoner. At last, I realized there was nothing I could do to discourage him, so I decided to leave Town. However, I knew I must do so in secret or Lord Berkley would only pursue me.

"I arranged to leave in the middle of the night. It was the evening of his cousin's coming-out ball and he was expected to attend for the family's sake. I was vastly pleased with the success of my plan until a wheel on my coach broke. We were near Wakefield when the accident happened. The rest is as I related previously."

Elliot opened his mouth to speak, but Catherine held up her hand to silence him.

"There is one more thing," she said. "I do not believe Lord Berkley is traveling through to London as he told you. I'm convinced he followed me here to once again attempt to force me into marriage."

Catherine's angry tones sounded a discord in the garden and clashed with the peace and spring beauty around them.

"It's true I'm not a close friend of Lord Berkley," began Elliot. "But I have been acquainted with him for some years now and I have never known him to act in such a manner."

Catherine heard the disbelief in his voice, and realized that the warmth of his hand had disappeared from hers. "You don't believe me, do you?" Her voice was weighed down with hopelessness. She had allowed herself to believe in him when she should have known better; She could rely upon no one but herself.

Although Elliot wanted to accept that Fitz was an absolute blackguard, culpable of all Catherine accused, he felt compelled to give him the benefit of the doubt. After all, Fitz was born a gentleman, a man of honor, and should have been incapable of such scurrilous deeds. Then there was the matter of Elliot's guilt in attempting to steal the woman Fitz hoped to wed. Elliot felt he should be generous to Fitz under the circumstances. It would, no doubt, ease his conscience later.

"Perhaps he was completely besotted by you and became a little overzealous. Surely you could understand that," reasoned Elliot.

"Although I have had men profess their affection toward me, I have never had one as persistent as Lord Berkley. I said all that I could, from gentle to blunt, but none of it mattered." She studied Elliot's face too closely for his comfort. "I wonder why I expected you to believe me?" she finally said. "You didn't accept that I was innocent of robbing your aunt's estate. Why should you accept what I say about Lord Berkley?"

"It isn't that I don't trust what you say," said Elliot. "I merely suggested that you might have overreacted. Surely if he were convinced you didn't welcome his attention, he would no longer press his company on you."

"Are you completely addlebrained?" burst out Catherine. She had held in her emotions as long as possible, but Lord Gage's attempts to explain away Lord Berkley's actions were too much. "I have told you I have done all I can to discourage the man and it's as if I had never spoken. He has begun again since his arrival. Oh, he is subtle, I'll give him that, but surely someone has noticed. I don't know what to do but escape again and hope he doesn't find me."

Elliot did not want her to leave until he had a chance to straighten out the misunderstanding between them. He realized too late that he had completely mishandled their interview, and frantically searched for some way to turn the conversation to his advantage.

"Lady Catherine, please listen to reason. I'm sorry if what I said caused you to think I did not believe you. Give me time to observe Fitz, and if he is doing what you say, I'll handle the situation."

"*If* he is doing what I say? You tell me you believe me in one breath and question me again in another. I am done with protesting my innocence for everything I say and do. I owe neither you, nor Bernice, nor Lord Berkley a single thing. And I no longer intend to live my life as if I do. You should be thanking me for taking care of your aunt when none of her family could tear themselves away from their activities to do so. Instead, I am made the scapegoat for everything that has gone wrong in your life since you were in leading strings. Enough is enough."

Elliot could see she was trembling. He did not want her to leave in such a taking. "Lady Catherine . . ."

"No! No more, my lord. I am finished with you! All of you."

There was nothing more he could do to stop her or she would claim he was as persistent as Fitz. He hoped he would be able to reason with her later. Although if everything had happened as she said, he could not blame her for being angry. Elliot walked back toward the house, his head down, completely oblivious to the beauty that had held his admiration only a short time earlier.

"Did you lose Lady Catherine?" asked a voice from the gathering twilight.

"Fitz," greeted Elliot. "She had an attack of megrims and excused herself for the evening."

"Evidently the country air does not agree with her. She never suffered ill health in Town."

"Fitz, what happened to your betrothal? I never asked, for it was none of my business, but things have changed now and I need to know. The woman is in charge of my aunt's estate and if there is any instability involved, I should be apprised of it."

Fitz laughed and waved a dismissive hand. "She is a woman. That should explain it all," he said. "Catherine has not experienced family and social ties as we have, and I believe she took fright at the thought of marrying and living with a man. I attempted to explain that she would adjust quickly, but she would have none of it. I left her alone for one evening and she disappeared."

"There was nothing else to cause her flight?" asked Elliot, attempting to draw Fitz out.

"You mean theft? Bernice told me what was happening." He paused a moment before continuing. "No, Catherine is innocent of everything but an active imagination and the ability to know what is best for her. I'm certain she'll be cured of both as soon as we're wed."

"Wed?" questioned Elliot, shocked into questioning Fitz. "You mean you are still set on marrying her?"

"Of course. Why do you think I'm here? I'll admit I haven't been completely honest. I wasn't just traveling to London. I've had men searching for Catherine since she disappeared and I finally found her. I was going to stay at the inn until I found a way to approach her, but your invitation solved the problem."

Fitz sounded pleased with himself, and Elliot felt a fool by falling in with his scheme even though he had no way of knowing what was going on at the time. That Fitz would use his friendship in such a way angered Elliot, but he attempted to keep the emotion in check until he learned everything he needed to know.

"Has Lady Catherine changed her mind about the marriage?" Elliot asked, wondering how Fitz viewed Catherine's reaction to his arrival.

"Not yet, but it's just a matter of time until she does. I don't intend to allow her to slip away again," said Fitz, his tone growing hard.

"And I suppose you'll take her prisoner if she doesn't," said Elliot, attempting to sound light-hearted enough to avoid suspicion that he was searching for information.

"If need be," agreed Fitz with a smile. "If need be."

To Elliot, Fitz sounded as serious as a man could be. He had been wrong to question Catherine's appraisal of Fitz. She had been right after all.

When Catherine left Elliot, she avoided the drawing room and hurried around the house to the back entrance, hoping to reach her room without encountering anyone else. She felt brittle to the bone, as if she would shatter into a thousand pieces if she was forced to explain her actions to one more person this evening. Reaching the back hall, she took the ser-

vant's stairs to her rooms. Betsy was sitting at the
small table with a book before her. She looked up
with a smile.

"He was all over the room tonight," she said, motioning toward the bed where the kitten was curled
up. "I think he was looking for you. He finally wore
his self out."

Catherine walked over to the bed and looked down
at the small bit of white fur that had caused her life
to become so complicated. There had to be a way to
keep her promise to Jane, and to remain sane at the
same time. She would think on it overnight.

Catherine faced the morning with only one idea
for escape from her situation. It was not one she welcomed, but she was determined to use it if no other
occurred to her. She descended the stairs slowly, not
eager to face another day filled with antagonistic people hurling accusations at her, or Fitz stalking her
every move.

She had taken breakfast in her room and had come
down after hearing the gentlemen leave for what she
assumed was a morning ride. Bernice seldom rose
before noon, so she hoped to have some peace in
her day.

"So you had an attack of megrims last night," said
a familiar sarcastic voice. "You certainly know how to
catch the gentlemens' attention."

Why, today of all days, had Bernice chosen to arise
early? thought Catherine with a silent groan. "I have
had some difficult days dealing with the estate and
your cousin's investigation."

"No more than you've deserved," said Bernice.
"Elliot continues to question why you're here even

though he hasn't yet found any wrongdoings. I'm certain it's only a matter of time before something comes to light."

"Can't you accept that I was your aunt's friend? That she put me in charge because she felt it was the best thing to do?"

"No, I can't," spat Bernice. "Aunt Jane always gave me anything I wanted. Why would she give my inheritance to you?"

"She hasn't given it to me. It is to be used for the cats, then it will come to you," Catherine explained patiently.

"I don't know what you did to her—perhaps you caught her when she wasn't in her right mind—but this is not something she would do," Bernice insisted stubbornly.

Catherine had known discussing the situation with Bernice would yield nothing, but she felt she had to try one last time. As far as she was concerned, she had done all she could. She was saved from any further conversation by the sound of wheels on the drive.

"It seems we are having visitors," Bernice remarked. "Did you invite some of your friends to enjoy your windfall?"

Catherine ignored the jibe. "Who is it, Harrison?" she asked the butler as he came from the breakfast room into the hall.

"I don't know, my lady." He opened the door just as the coach came to a stop at the bottom of the steps.

"Mama. Papa," whispered Bernice, a hand held to her mouth.

"Your parents? Why, I would think you would be overjoyed to see them," commented Catherine dryly.

"Why now? It's the wrong time," replied Bernice, without seeming to realize she was speaking out loud.

Catherine stared at Bernice but had no time to say anything more before George and Elizabeth, Lord and Lady Huntley, stepped down from their crested traveling coach.

The greetings and introductions had been exchanged, and Lord and Lady Huntley had been shown to their rooms to refresh themselves after their journey. Luncheon would be served soon and Catherine prayed that the gentlemen would return in time to join the party, for she did not know whether she could manage an entire meal alone with Bernice and her parents.

Catherine was certain she greeted Elliot with an excess of enthusiasm, for he looked at her in a questioning manner. However, she paid him no mind; she was too relieved to have someone else at the table.

Conversation at luncheon concerned the latest on-dits from London, and called for Catherine to do no more than nod and smile occasionally. However, the atmosphere changed once the party moved to the drawing room, and the servants were no longer present.

"Lady Catherine, we were surprised to find a lady of quality here. Bernice had informed us that a Miss Webster was in charge of Jane's estate," said Lord Huntley.

Catherine was so weary from answering the same questions that she sat silent for a moment too long.

Elliot observed her expression and decided to deflect Lord Huntley's interrogation. "Perhaps we should discuss this in private, Uncle. I believe I can explain everything to your satisfaction."

"Why?" asked Bernice, a satisfied smile on her face. "We are all family here; or nearly so," she said, shooting a glance toward Drew and Fitz.

"Would welcome a game of billiards," said Drew.

It was apparent Fitz was not eager to leave the gathering, but he rose and followed Drew from the room, looking back over his shoulder at the tense group gathered in the pleasantly appointed drawing room.

"Lady Catherine is not a stranger," began Elliot, then he went on to tell what he knew of Catherine's relationship with Jane and how she came about caring for the cats.

"I remember seeing you last Season," remarked Lady Huntley. "However, we never met. I was told you were only recently out of mourning."

Catherine looked down at her folded hands resting in her lap, resenting the interrogation. "Yes, for my grandmother. She raised me after my parents died."

"How distressing," murmured Lady Huntley. "I'm sorry."

Catherine met Lady Huntley's gaze and saw that she was sincere. It took the sting from the questioning she had endured. "Thank you, my lady."

Bernice did not at all like what was happening. "Ask her about the cats," she demanded petulantly.

"All the cats are gone but one," said Elliot. "Lady Catherine had conducted an exhaustive search before we arrived, but Drew and I also tried our hand and found nothing."

"Do you suspect someone took them?" asked Lord Huntley.

"Or did away with them," added Bernice, staring at Catherine.

"We have no evidence as to what has happened to them," qualified Elliot, favoring his cousin with a scowl. "As to the rest, at Bernice's insistence, I have been through the estate books and have visited with the solicitor. Nothing is amiss."

"It seems we have made a trip for nothing," said Lord Huntley, also directing a frown of discontent toward his daughter.

"I tell you, she has killed the cats," insisted Bernice.

"Cats come and go. It's their nature," replied her father. "And if they have met some worse fate, then you are richer all the faster. What is your complaint?"

What her father said was true and everyone in the room knew it. "No matter," she said stubbornly. "She should not be allowed to get away with it."

Catherine was tired of being talked about as if she wasn't present. "I have gotten away with nothing, for I've done nothing untoward. I've attempted to convince you of it time and again since you arrived and you wouldn't listen. I will say this once more in front of your parents. I have taken nothing from Lady Wakefield's estate. I have done the best I can to continue as Jane would have wanted. I have also cared for her cats to the best of my ability. I am as distressed about their disappearance as anyone here, but it cannot be laid at my feet, for I had nothing to do with it."

Catherine had had enough of this family squabble. She rose from her seat determined to have some peace that day. "Now, if you will excuse me, I have matters that need my attention."

After she had marched from the room, Elliot spoke. "She has a right to be on her high ropes. We have done nothing but question her honesty, and have given not one word of thanks for the excellent job she has done since Aunt Jane's death."

"I will not thank her for keeping my money," complained Bernice.

"It is not your money yet," said Lady Huntley sharply. "Your aunt left her estate as she saw fit, and it is not up to you to question it. I am ashamed of your behavior. I thought you had grown out of your pettiness, but I see I was mistaken."

"I have done nothing wrong," replied Bernice, tears welling in her eyes.

"You accused Lady Catherine of misusing the estate without any proof," said Lord Huntley.

"But I didn't know who she was," said Bernice, a tear rolling down her cheek.

"It doesn't matter. If she had been Miss Anne Webster, you still had no evidence of wrongdoing," her father replied. "You must change your ways or you will never find a man who will have you."

"If they are all like you and Elliot, then I do not want one," she wailed, running from the room.

"Bernice. Bernice," called Lord Huntley. "Come here and apologize." But it was far too late, for the sound of her footsteps had already faded.

"I'm sorry, Elliot," said Lord Huntley. "You know how she is."

"I'm not offended," replied Elliot with a grin. "I've taken far worse than that from her. However, I wish she would let go of her animosity toward Lady Catherine. It's devilish uncomfortable when they are in the same room."

"She'll come round," judged Lady Huntley. "Just give her time."

"I hope you're right," said Elliot, thinking it would

be a far easier thing to accomplish if they could only
find the missing cats.

Bernice's headlong flight from the drawing room
didn't stop until she was safely behind a closed door
in her room. Dashing away tears, she paced the floor,
attempting to release her anger by stomping on the
floor. For the first time during her stay, she regretted
the thick Aubusson carpet that covered the polished
boards, for her exertions yielded only muffled thuds.

Throwing herself across the bed, she sought a way
to punish the people who had thwarted her plans
and embarrassed her. Suddenly she sat up, a smile
forming on her lips. She had the perfect answer. Rising, she straightened her dress, then moved to the
mirror to tame her disheveled curls. Walking softly
across the ill-used carpet, she closed the door behind
her with only a whisper of sound.

Catherine sat in the enclosed garden watching the
kitten stalk imaginary victims among the flowers. Although she did not allow it to show, she vowed the
confrontation after lunch was the last one she would
tolerate unless it would be a few well-chosen words
as she climbed into her coach.

As she listened to Lord Gage explain all that had
happened, she suddenly wondered why she was sitting there being humiliated beyond all bearing.
There was no stipulation that she must remain at
Wakefield. She could easily take the kitten and oversee the estate through the solicitor and the steward
in writing as well as in person. An occasional visit to
see that all was going well would suffice. Even in her

absence, Catherine could ensure there would be no multitude of gowns purchased at the estate's expense. Nor would there be funds to support house parties. Bernice could live there growing old and gray and lonely while waiting for her inheritance.

Surprisingly, Catherine felt a twinge of regret at leaving. She searched for the reason, and found it occurred when she thought of Lord Gage. It was incomprehensible that she still had feelings for the man after their encounters. It only confirmed her decision that she needed to rejoin Society.

She would return to the house and begin packing immediately. The more quickly her trunks were filled, the sooner she would be able to leave Wakefield and its accompanying complications behind. Picking up the kitten, she made her way back to the house.

"Harrison," she called as the butler crossed the front hall, "have my trunks brought down to my rooms, please."

The man hesitated but a moment before saying, "Right away, my lady."

As he walked down the hall with his usual measured tread, Elliot stepped out of the drawing room.

"Going somewhere, Lady Catherine?" he asked, an extremely unpleasant expression on his face.

"I cannot see that it is of any concern of yours," she replied, passing him and going into the drawing room to fetch the kitten's basket.

Elliot followed, closing the door behind him. "Since my aunt put you in charge of the estate, and I am the principal heir, I think it is my concern. Who will look after my interest if you are gone?"

"Have no worry on that count, my lord. I will uphold my responsibility to your aunt. Your inheritance will not suffer. Besides, Bernice will be here to keep you current on the situation if you choose not to remain."

"It is my aunt's and uncle's arrival that has sent you packing, isn't it?" he asked with sudden understanding.

"Can you blame me? Withstanding Bernice followed by your arrival was more than enough, but I stayed because of Jane. Now I am leaving because of her. I'm certain it wasn't her intention that I be subjected to the treatment I've endured. I was merely to ensure that her pets were treated as they have always been. Her instructions give me leave to travel with or without the cats if I choose. And this afternoon I decided to leave Wakefield."

"Where will you go?" he asked.

"It is none of your concern. I will keep in touch with the solicitor and the steward in case I am needed. I will visit the estate, but I will schedule my trips so there will be no contact with any of your family. That should please Bernice to no end."

An illogical bit of panic came from somewhere and lodged in Elliot's chest, forcing him to admit that he did not want to lose sight of her again. After her first disappearance, he had convinced himself she didn't matter; that she was merely an attractive lady who could just as easily be replaced by another. But that had not been the case. Meeting her again had proven he had not forgotten, and he realized the pain would be far worse this time than the last.

However, before he could put his feelings into words, an uproar arose in the hall. They both rushed to the door. Elliot flung it open, only to meet with a wall of smoke.

"What's going on?" he yelled into the murky haze.

"Harrison, where are you?" He waited a moment then turned to Catherine. "Go out through the French doors. Get away from the house," he commanded before charging into the smoke.

Catherine did not hesitate. She could not run away if the staff of Wakefield was in danger. They had treated her kindly during her stay and she would not desert them. Taking a deep breath, she placed her handkerchief over her nose and mouth and darted into the haze that had swallowed Elliot.

The smoke burned her lungs as she made her way down the hall. At this hour most of the staff would be at the back of the house. Keeping her hand on the wall as a guide, she moved as quickly as possible. As she neared the kitchen she could see the doors were open and a rush of fresh air was beginning to clear the smoke. She had found no one on her way down the hall but could not feel grateful until she knew whether everyone had escaped.

Elliot saw her stumble out of the smoke-filled house and ran to meet her. "Catherine, what the devil are you doing? I told you to leave by the French doors."

"I had to ensure everyone was safe," she said, coughing.

"Did it occur to you to go around the house instead of through it?" he responded angrily.

"How could I help anyone that way?" she argued.

"It would have helped me considerably," he replied, still too incensed that she had put herself in danger to be courteous.

"You are big enough to take care of yourself. I was worried about the kitchen maids."

"What? Not about your guests?"

Catherine felt a little embarrassed that she had given no thought to the others. Looking around, she saw Drew circulating among the servants, giving them a reassuring word or a comforting touch on the arm.

"I understand the others are riding. Probably too far away to even see the smoke. The rest are all safe. Harrison assures me everyone is accounted for," Elliot said, observing the people huddled in groups.

"What happened?" asked Catherine, finally catching her breath.

"I don't know. The smoke is clearing by itself, so the house doesn't seem to be burning. Perhaps it's just a clogged chimney."

"They were cleaned not more than a fortnight ago," said Catherine.

"We will soon find out for sure. Harrison," he called, "it's clear enough. Shall we find out what caused this?"

The butler appeared his usual calm self, despite a slightly rumpled appearance. "I should be happy to accompany you, my lord," he replied, pulling at the bottom of his coat to straighten it.

The two men returned a short time later looking a little worse for wear.

Catherine immediately went to Elliot. "What did you find?" she asked, her golden eyes observing him intently.

"A pillow," he replied. Seeing her look of disbelief, he continued. "You may see it if you like as soon as the smoke clears completely. We have opened additional doors and windows and it should be gone in a very short time."

"How could a pillow have caused all this?"

"Someone had dampened it down and stuffed it in a pail. Then set it on fire and left it under the stairs in the hall. Being wet, it smouldered, producing all the smoke we encountered."

"Why would anyone do that? What did it accomplish?"

"It disrupted the household. Made us think the house was burning down around us. It could have been a prank that got out of hand. If not that, then someone must carry a grudge against one of us at Wakefield."

"Maybe it's me," said Catherine. "Remember the bridge."

"I do, and I vow I'll find the person responsible for both acts," he said, his face a stern reflection of his thoughts.

The smoke had cleared and they were in the hall examining the offending pillow when Catherine exclaimed, "The kitten! I had forgotten all about him." She hurried down the hall to the drawing room and stepped inside, watching for one blue eye and one brown to peer up at her from under a chair or settee.

When he didn't appear, Catherine looked in his basket only to find it empty. She attempted to quell the alarm that began to spread through her, rendering her limbs icy cold. She searched the room as methodically as she could. She was standing abnormally still in the center of the drawing room when Elliot came to find her.

"Catherine? What is wrong?" he asked. When she gave no indication that she had heard him, he moved to her side and took her arm, turning her until she was forced to look at him. She appeared dazed, and he wondered whether she had inhaled too much smoke after all.

"Catherine, speak to me. Tell me what is wrong," he begged.

"He's gone," she answered in a whisper.

"Who?" Elliot asked, thinking they had missed one of the servants after all.

"The kitten. The last kitten is gone."

FIVE

"You've just overlooked him in all the excitement. He must be hiding here somewhere," said Elliot, glancing about the room.

"I've searched everywhere and he isn't here," Catherine replied dully.

"We'll search again," insisted Elliot. He returned to the door and called for Drew and Harrison. When the two men arrived they inspected the room from wall to wall without finding any trace of the kitten.

"Harrison, gather the staff. We must comb the entire house. Do so immediately," ordered Elliot.

"Could have gone out," said Drew, nodding toward the French doors.

"They were closed, both when I left and when I returned," said Catherine. "If only I hadn't panicked and remembered to take him with me when I left."

"It wasn't your fault," consoled Elliot. "You were thinking of the safety of the people in the house. No one can blame you for that."

"I should have remembered," insisted Catherine, her lip trembling.

"Nonsense. Only a saint is perfect, and as lovely as you might be, you are not one yet," replied Elliot, hoping to startle her out of her self-pity.

"I never claimed that," responded Catherine, a glimmer of battle in her eyes. "But I should have remembered the importance of the kitten no matter what the situation."

"Elliot's right," said Drew, returning from the French doors. "Someone must have come in and removed him in all the confusion. Left some fresh dirt on the terrace."

"So I was right all along about the cats being stolen," said Catherine.

"Appears to be the case," confirmed Drew.

Elliot's eyes narrowed. "The smoke was merely a diversion meant to draw us away from the house so the kitten could be taken."

"We must search the grounds and outbuildings. Surely whoever it was couldn't have gotten far," said Catherine, moving swiftly to the French doors and out onto the terrace.

"Could be miles from here by now," said Drew, after she was out of earshot.

Elliot's visage was grim. "Or they needed to have gone no farther than the stream," he added, thinking the kitten would not last long in the fast-flowing water.

"In any event, must help Lady Catherine search. Cannot allow her to think we have no hope," said Drew.

"You're right," agreed Elliot. "But I hold out little promise for finding the animal nearby."

The grounds and outbuildings had been searched. Catherine, Elliot, and Drew stood in the small walled garden where the kitten played each day.

"If he had gotten loose, I should think he would

come here," said Catherine, looking around. "But I don't suppose there is any chance of that."

"Don't give up, Lady Catherine. Still have men searching the park," said Drew.

"But he's so little and so easy to miss. I have failed Jane completely."

"Come now, you are feeling sorry for yourself," chided Elliot. "Aunt Jane would know that you have done all that you could to keep her cats safe."

Catherine searched his face and was almost convinced he meant what he said. "But it hasn't been enough, and now everyone will think I helped do away with them in order to inherit. I pleaded with Jane not to include that bequest, but she would have nothing of it unless it was done."

"Look who has arrived," remarked Drew, as Bernice and Fitz rode into the stable yard.

"Shall we go greet them?" suggested Elliot grimly.

"Do you think . . . ?" said Catherine, unable to finish the question that was in all of their minds.

"I don't know, but there is only one way to find out," replied Elliot.

They reached the stables just as Bernice and Fitz dismounted.

"What have you been doing?" asked Bernice, her nose wrinkling in disgust at their disheveled appearance.

"First, we were forced to find our way out of a smoke-filled house," said Elliot. "I suppose neither of you know anything about that?"

"How could we? We left not long after luncheon," replied Bernice. "There was no smoke at that time. Have you questioned Lady Catherine?"

"I assure you, I did not set a dampened pillow alight," said Catherine.

"We've also been searching for the kitten," said Elliot, never taking his gaze from the two.

"Oh, has it gone missing, too?" asked Bernice, her manner too innocent for Elliot's liking.

"You don't seem surprised," Elliot replied. "Perhaps you knew about it beforehand?"

"What are you saying? Are you accusing me of doing something to that animal? I've been riding with Lord Berkley, as you can well see."

"But where were you riding and what were you doing?" spoke up Catherine.

"I do not need to answer to you," retorted Bernice, with a look intended to cut her to the quick.

However, Catherine was beyond being intimidated by anyone. "You need to answer to everyone. Tell us where you have been. Prove to us you didn't fill the house with smoke and steal the kitten away," she demanded.

"Elliot, are you going to allow her to interrogate me in this manner?"

"If not Lady Catherine, I will be demanding the same information," said Elliot.

"What is going on here?" said Lord Huntley, stepping down from the carriage, which pulled to a stop in the stable yard. He helped Lady Huntley down and they both joined the group.

"Oh, Papa," cried Bernice, dabbing at her eyes. "They are accusing me of the most terrible things. They say I have set fire to the house and done away with the kitten."

"Fire?" said Lady Huntley, looking at Wakefield House in confusion.

"We've done nothing of the sort," objected Elliot. "At least, not yet, for we have no proof. The house was not afire but only filled with smoke. We are merely questioning where you and Fitz have been."

"And will you also question us?" asked his uncle indignantly.

"If it comes to that, yes. Something is going on here, and I don't think Lady Catherine is the guilty party. She's been a convenient scapegoat, but now we need to find the real culprit if we are to save Aunt Jane's kitten."

Drew had been quietly studying Fitz. "Need to talk to your valet," he said, interrupting the discussion.

"What? What are you talking about?" asked Fitz, completely bewildered by the turn of events.

The remainder of the company turned their attention to the two men, seemingly relieved that Drew had chosen to address a common remark to Fitz.

"Either that or turn him off completely. Wouldn't keep a man if he allowed me out of my dressing room looking like that," replied Drew seriously.

"For God's sake, man. Like what?" demanded Fitz.

"All that hair," said Drew pointing to the front of Fitz's jacket. "And white at that. Shows up like a beacon on that shade of blue."

Everyone's gaze followed Drew's to the front of Fitz's jacket. Now that their attention was drawn to it, the white hair was apparent. Nothing had to be said to know that everyone's conclusions were the same.

"Fitz had nothing to do with the kitten," said Bernice, before anyone could voice their suspicions. "He was with me the whole time."

"Bernice, how could you stand up for such a man?" asked her mother. "I have seen nothing else on the entire estate with white hair, unless you include the gatekeeper."

"Not his hair," judged Drew. "Too short."

"Can you explain?" insisted Elliot. He thought of
what Catherine had told him of Fitz's behavior, and
knew if the man could pursue a woman in the way
she claimed, he would not hesitate to do away with
a helpless kitten,. "Well?" he urged.

But before Fitz could answer, Catherine spoke.
"Lady Bernice, your face is smudged. Let me have
your handkerchief and I'll wipe it off." Before
Bernice could react, Catherine jerked aside the linen
square wrapped around the other woman's hand. A
scratch, thin as a kitten's claw, ran across the back of
Bernice's hand. "You were both involved, weren't
you?" she charged.

"It was not his idea," admitted Bernice in a subdued voice. "I asked for his help."

"The two of you could not be well acquainted. Why
would he risk his reputation for such a ruse?" asked
Lord Huntley.

Bernice stared at the ground, unable to meet anyone's gaze. "It was not a ruse, or a prank, or any such
thing. It was entirely serious. No one would listen
when I complained about my inheritance. Both of
you," she said looking at her parents, "told me to be
patient.

"And you, Elliot, were out of the country just when
I needed you most. When you finally arrived, I was
overjoyed. I thought surely I could count on you to
see how ridiculous Aunt Jane's will was by not giving
us our inheritance right away. But you did nothing
but fall under her spell," said Bernice, shooting a
dark glance at Catherine. "You didn't think anyone
noticed, did you? Well, I did. When you didn't order
her to leave, I knew you would be no help at all. What
else could I do but continue?"

"Continue with what?" asked Lady Huntley.

"Oh, Mama, you are such a slowtop. With getting rid of the cats, of course. It was the only way for me to gain my inheritance. It is foolish to tie up an entire estate, which in part should already have been mine, merely so a few cats could live in comfort."

Lady Huntley gasped when she heard the words fall from her daughter's lips. "Bernice, how could you? We give you everything you want."

"This was mine," Bernice insisted sullenly. "I thought my inheritance, along with my dowry, would appeal to an eligible gentleman."

"You would only attract money-hungry men who cared nothing about you," said Elliot.

"Oh, I don't think so," replied Bernice, glancing up at Fitz from beneath her lashes.

"Where do you fit in?" asked Elliot, directing his question to Fitz. But before he could answer Bernice spoke up.

"I met Fitz by accident when I was out riding one day. We began talking, and before I knew it I was telling him all about my troubles. He offered to do anything to help, so I asked him to do away with the cats."

"If the cats were gone, I thought you would rejoin society, and I would have another opportunity to persuade you to marry me," said Fitz to Catherine.

"Marry her?" said Bernice, in a disbelieving voice. "You never mentioned that at all. What of all the sweet speeches you made to me? Did they mean nothing?"

"Sweet speeches? Just what occurred between you and Berkley?" asked Lord Huntley.

But before either Bernice or Fitz could answer, Catherine spoke up.

"Where are they? Where are all the cats? What did you do with them?" she demanded.

"It's all your fault," accused Bernice. "If you hadn't held on to that kitten, it would have all been over and done with before Elliot even arrived. But don't worry. Despite what I told him to do, Fitz found them a home. I suppose they are all still alive," she said with a pout.

"It's true, Catherine," said Fitz, finally speaking for himself. "If the story came to light, I knew you would never forgive me if the cats were harmed. I would lose you."

"You never had her, you fool!" said Elliot, his patience at an end. "Now, tell me about the bridge. Were you behind that also?"

Fitz hesitated before speaking. "It was only meant to frighten her. I was going to be there to rescue her; to gain a bit of gratitude, which I hoped would turn into something more."

"But you were nowhere in sight," said Elliot through gritted teeth, his hands fisting at his sides.

"I had run into Bernice on my way to Wakefield. I couldn't get away without raising suspicion in her mind, so I prayed Catherine would choose that day to forgo her walk."

"Prayed?" said Catherine. "I doubt you know the meaning of the word. If you prayed at all, it was to keep you from being found out."

"Catherine, you must believe that everything I did was directed toward bringing the two of us together."

"I should call you out," said Elliot, holding himself back from attacking Fitz in front of everyone. "You could have killed her."

"I meant nothing of the sort. Catherine, you must believe me," he pleaded, extending his hand toward her.

"Nonsense! You are spouting this foolishness simply to protect me, and it isn't necessary," said Bernice, tugging his hand back before turning to Catherine. "I know you are jealous because Fitz no longer cares for you. He told me how you attempted to trap him into marriage. During the afternoons we spent together, he explained how you were forced to leave London due to the embarrassment when it became public knowledge."

"You spent afternoons with Berkley?" demanded her father.

"Every day the weather allowed," replied Bernice. "He is so understanding of my position. Then, when Elliot invited him to stay at Wakefield, I knew our meeting was meant to be."

Fitz shifted uncomfortably beneath the scrutiny of the company. "Er, it was all quite innocent," he explained.

"I'm certain it was," agreed Lord Huntley. "But as a man of the world you must agree it is most important to avoid the issue of Bernice being compromised."

"Papa, what do you mean? Lord Berkley has been all that is gentlemanly to me."

"Bernice, your father is looking out for your best interests," said Lady Huntley. "You must listen to him."

"Feel free to use Wakefield's chapel, if you wish," offered Elliot, hiding the satisfaction he felt at what was soon to be.

"I think we could arrange a special license in a few day's time," murmured Lord Huntley, looking at his wife for confirmation. She nodded and he turned back to Lord Berkley. "It is settled, then. You and Bernice shall be wed as soon as it can be arranged."

The discontent disappeared from Bernice's face,

replaced by an expression of total happiness as she clung to Lord Berkley's arm. On the other hand, Fitz appeared ready to bolt.

Catherine and Elliot walked toward Wakefield House, leaving the Huntleys and Fitz behind still discussing wedding arrangements. Drew had gone on ahead to make himself presentable once again. A coach was being made ready, and soon the three of them would collect the cats.

"You are glowing with happiness, Catherine," commented Elliot, thinking she was lovelier than ever.

"The cats are safe, and with Lord Huntley as his father-in-law, Fitz will no longer bother me. Also, I'm no longer branded a thief. I am not, am I?" she asked, looking up at him.

"Indeed, you are not," he agreed. "I apologize for what you have been through. It is still difficult to believe that Fitz would behave as he did. However, I am not questioning it," he affirmed quickly.

Catherine's laugh was carefree and floated away on the breeze. "It is over and done with. I have no energy to continue being at daggers drawn. Without the specter of Lord Berkley hanging over me, I can once again go about my life."

"And what will that be? You mentioned continuing your travels before all this occurred. Is that still your plan?" Elliot asked, wondering whether he could convince her to stay with him.

"I haven't given it much thought yet. Now that I am not running from anyone, I am much more free than I was before. First I must make certain that all the cats are safe. Then I will decide what to do."

"Will you leave the cats behind?"

"Jane gave me leave to take them with me if I

chose. She knew I might want to live somewhere else. I will decide what is best for them."

"You like Wakefield, though, don't you?"

"It's quite pleasant," she replied. "Before Bernice arrived, I was happy here. I felt at home."

"You could stay," he suggested. "Oh, not constantly, but in between your travels and the Season in London. You would be able to oversee the estate and the cats. The estate will eventually be mine, and I would not object at all to your remaining in residence. I would be assured that everything was being taken care of in good order."

"Thank you, my lord, but now that you're back I'm certain you'll want to visit on a regular basis. From what I understand, you practically grew up here. I would not want to keep you away."

"Let us put paid to this contretemps. We shall both reside here," he suggested, a satisfied gleam in his eyes.

"My lord! How could you suggest such a thing?"

"I apologize, my lady. It seems I forgot to ask you to marry me. Will you be my wife and live with me here at Wakefield?" he asked. "Or wherever else you may want to reside. I have several other estates and a house in London. If none of them suit you, then we'll find a place that does."

Catherine laughed at his speech. "I'm certain I could be satisfied in a house you already own."

"Are you agreeing to marry me?" he asked, almost afraid to hope.

"I . . . I suppose I am," she answered, stunned at her own swift reaction to his proposal. But she had thought of him for a year now, and had relived all of their encounters. Even through the time he had investigated her, she had respected his drive to see his aunt's wishes were carried out. She could not hold that against him.

Catherine had been silent too long for Elliot; she could be changing her mind. "I was attracted to you since we first met," he confessed. "I have carried your memory in my heart from the time you disappeared until I met you again here at Wakefield. When I saw you, I knew what I felt was not mere infatuation, but a deep and abiding love.

"I'm sorry I was the gentleman with Fitz and stepped aside when he told me you were to be betrothed. If I had not, perhaps none of this would have happened, and you would not have had to suffer as you did. But it's all over now. Both Bernice and Fitz will be out of your life, and the cats will return home soon."

"How do you feel about the cats?" asked Catherine, wondering whether he would resent having them around.

Elliot envisioned a lifetime of cat hair on his jackets and scratches on his boots. "I became accustomed to them when I visited here with Aunt Jane, but I fear I may lose my valet."

"I will ask Betsy to instruct him in removing cat hair from your clothes. Betsy is smart and pretty, and has had her eye on George since he arrived. It would be fitting that the kitten brings them together, too."

"You are a romantic, Lady Catherine," Elliot said, taking her in his arms.

"As are you, my lord," she whispered, as his lips claimed hers.

THE
ROYAL KITTEN

by

Kate Huntington

PROLOGUE

October, 1813
London

Arabella Comstock was two-and-twenty, which was embarrassingly old for a debutante. Only her betrothal of long standing to the eldest son of a viscount saved her from being established quite firmly on the shelf.

Finally, after three years on assignment to the Imperial Court of Russia as a diplomatic aide, the Honorable Cedric Wyndham was coming home. He and Arabella would appear as a couple for the first time that night at a ball in their honor, and Arabella's father would formally announce their engagement to all their friends. In the morning, an official announcement would be sent to the newspapers.

This was to be Arabella's evening of triumph, and so it was with painstaking care that her maid confined Arabella's unruly, flame-colored curls into a classic chignon and crowned it with her late mother's emerald tiara so only a few tendrils escaped to trail artlessly down the nape of her neck. The elegant, gold-embroidered column of her high-waisted white gown displayed her statuesque figure and shapely arms to perfection. More of her mother's emeralds glittered at her earlobes and around her throat.

She wanted to look *perfect* for him.

Since she had come up from the country for the little Season with her father and his excessively silly new wife, Arabella had thoroughly enjoyed regaling her friends with the details of the approaching nuptials. For years Arabella had watched these young ladies, one by one, proceed up the aisle at St. Paul's and into wedded bliss ahead of her.

Now it was *her* turn.

Arabella's wedding would be in April, and she was more than ready. She had put the long years of waiting to good use in embroidering hers and Cedric's initials with exquisite stitches on the fine household linens that filled an expensive cedar-lined trunk in her bedroom. The fittings for her trousseau were almost completed.

She would not be sorry to leave her father's house. Mr. Comstock's happiness in his pretty young wife and infant son was so complete that there did not seem to be any room left in his heart for his grown daughter. Arabella felt like an outsider. He was probably looking forward to getting her off his hands.

Arabella firmly pushed all those old feelings of hurt and bewilderment to the back of her mind. That was behind her now.

Soon she would establish her own home with Cedric. She would have her own children to love. And she would never be an outsider again.

As she took her place in the receiving line between her father and stepmother, Arabella was determined to savor every fragrance, every sight, every sound of this magical evening. Her heightened senses were ravished by the perfume of hundreds of pink and yellow hothouse roses arranged throughout the room. The crystal chandelier above her head blazed with light and reflected the glitter of the ladies' jewels. The sweet, muted notes of a violin and pianoforte floated in from the ballroom and formed a lovely counterpoint to the soft voices and laughter of the guests.

But something was dreadfully wrong.

Cedric and his father, Lord Barlowe, were grimfaced when they entered the reception room shortly after the first guests arrived.

Arabella's welcoming smile died on her lips when, instead of bowing over her hand in greeting, Cedric caught her father's eye and said gruffly, "A word with you, sir!"

He did not even look at her when she put a hand on his arm to stop him from walking right by her.

"Not now, Arabella," he said, shaking her off. He did not meet her eyes.

"Cedric, what is it?" she asked in alarm. He had come to their ball in traveling clothes still splattered with mud, as if he had just arrived in town. He refused to surrender his heavy greatcoat to the footman who tried to take it from him. Obviously, he did not mean to stay.

A lump formed in the pit of Arabella's stomach. What could have happened? While Mr. Comstock ushered the gentlemen to his study, Arabella forced a smile to her lips and replied mechanically to the pleasantries of the arriving guests.

Her mind whirled with speculation.

Had someone died and sent Cedric's entire family into deepest mourning, so that the wedding would have to be postponed? If so, Arabella could not bear it.

She soon found out the truth was worse than anything she could have imagined.

After a servant summoned her and her stepmother to Mr. Comstock's private study, Arabella watched with a nightmarish sense of horror as her father's lips formed the words that Arabella's frozen brain refused, at first, to comprehend. Arabella's stepmother sobbed softly in sympathy at her husband's side.

Then Arabella turned to Cedric, who was looking down at his hands in acute embarrassment.

"You are *jilting* me after I have waited for you for three years?" she cried out in disbelief. "How could you?"

"The betrothal was never officially announced in the newspapers, so technically it would be incorrect to use that excessively crude expression," Cedric said reprovingly in that finicky way of his that Arabella always had found mildly irritating. "Because of your changed circumstances, my father—and I, of course—have agreed that a marriage between us would not be an advantageous one."

"Speak plainly, Cedric! *What* changed circumstances?" she demanded. "I am just the same as I was when you proposed to me three years ago except for being rather older, and whose fault is *that*, pray? *You* were the one who wanted to wait until your diplomatic career was established."

"Miss Comstock," Cedric's father said sternly, "I can appreciate the inconvenience this must cause you and your family—"

"Inconvenience!" Arabella exclaimed. "I should rather think *so!* We have had the invitations engraved! And I have only two more fittings for my wedding gown!"

"Really, Arabella, this passion is quite unbecoming

in a lady of quality," Cedric said, frowning at her exactly as if *she* were the one who was being unreasonable. "Of course I understand that you must be extremely disappointed. But a gentleman in my position can hardly afford to enter into an alliance so disadvantageous to himself."

"You asked—no. You *begged* me to marry you. Right here in this room! On your knees!" Admittedly Cedric had expressed himself with an eloquence that owed more to self-consequence than passion on that occasion, but until now Arabella had believed his affection for her was sincere.

"My dear Arabella," Lord Barlowe said, fixing Mr. Comstock with an accusing stare, "that, if you will recall, was before your father chose to remarry and produce an heir to inherit his lands and the majority of his fortune. I approved the match with the understanding that as Mr. Comstock's sole heiress you would inherit his entire fortune and property, and in return you would, in due time, become a viscountess when my son inherits my title. If you will permit me to say so, the match even as it was originally proposed was more to *your* advantage than to ours. Now it is simply impossible."

"Papa, *do* something!" Arabella cried. She was finding it difficult to breathe.

"I have offered a dowry of sixty thousand pounds!" Arabella's father sputtered.

"Generous, indeed, in the common way of things," Lord Barlowe replied. "But it hardly compares to what your daughter would have brought into the marriage if you had not produced an heir."

"Ah, so it comes down to money," Arabella said, thoroughly disillusioned. "How perfectly *venal* of you, Cedric."

"Arabella, *darling,*" her stepmother said, rashly putting her arm around Arabella's shoulders. "Calm yourself."

"Get away from me, Emily," Arabella snapped. She faced each of her betrayers in turn. They seemed to be frozen in varying expressions of dismay as they stared back at her. Arabella's heart was beating too fast. She thought she might be dying.

But Providence was not so kind.

"You have ruined my life, all of you!" Arabella cried when something inside her seemed to snap and time began to flow normally again. "Do not *any* of you ever come near me again."

Then she rushed out of the room and past the blurred faces of the astonished guests to throw herself across her sprig muslin counterpane and wish she were dead.

ONE

April, 1814
London

Today should have been her wedding day, Arabella realized with a start. She was shocked that it had not occurred to her until now. Six months ago Cedric Wyndham had ruined her life by jilting her. She should be depressed and miserable.

Instead, she was just hot and a little bored.

"I only want to see her, then we will go back to the hotel," Arabella's godmother promised as she dragged Arabella willy-nilly into the press of people wanting a look at Her Imperial Highness Catherine, Grand Duchess of Oldenburg. For weeks the arrival of Tsar Alexander I's sister had been the food of gossips, and wherever the lady went, hordes of curious Londoners were sure to follow.

Arabella blinked against the strong sunlight and permitted her companion to lead the way. Her godmother, a diminutive lady with a friendly manner, had a talent for insinuating herself between larger persons in crowds, and so they soon found themselves in front of the curiosity seekers who lined the path on which the grand duchess's carriage would pass. Arabella herself had no particular desire to see the foreign noblewoman, but she could not deny her godmother the pleasure of satisfying her curiosity after all she had done for her.

She still felt a bit strange dressed for the City in her pretty new pomona green walking costume and stylish hat after spending the past six months alone except for servants at her father's country house. In the country Arabella visited no one, nor did she have many callers. She still rather tended to avoid public gatherings, certain that they were alive with gossips who alternately pitied and despised her. But after a few weeks in London, it became clear that her disgrace had been replaced long ago by new scandals.

She was healing, she realized. She no longer tended to weep for no reason. Her healthy country appetite had returned. And if she was not a woman of the world of three-and-twenty who knew all men were liars and scoundrels, her head might be quite turned by all the compliments that had been paid to her by attentive gentlemen at a ball the previous evening. She wondered how many of them knew about her dowry of sixty thousand pounds.

The London Season and the victory celebrations planned for the summer of 1814 promised to be the most splendid in all of history because the long war with Napoleon was over at last. There would never be a social season like it again, and Arabella would have missed it all if her wealthy widowed godmother and maternal aunt, Mrs. Augusta Peabody, had not dragged her out of her self-imposed exile and positively bullied her into being her guest at Grillon's Hotel for the Season.

"For darling," Mrs. Peabody had declared, "much as I hate to mention it, at three-and-twenty you are not getting any younger. If that ninnyhammer of a stepmother of yours will not exert herself to find you a husband, *I* will!"

Well, the last thing Arabella wanted or needed was a husband, particularly one of her stepmother's choosing! But she was delighted to be reintroduced to all her favorite London shops, and Mrs. Peabody was an entertaining companion except for this irrational curiosity about Grand Duchess Catherine. Mrs. Peabody apparently was not alone in her obsession. Arabella had been vexed to find that when the grand duchess stirred out of doors, shopkeepers were wont to close their establishments and join the throng following her around on her sightseeing excursions.

For herself, Arabella did not see anything so remarkable in the lady.

The Grand Duchess Catherine was six-and-twenty and a widow unabashedly on the hunt for a rich new husband, preferably one with a lofty title. She was not particularly attractive—in fact, if she were not a grand duchess, unkind persons might be tempted to call her ugly—and she was decidedly overdressed for such a hot day.

But Arabella's interest in the grand duchess's party revived dramatically when she saw the devastatingly handsome man riding beside the great lady's carriage on a sleek black horse. The man had dark hair a bit longer than was strictly the mode, which gave him a rakish air. His dark brown eyes lit with amusement at something the grand duchess said. Arabella assumed he must be an officer of some importance because of the gold epaulettes on his dark green uniform coat and the number of decorations pinned to the red sash across his broad chest.

When the grand duchess abruptly ordered her car-

riage stopped, Arabella was startled to find the handsome Russian officer right in front of her, looking
her over appreciatively with those wicked eyes of his.
Arabella averted her face from his gaze, as would any
young lady of good breeding; but this, fortunately,
did not prevent her from watching him out of the
corner of her eye. She had to remind herself, quite
firmly, that she was soured on men.

The grand duchess's retinue stretched as far as the
eye could see and resembled a royal progress more
closely than a casual spring outing. The tsar's sister
apparently spoke only French, and she seemed to be
gesturing angrily at some object on the seat beside
her. Despite Arabella's disinterest in gawking at the
Russian noblewoman, her curiosity was piqued.

Then she saw him—the man who had ruined her
life. There was no mistaking his slender, elegant figure and that full head of wavy, heavily pomaded
blond hair. Arabella would have noticed him at once
if she had not been distracted by the handsome Russian officer.

Cedric Wyndham stared at Arabella in dismay for
a moment and then quickly guided his horse to the
opposite side of the grand duchess's carriage, presumably in the vain hope that Arabella would not see
him. The coward! He was probably afraid she would
cause a scene.

If so, Arabella thought in disdain, he flattered himself.

She was about to suggest to her godmother that
they leave when she saw a tiny, bedraggled-looking
kitten leap up on the back of the carriage from the
seat beside the grand duchess. It raised its back and
hissed at its mistress when she reached for it. Appar-

ently *this* was the cause of the grand duchess's angry gestures.

Arabella had never seen anything like the tiny animal. It was covered all over in downy silver-blue fur. It had a delicate little face and big, brilliant green eyes. Arabella thought it was perfectly adorable.

To Arabella's indignation, the grand duchess poked at the kitten with a mean look on her face and got her hand scratched for her pains.

Good, thought Arabella in satisfaction. She richly deserved it. Then the grand duchess drew her lips back in a snarl and brought her arm back as if to strike the helpless creature.

"She is going to kill it!" Arabella exclaimed in horror. "It is just a baby!"

"Arabella!" Mrs. Peabody cried out in alarm when the outraged Arabella darted around the handsome Russian officer's horse to rescue the kitten. Fortunately, the kitten had a strong sense of preservation. It hissed again at the grand duchess and leapt off the rim of the carriage right into Arabella's waiting arms.

"There, there," Arabella said soothingly as she petted the bristling little feline and cuddled it against her breast. It was so soft and warm. The duchess stared at her in outrage. The Russian officer laughed. He had a deep, rich voice, exactly as Arabella would have expected.

"Who *is* this girl!" the grand duchess demanded in French.

The Russian officer smiled at Arabella and answered the grand duchess in the same language. His teeth were blindingly white in his tanned face, and there were attractive little creases at the exotically upturned corners of his eyes that suggested that he laughed deeply and often. "I shall ask her, Catherine Pavlovna," he replied, "if you will permit."

The grand duchess favored him with an impatient little gesture.

"Mademoiselle, what is your name, please?" he asked Arabella in his lightly accented but otherwise excellent English. He was still on horseback, so she had to crane her neck up to look at him.

"Arabella. Arabella Comstock," she replied. "And you will give me leave to tell you," she continued, facing the grand duchess defiantly, "that *you* are not a fit person to care for a kitten."

"What is she saying?" the grand duchess asked disdainfully in French. "Tell her to give me my cat at once!"

"Tell *her,*" said Arabella, whose rather inferior schoolgirl French unexpectedly rose to the challenge before the officer could translate, "that she will get this cat over my dead body!"

When the officer translated, the grand duchess gave a scream of outrage and, leaning precariously from the carriage, made a grab for the kitten. Her lips were drawn back in a snarl and her fingers flexed as if she longed to wring the poor creature's neck.

Arabella gave a faint shriek and ran into the stunned crowd with the kitten.

"Bring me the head of that peasant!" the grand duchess commanded. She tended to get a bit overwrought when her will was crossed. "Why do you hesitate, Konstantin Mikhailovich? Send your men after her!"

"We dare not, your highness, for fear of injuring these people," replied Prince Konstantin Mikhailovich Obolensky, the grand duchess's cousin several times removed and the officer responsible for the grand duchess's safety while she was in London. "The crowd is too large."

"What does it matter if some insignificant nobodies get a few bruises?" she said, giving a sigh of pure exasperation. "Well! You have lost her now. Make inquiries. Find this girl. And bring me my cat!"

"Your highness," said that unpleasant Englishman who had been with them since the grand duchess came to London at the end of March, much to Konstantin's annoyance. This Cedric Wyndham was attached to the British diplomatic service, which told Konstantin that his host country's affairs were in a deplorable state. Mr. Wyndham dressed well and spoke like an educated man, but Konstantin did not like the insinuating tone he adopted with the grand duchess.

"I know the girl, your highness," the man said in his competent French, putting himself forward.

"Well, then, Mr. Wyndham," the grand duchess said through gritted teeth, "go after her and bring me my cat. Konstantin! Go with him and take some of the soldiers, so she will know that stealing what is mine is no small matter."

"I will not fail you, your imperial highness," Cedric said ingratiatingly.

Konstantin gave him a bland look as he remembered the fire in the lovely red-haired girl's eyes. He thought the English *jeune fille* would be more than a match for this mincing English mushroom, and he looked forward to the confrontation.

TWO

Mrs. Peabody found her errant goddaughter sitting on her bed at Grillon's Hotel, watching the kitten lap up a bowl full of water.

"My girl, what do you think you are going to do with that kitten?" Mrs. Peabody demanded, putting her hands on her hips.

"Give it some fish to eat when Mary comes back from the market," Arabella said serenely.

"*If* the whole of the Russian army does not beat down our door looking for you first! What were you *thinking* of?"

"The kitten, of course," Arabella said, looking down at the little feline lovingly. "You can tell the dreadful woman does not care for the poor thing. This is its second bowl of water, it was so thirsty. I wonder what its name is."

"Darling, you were recognized." Mrs. Peabody could not bring herself to mention the name of the faithless individual who had jilted her cherished goddaughter. "It is only a matter of time before they find us."

"I will not give the kitten up," Arabella said.

The expression on Arabella's face when she

looked at the kitten told the whole tale. Her darling girl was about to be hurt again.

Arabella could not keep the kitten. That cause was hopeless. But Mrs. Peabody was encouraged to hope the ice that had imprisoned Arabella's heart these past months was beginning to thaw.

Perhaps now was the time to introduce the sensitive subject that had remained unspoken between them since Mrs. Peabody brought Arabella to London.

Mrs. Peabody took a deep breath.

"Arabella," she said carefully as she sat beside her goddaughter on the bed and put an arm around her shoulders, "you are a sweet, compassionate girl. It does not surprise me in the least that you would defy a grand duchess and what appears to be half the Russian army to rescue a mistreated kitten. Is it not time to extend some of this generosity to the person who loves you most in the world?"

Arabella stiffened.

"You are referring to my father, I suppose," she said with a brittle laugh that made Mrs. Peabody's heart break. "You could not be more mistaken. He has no use for a grown daughter left over from his former marriage now that he has a young wife and son to complete his happiness, I assure you."

"My poor darling," she said, sensing the hurt behind Arabella's harsh words. "You are wrong, Arabella. He must miss you terribly."

"Hardly!" Arabella scoffed. "Do you know what he said to me on that horrible night? He said I had upset Emily dreadfully with my unladylike and undignified behavior, and I had embarrassed them both in front of their guests. *I* was subjected to the ultimate humiliation. *My* life was ruined. But he was only thinking about himself and *her.* He did not object when I said

I wished to go into the country alone. I have received no word from him or Emily since except for an invitation to visit them in town at Christmas, which I could not accept."

"Of course not. It was too soon. They understood that and thought it best to give you time to deal with your disappointment."

"Disappointment," Arabella mused. "Such a pale word to describe my feelings of betrayal. Being jilted was only part of it. After my father met Emily, I may as well have dropped off the face of the earth for all he cared. Please do not speak of his missing me."

A discreet knock sounded at the door, and Mrs. Peabody's maidservant appeared in the doorway with Arabella's maid in tow. At a signal from her mistress, Mrs. Peabody's maidservant returned to her duties in the other room.

"Mary!" Arabella exclaimed, taking in her maid's disheveled appearance and flushed face. "What happened to you? You were gone so long, I was afraid you had gotten lost."

"Miss Arabella! There is a powerful commotion in the street," the girl said, gasping. "It is full of soldiers and horses, and—"

"Yes, yes, Mary," Arabella said calmly. "Sit down and catch your breath. Then I shall need you to go to the back garden and fill a small box with loose soil. Perhaps one of the inn servants can provide you with one."

"Yes, Miss Arabella," the servant said, sending Mrs. Peabody a troubled look. Mrs. Peabody gave the maid a sympathetic shrug of her shoulders and an encouraging little nod.

Arabella took the packet of fish from her servant's basket, opened the paper tightly wrapped around it, and bent down to feed the fish to the kitten. "There you go, my pretty," she crooned. "My goodness! I wonder when that dreadful woman fed the poor little thing last!" The kitten had pounced upon the fish with such energy that Arabella dropped it on the floor for fear of having her fingers bitten. Then, as if determined to keep the fish from slithering away, the kitten trapped it with its paws and tucked into it as if it was starving, purring loudly all the while. The fish was gone in a twinkling, leaving the skeleton and head intact.

"I believe all young creatures eat as if they are ravenous," Mrs. Peabody said, fastidiously averting her eyes from the kitten's demonstration of its more savage nature. "One cannot assume it has been starved."

"That woman," Arabella said with real loathing in her voice, "is capable of anything."

Mrs. Peabody and the maid exchanged apprehensive glances when a loud knocking was heard at the door. Arabella petted the kitten and remained crouched down beside it as it groomed itself. The maid gingerly picked up the fish skeleton and wrapped it in the discarded fishmonger's paper, presumably so she could dispose of it later.

"I am Cedric Wyndham, here on the official business of Her Imperial Highness, Grand Duchess Catherine of Oldenburg, and the British Government," an all-too-familiar voice announced with its customary self-importance from the other room when Mrs. Peabody's maidservant opened the door. "Summon Miss Comstock *at once!*"

Arabella rolled her eyes and picked up the kitten.

"What are you going to do?" Mrs. Peabody asked, looking flustered.

"Tell Cedric what I think of the company he has been keeping of late, of course," Arabella said sweetly as she carried the kitten into the main room of the suite. Mrs. Peabody and Mary followed.

"Miss Comstock," Cedric said severely as soon as he saw her, "you have offended the Grand Duchess Catherine of Oldenburg, sister of Alexander I, Emperor of All the Russias."

"And a pleasant good morning to you as well, Cedric," Arabella said dryly. "If you have come to tell me I must give this poor creature back to that harpy, you have wasted your time."

The dark-haired Russian officer entered the suite behind Cedric and gave a smile of reassurance to the startled maidservant who had been about to close the door. Two Russian soldiers entered the room behind him and took up posts on either side of the doorway. Mrs. Peabody's maidservant went to stand protectively beside her mistress.

Well, Arabella fumed, if Cedric thought he could intimidate her with this show of power, he was wrong. How like Cedric to bring three armed men to confront four defenseless women and a half-starved kitten! She stiffened her spine and gave him a look she hoped would convey glacial indifference.

"Arabella! This could cause a very unpleasant incident," Cedric said, gesturing toward the kitten in her arms. "My career with the diplomatic service might be at stake. Surely you are not still so angry with me for breaking off our, ah, arrangement that you would take this sort of petty revenge."

"The word you are groping for, Cedric, is 'betrothal.' And my rescue of this poor, abused kitten from that *dreadful* woman's abuse has nothing to do with it."

The Russian officer, who until then had been enjoying the scene with all the relish of a ticket holder at an amusing play, appeared to be startled by her words and shot Arabella a searching look.

"Now, now, Arabella," Cedric said in a patronizing tone that made Arabella itch to slap him. "Just give me the kitten and—"

"Never!" Arabella cried, turning with the kitten in her arms so her back was to him.

"Unreasonable girl!" Cedric shouted. "You leave me no choice but to use force."

At that he spun Arabella around and roughly tore the kitten from her arms.

"Be careful," Arabella cried. "You will hurt him!"

"Be still, you troublesome little beast," Cedric snarled under his breath as the frightened kitten cried piteously. Cedric screamed when the kitten scratched him on the nose and vaulted out of his arms to land on Arabella's bosom.

"Why, you *nasty* little creature!" Cedric cried, rubbing his nose.

The Russian officer, who had been poised on the balls of his feet as if he would intervene, burst into rich, delighted laughter when the kitten scratched Cedric. Cedric gave him a hard stare.

"What are you standing there for?" he demanded of the Russian officer, apparently unwilling to tangle with the ferocious animal again. "Take the damned kitten away from her."

"Not *I*, my friend," he replied, his dark eyes alight with humor. "I would only earn myself a hard slap if I presumed to put my hands on the excellent portion of feminine anatomy the kitten, with impeccable taste, if mademoiselle will permit me to say so, has chosen as his refuge."

Arabella felt her face grow warm under the officer's frankly admiring regard. Once again she had to remind herself, very sternly, that she was done with men.

"Very well, then," Cedric said with an ugly look on his face. "Remember, Arabella, that you *forced* me to use violence."

When he bore down upon Arabella, she quickly thrust the kitten into her maid's arms and shoved the woman into the other room. She shut the door behind her just as an enraged Cedric reached her.

"Lock the door, Mary!" she shouted. Mrs. Peabody and her maidservant screamed. In a fit of temper, Cedric gave Arabella a shove that knocked her to the floor. She sat up, braced against one arm.

"Tell your maid to come out here at once and give me the kitten," he said menacingly as he knotted his fists and crouched over her, "or you will be sorry."

Arabella closed her eyes and tensed against the expected blow. She threw her free hand in front of her face to protect it.

Then she heard Cedric give a yelp of mingled pain and surprise. She opened her eyes to see that the Russian officer had her erstwhile fiancé by the collar and was shaking him like a rat.

"You have forgotten that you are a gentleman, Mr. Wyndham," the Russian said savagely. "You will do well to get out of my sight before I forget that *I* am one and beat you to a bloody pulp in front of these ladies!"

"See here," Cedric said, cowering. "You cannot talk that way to me."

"*Go!*" the Russian said, abruptly releasing Cedric and signaling Mrs. Peabody's maidservant to open the door.

Cedric rubbed his injured nose again, gave the Russian a black glare, and stalked to the doorway.

"The grand duchess will hear about this," was Cedric's parting shot. He made a hasty exit when the Russian took a threatening step toward him. The Russian then gestured toward the two soldiers who had accompanied them. The men saluted respectfully and followed Cedric.

The officer then turned to Arabella, who was still on the floor, staring at him with her mouth open.

"Here, *petite*," the Russian said as he assisted her to her feet with a solicitousness that suggested she might be made of spun glass. "Did he hurt you?"

His hair is so black it has blue lights in it, Arabella thought, momentarily dazzled.

"No," she said when she had found her voice. "Who are you?"

He gave her another of those smiles.

"Prince Konstantin Mikhailovich Obolensky, at your service, *mademoiselle*," he said, bowing over her hand. "You are Miss Arabella Comstock, I know, and this lady?" he added with a smile at Arabella's godmother.

"My aunt, Mrs. Augusta Peabody." The Russian bowed over the elder lady's hand with courtly grace.

"I still will not give you the kitten," Arabella said, just so there would be no misunderstanding.

"When I left the grand duchess, she was demanding your head on a pike," he said dryly. "Although I persuaded her that the English authorities might have strong objections to this expedient solution to her complaint, you would be wise to give the kitten to me now, *mademoiselle*."

"She will have it over my dead body!"

"I believe you have made that statement before,

and I would warn you not to say it in front of the grand duchess again. She would be only too delighted to arrange precisely what you suggest."

"Are you threatening me?" Arabella said with narrowed eyes.

"Not at all," he said, raising one eyebrow. "Merely offering you advice that I think you would be wise to consider."

"I do not understand," Arabella said with a sigh. "She obviously does not care for it. Why does she want it back so badly? It is only a kitten."

"On the contrary, this is a very valuable animal," the prince said. "A rare Archangel cat. It is named for Arkhangelsk, a city in Russia located on the White Sea that is said to be where the cat first roamed wild in olden times. The breed has been a favorite with the Russian royal family for centuries. Before that, it was hunted—" He broke off with a look of dismay, obviously realizing this admission was not a fortuitous one.

"Hunted!" Arabella cried out in horror. "They *ate* them?"

"Er, no. They, ah, wanted the pelts. In the adult, the fur is even more luxurious, with a texture as fine as sable."

Arabella ran to the door through which she had thrust her maid and the kitten. She blocked it with her body, prepared to fight to her last breath if necessary.

"That is *barbaric!*" she said in a voice of loathing. "Prince or no prince, I think you had better leave now."

He lifted one dark eyebrow.

"Fortunately for you," the prince said as he walked to Arabella and loomed over her, "it is against my principles to use force against a lady." His dark eyes promised all sorts of wicked things, and suddenly Arabella found it hard to breathe. "Otherwise, it would take more than a few scratches from a frightened kitten or a passionately angry woman to stop me from taking what I want," he added softly.

He stopped to let his words sink in. Arabella was glad she had the door at her back because her knees had gone all wobbly.

"Good day, mademoiselle and madame," the prince said, all courtliness and charm again as he stepped away from Arabella and went to the door. He smiled at Mrs. Peabody's maidservant when she opened it for him. "I regret to say you have not heard the last of this."

He bowed to both ladies, smiled again at the maidservant, and turned to leave.

"His name is Raphael," he said to Arabella over his shoulder.

"Raphael," Arabella repeated blankly.

"After the archangel."

Then he was gone.

Arabella opened the door to the bedchamber so Mary could come out. Arabella sank into a chair and accepted the kitten from the maid's arms. The kitten permitted itself to be petted for an instant, then it sprang to the floor to explore the room with bright, curious eyes and judicious sniffs.

"What a *man*," Mrs. Peabody said, sinking into a chair and fanning herself with her handkerchief.

She could not have summed up Arabella's sentiments more precisely.

* * *

What a woman, mused Konstantin as he rode back to Piccadilly.

The memory of the way the girl's indignant eyes had flashed green fire at that imbecile Cedric Wyndham made Konstantin want to go back to Grillon's at once and annoy her again.

Konstantin had been startled to learn that this was the fiancée the despicable Mr. Wyndham had discarded. In his cups he had boasted of his ambition to marry the grand duchess and promote friendly relations between their countries.

Cedric Wyndham apparently thought he was such a splendid fellow that the Russian Royal Family would welcome him with open arms. He had talked of the unpleasant necessity of breaking the heart of his fiancée, a young English lady, so he would be available for the honor he expected the grand duchess to bestow upon him. According to Wyndham, the disappointed girl had retired to her father's country house, presumably to shrivel into a pathetic spinster from unrequited love.

At the time, Konstantin more than half believed Cedric invented this fiancée to impress his drinking companions with what a devil he was among the ladies. Konstantin had several times caught Cedric out in minor falsehoods of the type that did little outward harm but pointed to a serious defect in character.

Konstantin found it difficult to believe a young lady as beautiful and obviously intelligent as Miss Comstock had lost even a single night's sleep over an imbecile like Mr. Wyndham. He was handsome, Konstantin conceded, in that vapid, blond style the English seemed to admire so much. But Konstantin thought he was too much in love with himself to have any passion to spare for a bride. In addition, he was a coward. He wore it upon his person like a stench that no amount of expensive cologne could hide.

Fortunately for the Romanov Dynasty, it was unlikely that Catherine Pavlovna would demean herself to marry a mere British commoner.

Catherine Pavlovna had quite as high an opinion of her own consequence as Cedric had of his. Irritating as the grand duchess often was, not even she deserved Cedric Wyndham! Despite her faults, Konstantin generally was quite fond of his cousin, for she could be amusing and generous when it suited her.

Unfortunately for the lovely Arabella, Catherine Pavlovna also was a stubborn and possessive woman. She would not give up her kitten easily, even though she had more than once complained that traveling with a young animal was a dreadful nuisance. She had brought the creature to London on impulse, merely because some flatterer had complimented her on the delightful picture she made one day in a charming blue ensemble with the kitten on her lap. Even so, Konstantin did Catherine Pavlovna the justice to believe she probably would not have lost her temper with the kitten if it had not, er, exercised its animal nature on the cushions of the grand duchess's carriage and soiled the skirt of one of her favorite gowns.

Catherine Pavlovna could not endure opposition, and she was capable of crushing anyone who got in her way. The pretty English girl would find her a formidable enemy if she insisted upon having her kitten back. On the other hand, Konstantin reflected, the volatile grand duchess was equally capable of forgetting all about the kitten if a fresh grievance presented itself.

Konstantin sincerely hoped the latter case would prevail, even though, unhappily, it would leave him without an excuse to see the enchanting Arabella Comstock again. The girl would make a much more compassionate mistress for Raphael than the grand duchess.

However, Konstantin's duty was to Catherine Pavlovna by order of the tsar himself, so he reluctantly thrust the image of shining red curls and defiant green eyes out of his mind.

THREE

"Your highness, I implore your forgiveness," Cedric said to the furious grand duchess. "The girl has clearly gone quite mad from unrequited passion for me."

Cedric Wyndham appeared determined to put himself at the center of this particular drama.

"Then she shall realize her mistake in defying *me*," said the grand duchess through gritted teeth. Catherine Pavlovna took second place to *no one* when it came to histrionics, thought Konstantin appreciatively.

"Gentlemen," she said imperiously, turning to the long-suffering Russian ambassador, Count Lieven, and Sir Gregory Banbridge, a senior British Embassy official who had presented himself at the grand duchess's bidding. Konstantin knew that the presence of his superior was a great source of chagrin for Mr. Wyndham, who had been bristling ever since he saw the man. "You will go at once and arrange for this Miss Comstock"—she wrinkled her nose in disdain—"to be arrested and thrown into the darkest and most disagreeable of London's prisons! You will then search her house and find my kitten!"

"Your highness," the Russian ambassador said. A

film of perspiration was beginning to form on the
usually unflappable gentleman's brow. "Surely you
would not wish to precipitate an embarrassing international incident over a kitten."

Count Lieven was being tactful. What he really
meant, Konstantin knew, was *another* embarrassing international incident. Upon her first official visit to
Carlton House to dine with the Prince Regent, the
grand duchess had shocked the dignitaries assem-
bled to do her honor by insisting that the finest mu-
sicians in England engaged for the evening's
entertainment be sent away.

Music made her vomit, she loudly insisted to her
bewildered host. The gossips fortunate enough to witness the incident had dined out on the story for
weeks. The Prince Regent, who prided himself upon
the elegance of his entertainments, was not amused.

The Prince Regent was further insulted to find that
the grand duchess's idea of pleasant dinner conversation was to berate him before his other guests for
his harsh treatment of his headstrong daughter, Princess Charlotte, whom he had ordered confined to
her apartments for defying him in the matter of her
arranged marriage to Prince William of Orange. It
was common knowledge that the grand duchess had
visited the disgraced princess and encouraged her in
her rebellion.

There was nothing Catherine Pavlovna enjoyed
more than a piece of high meddling.

"I am certain," Sir Gregory said, giving Cedric a
look that made him squirm, "that we will be able to
resolve this matter without employing such drastic
measures."

"Do so, then," the grand duchess said crisply. "And
do it quickly, before I lose my patience with the in-

competence of the British Government to deal with what is really a very simple matter. My pet was stolen and you know where the thief lives. Get it back!"

Then she swept magnificently out of the room with her ladies following.

As soon as she was gone from sight, the ingratiating smile melted like wax from Sir Gregory's face.

"Mr. Wyndham," he snapped in English, obviously assuming that none of the grand duchess's staff members spoke their host country's tongue, "need I tell you that it is of the utmost importance for you to get that wretched animal back for her imperial highness *immediately?*"

"No, Sir Gregory," Cedric said humbly.

"Well, see to it, then! If the grand duchess has cause to make an official complaint to his majesty's government about this matter, I will be called into account for it. If that happens, you will find yourself posted to the most unpleasant, disease-infested backwater that has the honor to enjoy diplomatic relations with the British Government. Do I make myself clear?"

"Perfectly, Sir Gregory," Cedric declared. "I stand ready to make the ultimate sacrifice for my country—I shall offer to marry the girl. I am afraid that nothing less will appease her."

"If that is what it will take, then go at once to inform the young lady of her good fortune," Sir Gregory said dryly. "You can always break it off again once the kitten has been restored to the grand duchess." He paused to accept his hat and cane from a footman. "Good day to you, sir. I expect to hear before nightfall that this tedious matter has been resolved."

"Yes, Sir Gregory," Cedric said when that gentleman left the room. He gave Konstantin a look of disfavor.

"I am pleased to see you find the matter so humorous, Prince Obolensky," he snapped.

Konstantin did not bother to wipe the grin off his face.

"Do permit me to serve as your escort to Miss Comstock's hotel," Konstantin said. "I would not miss this for the world."

Cedric gave an affronted sniff.

"I suppose you were fooled by Arabella's behavior toward me this morning," Cedric said in a vastly superior tone. "Obviously you know nothing of women."

Konstantin lifted one dark brow.

"Indeed?" he said encouragingly. "Then I would consider it a great favor if you will take me along so that I may witness the hand of a master at work."

Cedric was about to annihilate Konstantin for this effrontery when the grand duchess unexpectedly came back into the room.

"What is this?" she demanded in French. "What are you saying?"

The grand duchess disliked it excessively when people had private conversations in languages she did not understand. She was convinced, in the manner of all self-centered persons, that the conversation had to be about *her.*

"Monsieur Wyndham is about to lay his heart at the feet of Mademoiselle Comstock, Catherine Pavlovna," Konstantin said smoothly in French. "He is persuaded the young lady will refuse to relinquish the kitten until he makes good his promise to marry her."

"You would offer to marry that girl for my sake?" the grand duchess said, obviously intrigued.

"I would do anything to please you," Cedric said fervently, daring to kiss her hand.

"Excellent," she said. "Go at once and get my kitten!"

Cedric bowed, frowning when Konstantin followed him to the door.

"I do not require your escort, sir!" he said just under his breath in English.

"What is this?" the grand duchess demanded in French. "What are you saying?"

"I was just offering to provide an escort, but Monsieur Wyndham has said he does not wish it," Konstantin replied.

"You will go with him, Konstantin Mikhailovich," the grand duchess said, raising one brow. "And you will report to me afterward."

"Yes, Catherine Pavlovna," he said, imperfectly hiding his satisfaction.

Arabella sat on the sofa, watching the kitten peek in and out of her best straw bonnet and feeding it little tidbits of the cheese that the management of the hotel had sent to the room of so valued a guest as Mrs. Peabody.

"Child, why are you not dressed?" Mrs. Peabody exclaimed, throwing up her hands at the spectacle of her goddaughter sprawled in an extremely unladylike posture with the skirt of her green walking costume crushed beyond repair, her jacket missing, and several buttons of her dainty blouse of lace-trimmed white lawn undone to reveal her exquisite collarbones and rather too much of her firm young bosom as a concession to the warmth of the day. "We were to go calling this afternoon!"

"Must we?" Arabella asked with a look of dismay. She gave a startled gurgle of laughter when the kitten suddenly abandoned the hat and sprang up on the sofa to land on Arabella's stomach. Arabella petted the kitten's head with a gentle finger as it batted at the lace on her blouse.

"I suppose not," Mrs. Peabody said, pleased to see that the sad look that had shadowed her cherished goddaughter in the days after Cedric Wyndham had repudiated their engagement was gone from her goddaughter's eyes. The girl was healing at last, praise heaven.

Of course, Mrs. Peabody wished an eligible suitor had put that soft, glowing look in Arabella's eyes instead of a kitten, but one could not have everything.

At that moment, there came an imperious rapping at the door, and Mrs. Peabody's maid opened it to reveal Cedric Wyndham, Prince Obolensky, and the same two members of the grand duchess's personal guard who had called with those gentlemen earlier in the day.

Mrs. Peabody stiffened. She had heard about the sort of rough justice employed by foreigners, and she feared for her goddaughter's safety.

Instead of threatening the girl, though, Cedric dropped gracefully to one knee before Arabella, who hastily sat up on the sofa and put one hand up as if to fend him off.

To Konstantin's everlasting regret, the lovely Miss Comstock hastily buttoned the top of her blouse with the other hand to hide a delectable glimpse of creamy young flesh from the gentlemen's view.

"See here!" the girl said sharply when Cedric took

the hand lifted against him in both of his. She pulled it away and put both her hands behind her back. "What do you think you are about, Mr. Wyndham?"

"I am here to lay my heart at your feet," he said in the congratulatory tones of someone delivering tidings of exceedingly good fortune.

"Are you *mad?*" Arabella demanded. "What nonsense is this?"

"I will marry you if you will give the kitten to me."

"Why you arrogant, conceited—" She stopped to draw breath when adequate words failed her. "Do you think I want to marry you after what you have done?"

Cedric looked at her in blank astonishment. It was plain that he did.

"Get out!" she cried, jumping up from the sofa. "Get out of my sight!"

She gave him a shove that made him fall on his backside with a thump.

"I would not marry you if you were the last man on earth!" she declared, drawing her foot back as if she would kick him. A cry of distress from Mrs. Peabody made her think better of it, though; instead, she carried the kitten to the window that overlooked the street and turned her back on him.

It was obvious from the expression on Cedric's face that he could not believe he had been rejected.

"But Arabella, you have *always* wanted to marry me," he persisted as he rose to his feet. He glared at the prince when he extended a hand to assist him.

"That was a long time ago, Cedric," she said without turning around. "I think you had better go now."

"You spent six miserable months in the country, shunning all company," he protested. "Why would you do so if you did not still love me?"

"Because I was utterly humiliated, you *idiot,*" she said, turning around at that. "I had been planning the wedding for three years. All of my bride clothes had been ordered. All of my friends knew we were to marry in April, and that I had been jilted. How could I face them and their pitying looks?"

"Ah, I understand," he said with an odiously superior smirk. "You wish to punish me a little for hurting you."

Unbelievably, he was unwise enough to cross the room with an impetuous stride and take Arabella in his arms. Apparently he thought he could resolve her maidenly qualms with a manly kiss. The kitten jumped out of her arms as soon as Cedric approached.

"Stop that!" Arabella snapped as she turned her face away to avoid Cedric's questing, slightly moist lips. Her nose was wrinkled in distaste.

"Mr. Wyndham!" Mrs. Peabody said, wringing her hands in distress and casting a look of helpless appeal at Konstantin. "I must insist—"

Konstantin was about to intervene, but the kitten was faster. It gave an outraged snarl and sank its teeth into Cedric's ankle, right through his silk stockings.

Cedric let go of Arabella abruptly; she picked up the kitten with a little crow of triumph and held it against her cheek.

"My hero!" she said with a laugh as she kissed the kitten on its little pink nose. "You shall have something delicious for your supper, Raphael, I promise you."

Konstantin found, not entirely to his surprise, that he envied that cat with all his heart.

"Arabella!" snapped Cedric. "Stop talking to that stupid cat when I am paying my addresses to you!"

"Your addresses are unwelcome, sir," she said coldly. "I wish I could express some gratitude for the honor you have done me, but I am afraid I cannot. You are only engaging in this ridiculous charade because you want me to give you the kitten."

"What of it? Is this kitten more important to you than becoming the future Viscountess Barlowe?" he asked archly. "As my wife, you would move in the highest circles."

"I move in the highest circles *now*, you silly man! And not even the honor of becoming the queen of England would be worth the irritation of being married to you."

"Bravo, *petite!*" exclaimed Konstantin.

"You stay out of this!" Arabella snapped.

Konstantin gave her a mocking little salute, but he could not wipe the grin off his face. The little English spitfire was magnificent!

Humiliated, Cedric gave Arabella a look of pure loathing, snatched his hat from the maidservant, and turned from the door to deliver his parting shot.

"You will be sorry for this day's work, Miss Comstock," he said with stiff dignity.

As soon as the door was closed behind him, Konstantin erupted into gales of laughter. The guards on either side of the door managed to keep straight faces, but one of them was quivering with the effort. Cedric Wyndham was universally disliked by all the members of the grand duchess's household.

"You," Arabella demanded, putting the kitten on the floor and rounding on Konstantin. "What have you to say for yourself?"

"Nothing. Absolutely nothing. I have no excuse for my existence," he said, hanging his head. "I am a worm, a maggot, an *insect* too low for mademoiselle's regard."

He was rewarded for this outrageous statement with a quirking of the young lady's soft pink lips. The anger had quite died from her eyes and left them sparkling with amusement.

"Quite right," she said, mollified. "What *possessed* the man to think his suit would be at all acceptable to me?"

"Overweening conceit?" Konstantin hazarded.

Just then the kitten raised itself on its hind legs, batted a flounce on Arabella's skirt, and gave a loud meow. In fascination, Konstantin watched Arabella's heart melt. That was the only explanation for the expression on her face. If she ever looked at Konstantin that way, he would die a happy man.

She bent down and lifted the kitten into her arms.

"Poor baby Raphael," she crooned. "Is he hungry?"

Konstantin reached out to touch the kitten's head and the little creature leaned rapturously into the caress.

Arabella had stiffened, but now she looked at the prince in surprise. He marveled at the beauty of two pairs of lovely, wide emerald eyes, identical in hue and brilliance, fixed upon him.

"He likes you!" she said in astonishment.

"Of course he does," he said softly. "I used to feed him caviar when the grand duchess was not looking."

"Caviar!" exclaimed Mrs. Peabody. "You fed caviar to a *cat*?"

"Yes, madame," Konstantin said. "Raphael is quite fond of a meal of caviar and toast points."

He gave Arabella a smile and, since she could not push him away without dislodging the kitten, decided it was safe to kiss her fingertips. They smelled vaguely of fish. He was absolutely enchanted.

"Good afternoon, Miss Comstock. Caviar to the contrary, I can see Raphael is much more contented with you than he was with us. I will do my best to persuade my cousin to let him remain with you."

"Thank you," Arabella said, her beautiful eyes glowing with gratitude. "I could not bear it if Raphael was taken from me now."

"Do not worry, *petite*. I am sure that in time Catherine Pavlovna will forget all about the kitten."

He devoutly hoped he was right.

"Good afternoon, Madame Peabody," he said to Arabella's godmother with a bow.

Then he hurried off to the Pulteney. Not for all the world would he miss the tongue-lashing Mr. Wyndham was going to get from the grand duchess for failing in his mission.

FOUR

The grand duchess coldly regarded the utterly broken man begging her for mercy in impassioned and, in his agitation, excruciatingly ungrammatical French.

Naturally the little English nobody had thrown the Englishman's proposal of marriage back in his face. The grand duchess could have told him the tiresome girl had not committed the grave faux pas of offending the sister of the Savior of Europe merely to punish Cedric Wyndham for not marrying her.

Really, the conceit of the English was quite incomprehensible.

The wretched girl's design from the beginning was to attract the grand duchess's attention, of course. Nothing, she was sure, would give the little nobody greater satisfaction than forcing Her Imperial Highness Catherine, Grand Duchess of Oldenburg, to demean herself by calling on her at her hotel to request the return of her pet. What better way for a social inferior to bring herself to the notice of someone so far above her?

Well, the grand duchess obviously could not trust the incompetent members of the British Government to resolve this rather tiresome matter for her, so she might as well do it herself.

"Daria," she said to her head waiting woman, "I wish to pay a call. Arrange it."

She regarded her cousin, who was having a difficult time keeping an impassive countenance, with a look of glacial disapproval.

"Since this affair amuses you so much, you may accompany me, *Colonel* Obolensky," she said, making her displeasure known by using his military rank instead of his patronymic.

"Yes, your imperial highness," he said gravely.

As expected, her arrival at Number 7, Abemarle Street, caused a sensation among the gratified staff and guests fortunate enough to witness the event.

"Tell that silly woman to stop standing there as if a fly had flown into her mouth and summon that dreadful girl at once," the grand duchess rapped out in French to Konstantin shortly afterward, when a dumbstruck maidservant admitted them to the dreadful girl's suite at Grillon's Hotel. A wide-eyed younger maidservant curtsied and ran into an adjoining room, presumably to do her bidding.

The grand duchess then proceeded to install herself in what appeared to be the most comfortable of the chairs in the main room of the suite and indicated with an impatient gesture that her ladies should arrange themselves around her as if she were about to give an audience to some of her brother's more humble subjects. Konstantin, as interpreter, took up a station at her right hand; the guards took up their positions on either side of the door.

An elegantly dressed middle-aged woman was the first to reply to the summons. She sank into a graceful curtsy before the grand duchess and began nattering excitedly in that clumsy, grating language of hers.

"Who *is* this person?" the grand duchess demanded of Konstantin.

"This is Madame Peabody, your imperial highness. She is the aunt of Mademoiselle Arabella Comstock, and your hostess."

Konstantin said this with a look of mild reproof that quite exasperated her. Did he actually think she was going to permit the woman to be introduced to her? She stuck her nose in the air and turned away to indicate that she did not wish to converse with this inferior person.

Her hostess, as Konstantin was pleased to style her, seemed to deflate as the grand duchess continued to ignore her. The woman asked Konstantin a question. He nodded and turned to the grand duchess to translate.

"Madame Peabody asks if you would condescend to take tea and cakes with her and her niece, your imperial highness," Konstantin said in a perfectly level tone that ill-concealed his disapproval of her manner.

"Konstantin Mikhailovich," she said in exasperation as the Englishwoman patiently waited for the prince to translate, "these people are *beneath* me."

"Aunt Augusta!" an amused female voice called from another room. "Who has arrived? Mary is somewhat incoherent, and—"

Arabella's smile faded and her words broke off when she entered the room in time to witness her aunt being thoroughly snubbed by their distinguished visitor. She sent Konstantin a searching look. He gave her a rueful smile and a self-deprecating little shrug to deny responsibility for whatever was about to happen.

Arabella was wearing a fetching pink walking costume; the kitten was riding on her shoulder so that it could bat at the frilly trimmings on her pink straw bonnet. The kitten saw the grand duchess, leaped from Arabella's shoulder to the floor, raised its back, hissed in the outraged grand duchess's direction, and streaked out of the room with a screech that made Konstantin's teeth hurt.

Konstantin clamped his jaw tightly to keep an unseemly burst of laughter from escaping. He knew it would not be well received. His eyes were starting to water.

The grand duchess's outraged cry of "Come back, you miserable cat!" in French required no translation. Her voice was shrill with anger.

"Do not stand there like blocks," she said to her ladies with an impatient gesture. "Fetch my cat at once!"

When they would have obeyed, Arabella moved to bar the doorway. One of the determined ladies reached out to shove Arabella out of her path, but the prince caught the woman's arm and walked around her to range himself protectively at Arabella's side.

"Catherine Pavlovna, may I remind you that you are a guest here?" Konstantin said in French, giving the grand duchess a look of deep reproach.

"You forget yourself, Colonel Obolensky," the grand duchess said forbiddingly. "I *will* have my cat."

"Possibly, my cousin. But not like this, I beg of you. Let us take our leave. We waste our time here."

He walked to her chair and offered her his arm.

After a moment of indecision, she stood and accepted it.

In the carriage, she faced him with anger in her eyes.

"I have demeaned myself to wallow in this *squalor*," she said, dismissing the Grillon's elegant facade in one comprehensive sneer, "to no avail. What have you to say for your behavior, Colonel Obolensky?"

"Catherine Pavlovna, I could not permit you to compromise your dignity by engaging in an unseemly argument with commoners," he said, knowing that this was the only approach likely to pacify her. "I thought we had agreed that you would ask the young lady civilly for the kitten."

"That was before the creature *hissed* at me."

Konstantin knew that for all her arrogance, his cousin was capable of being hurt. The kitten's rejection in front of these foreign gentlewomen had surprised and embarrassed her, and she had reacted with anger, the only defense her pride would allow her.

"Why do you not let the girl keep the kitten?" he said. "You have said often enough that it is a nuisance."

"But it is *mine*," she said stubbornly. "This is all your fault, Konstantin Mikhailovich!"

"*My* fault?" he exclaimed.

"Do not put on that innocent face for *my* edification. You are interested in that wretched girl. I saw how you looked when you thought Daria was going to strike her."

"Catherine Pavlovna," he said reproachfully.

"Well, perhaps your *deplorable* taste in females can be put to good use. I am charging *you*, Konstantin Mikhailovich, with full responsibility for retrieving my kitten. You seem to think that a more civilized approach is required, even when dealing with creatures quite below one's notice. Very well. Approach this girl and persuade her to return what is mine by any means necessary."

"But—"

"If you do not—" She raised her eyebrows when he would have interrupted her, and he lapsed into resigned silence. "If you do not," she repeated, "I will persuade Alexander to relieve you of your military rank and send you home to Russia in disgrace. And I will have that girl arrested for good measure."

Konstantin knew that she could make good on both of these threats. It was well known that the tsar valued his sister's opinion over that of any of his counselors, and that she was first in his affections even before his beautiful wife, the Tsarina Elisabeth. Catherine Pavlovna, for all that she cherished a tepid cousinly affection for Konstantin, would ruin him and possibly his entire family as well without the least compunction if he failed her.

She did not forgive disloyalty.

Ever.

Although the British authorities would be reluctant to arrest an English girl of good family on such a trivial matter, Konstantin knew they would not hesitate to sacrifice Arabella Comstock on the altar of international diplomacy.

"Seduce her if you must," Catherine Pavlovna said with a thin smile. "You may think of it as a souvenir of your English visit. But get my cat from her."

"Yes, Catherine Pavlovna," he said, because he could do nothing else.

* * *

Arabella's godmother had insisted that they go to Almack's, even though Arabella was reluctant to leave the kitten behind with her maid. She told Mary to open the door to *no one* before their return.

"My dear girl, it will be a complete waste of a perfectly good Season in London if you do not make the least attempt to meet suitable gentlemen. And one does *not* fail to use vouchers for Almack's when one of the lady patronesses has been kind enough to provide them."

"I have met gentlemen," Arabella said archly. "See? Here is one now."

She smiled at the young man who had approached and bowed to her. She accepted his invitation to dance, and so she was on the way to the dance floor when she saw Prince Obolensky enter the room with the grand duchess, several of her attendants, and Cedric.

Arabella gasped, came to an abrupt stop, and dropped her fan, almost causing a collision with several other pairs of dancers who were also on their way to the dance floor. Arabella's partner obligingly picked up the fan as the prince walked right up to them.

"Good evening, Miss Comstock," he said, taking her hand and kissing it.

"Good evening, Prince Obolensky," she said. "Oh, forgive me!" she added to her partner, who was standing patiently by to present her with her fan. Flustered by the unholy amusement in the prince's dark eyes and the pleasant sensation of her chilled hand being held in his warm one, she took a step back and accepted the fan from her partner with a word of thanks. "If you will excuse me," she added to the prince, recovering a bit of her composure now that he was no longer touching her, "I am engaged at the moment."

"Of course," he said, smiling. He bowed to her dance partner and sauntered off.

"Prince Obolensky!" Mrs. Peabody said, turning pink with pleasure when he seated himself beside her. "How delightful to see you under less trying circumstances!"

"Good evening, Mrs. Peabody. I hope you will permit me to keep you company while Miss Comstock is dancing. The grand duchess is occupied with her many admirers, so I am quite *de trop.*"

"Well, I rather hope you will dance with Arabella yourself after causing that very odd scene on the dance floor just now," she said frankly. "The gossips have fed quite enough on my darling girl as it is."

Konstantin gave her a curious look.

"When that dreadful Cedric Wyndham broke off their engagement, I mean," she explained. "For all that it was not precisely official, as the wretched man never tires of pointing out, my poor girl waited for him for three years only to be jilted in the most ungentlemanly manner! I quite feared for her reason."

"She was in love with him?" Konstantin asked, frowning.

"She thought she was, which is the same thing to an impressionable young girl." She called Konstantin's attention to the waltzing couple. Arabella was laughing at some remark of her partner's and her color was heightened from the exercise. The folds of her pretty yellow voile gown fluttered around her. "It is such a relief to see her happy again. She always had such sunny spirits as a child."

"She is very beautiful."

"*I* think so," Mrs. Peabody said, obviously pleased with this praise of her protégée. "I want to thank you for not letting the grand duchess take the kitten away from us. Arabella has had so much disappointment in her young life."

Konstantin squirmed a bit under the lady's assumption that the grand duchess had withdrawn her claim to the kitten, but he could hardly correct her.

"And how is my little friend Raphael?" he asked instead. "In good health, I trust?"

"Thriving. Arabella and I quite dote on him."

"I am glad. I was wondering, Mrs. Peabody, if I may call on you and Miss Comstock tomorrow."

"We would be pleased to receive you," Mrs. Peabody replied, giving the prince a coy look.

"Splendid," said the prince. "I am glad you do not object to my company after all this."

"Of course not," Mrs. Peabody said warmly. "You understand, though, that I am not Arabella's guardian, do you not?"

"Yes. Her father has a town house in London. I know this because Mr. Wyndham went there first to look for Miss Comstock before we found you at Grillon's."

"Of course," said Mrs. Peabody. "I vow I could *shake* the wretched man!"

"Mr. Wyndham?" Konstantin hazarded.

"Him, too," she said. "But I was speaking of Arabella's father, Mr. Comstock. First he marries this absolutely useless young woman and quite shuts Arabella out of his life. Then he treats her as if *he* is the injured party when her engagement is broken."

Mrs. Peabody fixed the prince with a look so fierce he almost recoiled.

"I am delighted by your apparent interest in my niece, Prince Obolensky," she said crisply. "There is nothing like a handsome new admirer to perk up a girl's spirits. But I warn you that you will answer to me if you hurt her."

In her vehemence she reminded him unpleasantly of the grand duchess.

"I assure you, dear lady, that I would not hurt her for the world," Konstantin assured her.

He hoped very much that he would not have to.

When the dance was over, Arabella found with dismay that Prince Obolensky was sitting next to Mrs. Peabody, saying something to her that made the older lady giggle coquettishly.

"Ah, Miss Comstock," the prince said, standing when she hesitantly approached with her partner. That gentleman bowed politely to them all and took his leave. Konstantin offered his arm to Arabella. "May I?"

Arabella looked to her godmother for support, but Mrs. Peabody only said with a complacent smile on her face that made Arabella's heart sink, "Run along, dear. I was about to go into the card room."

Feeling trapped, Arabella lay her hand on the prince's arm and was uncomfortably aware of every eye fixed upon her.

"There is no need to look at me as if I were an ogre," he whispered. "I do not bite, I promise you. At least not in front of so many witnesses."

"Will the grand duchess not punish you severely for talking to the enemy?" Arabella asked as he escorted her to a set that was just forming.

"No. She thinks I am trying to charm you on her

behalf into giving the kitten back," he said gravely. He paid Arabella the compliment of believing she was far too intelligent to swallow a lie.

Arabella's eyes narrowed.

"I will *never* give Raphael back, you know."

"I know. But I see no reason not to enjoy a flirtation with a charming young lady with her imperial highness's goodwill while I may. She will even give me leave from my duties to call on you tomorrow."

"Do you really want to?" Arabella asked, feeling flattered and alarmed all at once.

"With all my heart," he said with a smile that made her bones melt as he bowed and took her hand to lead her into a movement of the dance. Arabella's mind was awhirl when she curtsied to the gentleman opposite and circled him in small mincing steps according to the pattern.

"I think it only fair to warn you that I am quite soured on men," Arabella said when she and the prince came together again.

"Perhaps I can change your mind," he said hopefully. "I am generally rather popular with the ladies."

"I will wager you are," she said out of the corner of her mouth as she left him to approach the opposite gentleman again.

Then she saw her father and missed a step.

"May I bring you a glass of wine?" Konstantin asked when he had escorted her to a chair. She seemed so uncomfortable that he did not have the heart to inflict his presence on her any longer.

"No," she said hastily. She reached out and grasped his wrist when he bowed and would have excused himself to return to the grand duchess. "Do not leave me!"

He raised one eyebrow.

"Certainly not, if you wish it," he said, preparing to seat himself beside her.

That was when a middle-aged gentleman with obviously dyed auburn hair and a flamboyant manner of dressing quite at odds with his years and dignity bore down upon Arabella.

"Arabella," he said stiffly.

"Father," she replied, matching his tone. She turned to Konstantin. "Prince Obolensky, may I present my father, Mr. Comstock?"

"Your servant, sir," Mr. Comstock said, sketching a bow in Konstantin's direction. Konstantin solemnly returned it. "Arabella, I, ah, wanted to be sure you are well."

"Quite well, I thank you."

The gentleman nervously cleared his throat.

"Er, I was worried about you. Wyndham showed up on my doorstep this morning and demanded to know your whereabouts. He did not seem to be in any sweet temper. He had some Russian soldiers with him and put the house in an uproar." Mr. Comstock squinted at Konstantin. "I say, you were with him, were you not?"

"I was," the prince conceded warily.

"Anyway, Arabella," Mr. Comstock continued, "he said he was searching you out on behalf of the grand duchess of Oldenburg. I know I should have come to Grillon's at once to make sure you were not in some sort of trouble, but Emily was so upset by the visit of those soldiers to our home that she begged me not to leave her and young Gilly unprotected." He turned to Konstantin to include him in the conversation. "Gilly is my son," he said proudly. The mere thought of his heir quite transformed his face. "Fine young rascal. Almost a year old. The day he was born was the happiest day of my life. It is a wonderful thing for a man to have a son when he almost has lost hope."

"I am certain it is," Konstantin said politely.

"Anyway," Mr. Comstock said, turning once more to his daughter, "I could hardly leave Emily when she was in such a taking."

"I quite understand," Arabella said, forcing the corners of her lips to turn up. Her beautiful eyes were so sad. "Pray do not give it another thought, Father. If you will excuse us, Prince Obolensky has requested the next dance, and—"

"Arabella, this estrangement between us must come to an end!" the older man blurted out.

Arabella's face softened and her lips parted. But before she could speak, her father went on in a huffy tone.

"It is not fair to Emily, for people have been saying behind her back that she is a wicked stepmother, and she has driven you from our home. The least you can do is call upon us occasionally for appearances' sake if you cannot bring yourself to live with us. You know how sensitive Emily is to any slight."

"Good-bye, Father," Arabella said sadly, taking Konstantin's arm and starting to lead him away.

"She is in the ladies' withdrawing room at present. But when she sits down again, I would be obliged to you if you would come over and chat with her awhile," Mr. Comstock persisted.

He gave Konstantin a speculative look.

"You could bring the prince along with you," he added, as if he had just been struck with a happy inspiration. "And if you are on calling terms with the grand duchess, perhaps you can present Emily to her."

"No, Father. I am not on such intimate terms with the grand duchess, I assure you," Arabella said wearily. She gave a little tug on Konstantin's arm to get him moving toward the dance floor again. "As for expecting me to fawn all over Emily for the benefit of the gossips, I am afraid it is quite impossible."

"Arabella!" her father called after her, sounding quite put out.

She kept walking.

"Thank you, Prince Obolensky, for lending me your support through . . . that," Arabella said to Konstantin with a sudden, painfully bright smile. Her eyes were suspiciously moist. "I am sorry to have kept you from the grand duchess for so long."

Obviously she expected him to just walk away from her. Poor girl. No wonder she was quite soured on men, as she put it.

"Not at all," he said, masterfully taking her in his arms and swinging them both into the waltz.

FIVE

Arabella bit her lip and reflected that the note was so typical of her stepmother.

Dear Arabella,

I do hope you will attend Gilly's first birthday party on Sunday next. You have been a stranger to your little brother, and to your father and me, for much too long. And, dearest, if you should wish to bring that divine Russian prince who was dancing with you at Almack's last night, your father and I would be most pleased to receive him! It would be quite a feather in my cap to be able to introduce him to all my especial friends. Do you think your prince can arrange for me to be presented to Grand Duchess Catherine? If so, I can go calling with you on any day you would find convenient.

With a wry look, Arabella passed the note on to her godmother.

"How surprising that Emily has remembered my existence now that I appear to be on polite terms with a member of Grand Duchess Catherine's party," she observed.

"Polite terms? Is that what you would call it?" Mrs. Peabody said quizzically. "I had to be on my guard every moment for fear the prince would drag you out on the balcony to have his wicked way with you. It was quite apparent that *you* would not put up any great show of maidenly shrinking!"

"Never mind that," Arabella said hastily. "It is apparent that Emily got the wrong impression."

"You had better hope *the prince* did not get the wrong impression," Mrs. Peabody said archly.

"Nonsense," Arabella scoffed. "Prince Obolensky could have any woman in London he chooses. Do you think I cannot see how they *look* at him?"

"I can see how *you* look at him, darling," Mrs. Peabody said. "He is a very nice young man. It is too bad he is a foreigner, for he will leave at the end of the summer with the grand duchess's party, I imagine."

Arabella took a hasty step away from her godmother and turned to stare fixedly at a charming arrangement of fresh yellow roses in a porcelain vase. "I do not wish to discuss this any further."

"Very well," said Mrs. Peabody agreeably. "Let us discuss instead this invitation to your half-brother's birthday party."

"I am not going," Arabella said around the lump that formed in her throat every time she thought of her father. "Of course, *you* may go if you choose."

"Do not be hasty, dearest," said Mrs. Peabody, looking troubled. "I am certain your father deeply regrets his estrangement from you. Can you not reconsider?"

"I think not," Arabella said bitterly. "I swore I would never enter my father's house again, and nothing in Emily's note persuades me to change my mind.

Do not be concerned for my father's feelings. I do not flatter myself that my absence from his cozy new family circle has bothered him overmuch."

"Perhaps not, but it bothers *you*," Augusta said, touching Arabella's shoulder sympathetically. *"That* is what concerns me."

A rap sounded at the door and Konstantin soon joined the ladies with a smile on his face that made Arabella forget the heartache that any thought of Emily or her father inevitably brought her.

"Good afternoon, Miss Comstock," he said politely. His eyes were dancing with mischief. "I hope you did not forget you are promised to me today. I have brought a hamper of delicacies pilfered from Catherine Pavlovna's larder, some blankets, and a hired carriage for an excursion to the park. May I have the honor of sharing them with you? And with Madame Peabody and Raphael, of course?"

"My aging joints are much too cranky to make sitting on the ground for any length of time an agreeable experience, young man, so I must beg to be excused," Augusta said with a twinkle in her eye. "Raphael would probably enjoy some fresh air. I shall fetch him, shall I?"

"Aunt Augusta!" Arabella said after her godmother as she briskly left the room, presumably to find the cat. "It would hardly be proper—"

When Arabella started to follow Mrs. Peabody, Konstantin caught her shoulders in his hands and drew her back to rest in the protective cradle of his chest with one strong arm wrapped around her waist and the other playing in her hair. Arabella closed her eyes as his warm lips explored the sensitive skin just above her ear. She could feel his breath against her temple.

"My dear Miss Comstock," Konstantin said. His

voice sounded lazy and amused. "One would think you were afraid to be alone with me. You were not so shy last evening."

"That was different," she said, covered with shame at the memory of how she had flirted with the prince. She had stayed within the boundaries of propriety by dancing with him only twice, but she went into supper on his arm and accepted his escort back to the hotel on behalf of herself and her godmother with every appearance of pleasure. "We were not alone then—Oh!"

He suddenly turned her around in his embrace so they were face to face.

"True," he agreed, slowly drawing his thumb across her cheekbone as he cupped her face with one warm hand. "Mr. Wyndham was there to see us, was he not? How charmingly you blush when a man touches you, *ma belle.*"

Arabella was mortified.

"I did not mean—"

"Naturally you wished to show Mr. Wyndham, your father, and all your friends that you are not a pathetic spinster wearing the willow—is this the correct expression?—for your faithless fiancé. Now you fear that after receiving such encouragement from you last night in a crowded ballroom, I may forget myself and take liberties today. Ah, but I must admit I am tempted."

"Prince Obolensky, I do not know what to say," she stammered. She sounded like an idiot.

"Say nothing then," he said as he bent to kiss her.

She knew she could have stopped him with a word, but the way he touched her sent her senses reeling. She admitted to herself that she *wanted* him to kiss her. She had the surprising thought that here was a good man, a chivalrous man she could depend upon.

Then she found it impossible to think at all.

She had experienced her share of innocent forays into the gardens with various youths of good family before she was betrothed to Cedric, but they had not prepared her for anything like the heat of Konstantin's kiss. She gave a little whimper when his tender assault forced her lips open. The intimacy of his tongue in her mouth almost made her knees buckle.

To her shame, her arms had wound themselves quite of their own volition around his neck by the time Konstantin broke off the kiss, gave her a chaste salute on the forehead, and stepped back from her. Half afraid of what she might see, she looked into his eyes. She expected triumph or, worse, his usual lazy amusement. Instead, he looked solemn.

"You are right, *ma belle,*" he said, taking a deep breath. "It is *not* a good idea for us to be alone."

"I am sorry I was gone so long, my dears," Augusta said as she entered the room with Raphael in her arms. Mary followed with the kitten's water and food bowls, a jug of fresh water, the inevitable box of sand, and other supplies for the kitten's comfort. "I vow, Raphael," Augusta said, stroking the kitten's fur and looking down lovingly into his pert, smiling cat face, "you are almost as much work as a human infant when you go on an outing."

Arabella turned to look out the window to give herself time to recover her composure. She could not breathe normally, let alone organize her thoughts well enough to utter a single coherent sentence.

"We have changed our minds," Konstantin said to Mrs. Peabody. "We are not going out after all."

"Oh?" said Mrs. Peabody, sounding surprised. Arabella could positively feel the older lady's concerned eyes focused on her back.

"We would not enjoy ourselves half so much without your company," he said smoothly. "If you will not come to the picnic, Madame Peabody, we will bring the picnic to you."

Arabella turned around to give him a look brimful of gratitude. He must have known he could have taken any liberty that he chose with her reputation now, and she would have been powerless to resist once he got her alone. He had done this to give her time to recover her wits.

"Excuse me for a moment, ladies, if you will," he said as he bowed to Mrs. Peabody with a flourish.

When he looked at Arabella, she could see that hers were not the only defenses that had been shattered. His lips were smiling with their usual mocking amusement, but the open, vulnerable look in his eyes made Arabella tumble helplessly over the edge of sanity and into love with him.

When Arabella wrinkled her nose at the dark little mound of caviar Konstantin had spread on a toast point and held temptingly before her lips, he fed it to an ecstatic Raphael instead.

"Enjoy it while you can, Raphael," Mrs. Peabody said with a laugh. "Fond as I am of you, I draw the line at feeding caviar to a cat."

Konstantin noticed that all of them—including himself—had begun talking to Raphael as if he might talk back. And, in a way, he did. The Archangel kitten had the most extensive repertoire of cat expressions Konstantin had ever seen.

He reflected that the time he had spent with Arabella, her aunt, and, yes, Raphael the cat, were the happiest he had spent since he was home at his father's palace in the Volga River Valley.

Konstantin envied Raphael now as the kitten began a slow, crouching ascent up Arabella's exquisite, half-reclining body. She was wearing a simple high-waisted blue dress with small puffed sleeves. Konstantin, Arabella, and Raphael were having their picnic on the blankets Konstantin had spread out on the floor of the parlor. Mrs. Peabody, who Konstantin did not believe for a moment was plagued with creaking joints, nibbled at a pastry from a comfortable chair.

When the kitten pounced suddenly and landed on Arabella's breastbone, she leaned on her elbows, laughing, and tossed her head back so her tantalizing riot of curling, flame-red hair pooled on the polished hardwood floor. Because she was dressed for an afternoon at home, her hair was tied loosely with a ribbon so the mass of it was allowed to flow down her back instead of being all gathered up in its usual elegant chignon. Konstantin remembered how the fragrant curls had clung to his fingers when he kissed her, and he wished he could kiss her again. Immediately. Arabella closed her eyes when the cat put its paws lovingly on each side of her face, and it took all the discipline at Konstantin's command not to moan.

As the blood pounded in his temples, Konstantin reminded himself that Arabella was not deliberately trying to torture him. He dared not look at Mrs. Peabody.

"Phew! You smell all fishy," Arabella said suddenly to Raphael, laughing, and broke the spell. She rolled to her side so the kitten could spring to the floor in safety and sat up.

Knowing he was playing with fire, Konstantin dipped a ripe strawberry into a bowl of cream.

"So you will spurn Russia's best caviar, will you?" he said, hoping he sounded debonair and teasing rather than like a besotted idiot. "Here is something you will like."

He held the strawberry to Arabella's smiling lips, and she delighted him by opening that soft pink mouth and closing her eyes as she received it. The look of sensual pleasure on her face when she chewed the morsel almost undid him.

"Well," said Mrs. Peabody, a bit more loudly than was necessary. "That was very diverting! It was very kind of you to share your picnic with us, Prince Obolensky."

She gave Arabella, who had opened her eyes and was looking into Konstantin's with a bemused expression on her face, a pointed look.

"Was it not kind of Prince Obolensky, Arabella?" she prompted.

"Oh, yes," the girl said hastily. She looked down at her lap and reached for Raphael, who was sniffing about the remains of the caviar bowl. "Most kind. Thank you, Prince Obolensky."

"It was my pleasure," Konstantin managed to say with creditable composure. He started gathering dishes into his basket, and Arabella started to help. Their hands touched when they reached for the same bowl, and Arabella gave a little gasp and shied away. A delicate pink flush tinted her cheeks.

Konstantin was, he thanked God, more adept at hiding his feelings than she was. Still, he could not look either lady in the face for fear of what his eyes might reveal. What had started as an innocent flirtation was becoming quite another thing entirely. He began to wonder what his father would say if he brought home an English bride.

"I must return to the Pulteney at once," he said hastily. "The grand duchess has several engagements this afternoon, and I will be expected to accompany her."

Arabella had by this time regained her composure and helped him finish putting the broken meats of their feast in the basket. She had to hold Raphael back so he would not leap into the basket after the last of the food.

God bless inquisitive little kittens for providing timely distractions, Konstantin thought fervently.

Konstantin stood with the hamper in one hand and the blanket draped across his arm. He extended his free hand to Arabella to help her to her feet. His skin tingled where their hands touched exactly as if he were an awkward, lovesick youth, he thought in exasperation.

"I wish you a pleasant afternoon, Mrs. Peabody, Miss Comstock," he said, bowing. Then he left before he could make an utter fool of himself.

SIX

One minute Arabella was standing by the French doors to the terrace, sipping a glass of champagne. The next, she found herself braced against a decorative flowering tree in her hostess's garden while Konstantin kissed her as if she were the only woman on earth.

It occurred to Arabella for just an instant that the ravishing sea green gauze ballgown trimmed in silver lace that had arrived only that afternoon from the seamstress's was likely to be snagged on the rough bark of the tree if she did not take care. All thought of preserving her finery, however, fled from her mind when Konstantin released her lips and began raining ardent little kisses all over her upturned face.

"I have been waiting all evening to do that," Konstantin admitted when he had completed the task with his usual thoroughness.

It took Arabella a minute to speak. When she did, her voice sounded an octave higher than usual. Konstantin had called on Arabella and her aunt every day for the past week, often escorting them on walks to Green Park and *ton* parties. But until tonight Konstantin had made no attempt to be alone with her.

"Konstantin, we had better go back in," she said,

shamelessly hoping he would try to talk her out of it. Arabella had seen Mrs. Peabody's worried look when Konstantin carefully took the champagne glass from Arabella and gave it to a passing waiter. Then Konstantin had seized Arabella's hand and pulled her, laughing breathlessly, into the darkness beyond the flower-decked ballroom.

"Not yet," he said. "Arabella, when the grand duchess's party returns to Russia, I would like for you to accompany me. Either as my wife or as my fiancée. My parents will wish for me to be married from our old church in Russia, but I will be just as happy to be married in England if it means we can marry sooner."

Words failed Arabella as her eyes filled with happy tears.

"Arabella?" he said, sounding anxious. "Is it too soon?"

She could not have spoken to save her life, so she hugged him instead.

"Does this mean yes?" he asked with a shaky laugh in his voice as he tightened his arms around her. Arabella wanted to stay with him in the mysterious, flower-scented darkness for the rest of her life.

"You have not answered me," Konstantin pointed out after a moment, kissing her cheek. "Not in words."

"Yes. The answer is yes, of course," she said. "But you will have to take Raphael, too."

Raphael.

Catherine Pavlovna.

Konstantin sobered instantly. He had a feeling that Catherine Pavlovna's reaction to this sweet madness was likely to blister his ears.

"Is something wrong, Konstantin?" Arabella asked shyly. "You have not changed your mind, have you?"

"Never," he said vehemently as he crushed her to his chest again. "Never so long as I live."

Arabella knew that even so unexacting a chaperone as Mrs. Peabody was likely to be scandalized, but she cast caution to the winds and danced with Konstantin a third time, and then a fourth.

What did it matter if the gossips ran wild with speculation? Konstantin had asked her to marry him.

She wanted this night to last forever; she wanted it to end immediately so she could become his bride all the sooner.

Once Arabella would have considered an elopement to Gretna Green a disgraceful affair, but now she wondered if she might convince Konstantin to embark upon one, preferably tonight.

Probably not. He was most truly the gentleman and would refuse to compromise her in any way.

Blast it!

"I shall call upon you tomorrow, my love," Konstantin whispered as he prepared to hand her into Mrs. Peabody's carriage. His eyes were full of sweet promise. "After I call on your father."

"Arabella!" called Mrs. Peabody, sounding impatient. Arabella could have lingered before the carriage until dawn, just looking at his handsome face. *"Do* get in!"

After Arabella had settled herself inside, Konstantin bowed to Mrs. Peabody, who was already seated in the carriage.

"Good evening, Prince Obolensky," Arabella's godmother said with an unsmiling little nod of dis-

missal. She sounded vexed. As soon as the carriage
door was closed and they began moving through the
street, she rounded on Arabella.

"What were you *thinking,* my girl!" she demanded.
"There had better be a proposal of marriage in the
near future or you will be utterly ruined! The look
on his face when he dragged you into the gardens—"
She had to stop and fan her heated cheeks.

Arabella knew there was an excessively silly grin on
her own face. She could have put her godmother's
concern about Konstantin's intentions to rest, but for
tonight she would selfishly hug the delicious news to
herself and dream of him.

Arabella abruptly came awake from her pleasant
reverie when a tearful Mary met them at the door of
their suite.

"Miss! They *forced* their way in. They took him away,
even though he scratched that bad man again!" she
cried.

"Raphael!" shouted Arabella as she ran straight to
her bedchamber in the hope she would find him
curled up on the pillow she had put in a pretty hatbox
for him to sleep in. "No!" she cried, when she discovered he was nowhere in the suite. "Who took
him?"

"It was Mr. Wyndham, miss," Mary said, wringing
her hands. "He said if I did not hand over the kitten
at once he would have me placed under arrest. I refused, so he pushed me down and took Raphael, anyway."

"It is just as she says, miss," Mrs. Peabody's maidservant corroborated. "He came forcing his way in
here when I tried to shut the door again. Tore the
kitten right out of Mary's arms, he did, and it was
scratching him and crying something pitiful. He had

two of those big, burly Russian guards with him, and
they stared at me so fierce, I thought I would have a
spasm!"

"It was not your fault, Mary," Arabella said, patting
her distraught maid on the shoulder. She insisted
that she did not need Mary's help to undress and
suggested that the maid have a cup of tea to settle
her nerves.

Then she went into her bedroom and stripped off
the sea green gauze gown, heedless of the way the
delicate fabric shredded a bit when she tore at the
hooks that closed it in back.

She was shivering by the time she got into her
nightgown and burrowed under the counterpane.
She doubted she would ever be warm again as she
closed her eyes and wished Konstantin's strong arms
were around her.

"Catherine Pavlovna, what have you done?" Konstantin exclaimed when he found the grand duchess
regarding Raphael with every appearance of disgust.
He had forgotten his company enough to shout the
question in English. Raphael's ears were laid back
and he hissed at the grand duchess with a fury that
made his emerald eyes shoot sparks. His fur was
standing all on end.

Cedric Wyndham stood nearby, giving the kitten a
poisonous look as a lackey swabbed the multitude of
bloody scratches on his hands with some solution that
made his eyes water. Konstantin hoped the scratches
were *very* painful.

"Damned cat," Wyndham huffed.

"You did well, Mr. Wyndham," the grand duchess

said. "After a few days the creature will settle down
again."

She turned unhurriedly to Konstantin.

"Did you wish to make some comment, Colonel
Obolensky?" she asked. "You know I cannot understand a word of that barbarous tongue."

Konstantin had good reason to suspect the grand
duchess understood him perfectly, but he repeated
the question in French.

"I have done nothing but reclaim my property with
Mr. Wyndham's assistance," she said. "It seems he
has a better sense of what is owed to me than my own
cousin. While you were disporting yourself with that
girl, Mr. Wyndham went to her hotel and fetched the
cat, which is what *you* should have done days ago."

Konstantin wanted to wipe the superior smirk off
Wyndham's face, but that would wait.

"Where are you going, Konstantin?" the grand
duchess demanded when he turned and started to
walk to the door. "I did not give you permission to
withdraw!"

Konstantin kept walking.

"You are not to see that girl again!" she shouted
after him. "I *will* be obeyed in this matter, Konstantin
Mikhailovich!"

The grand duchess could convince her brother to
dismiss Konstantin from his post in disgrace, but that
was not nearly as serious a matter as failing to comfort
Arabella when she needed him.

The porter at Grillon's refused to admit him. "This
is a respectable hotel," the man told him in a
shocked tone. He would lose his position if he admitted a gentleman to the hotel at this indecent hour
to awaken two gentlewomen who were staying within.

"Where were you earlier tonight when an Englishman and two Russian soldiers forced their way into the gentlewomen's suite and stole a cat from it?" Konstantin demanded furiously.

"If you will not lower your voice, sir, I shall have to send for the manager!"

"Do so at once," Konstantin snapped. "I should like very much to hear what he has to say about this affair."

The manager was polite but firm. Grillon's would be pleased to admit Konstantin at a respectable hour in the morning, but nothing would persuade the manager to permit Konstantin to disturb the ladies now.

Not willing to give up, Konstantin skulked outside the building and threw a stone at a window he hoped belonged to Arabella's bedchamber.

It was with mingled relief and trepidation that he saw the window push open and a feminine white-clad figure lean out. Her face was all in shadows.

"Arabella?" he hazarded, hoping that this was not an unknown lady who would rouse the entire hotel with her screams at being accosted by a man in the middle of the night.

"Konstantin," she said in a voice choked with tears.

He held his arms up. The window was only just above him and he could catch her easily. The question was, did she have the courage to jump.

It seemed she did.

She landed solidly in his arms, and he almost lost sight of his mission with those warm, soft curves pressed against him.

He could have held her like this forever, but she pushed against his chest with such determination that he had to put her on the ground or risk dropping her.

"Cedric took Raphael," she said tearfully. She shivered, so he took off his uniform coat and placed it around her shoulders.

"Will you bring him back to me?" she asked in the shy, hopeful voice of a child who has been disappointed too often. "Please?"

"I am sorry, *douchenka,*" he said with a long sigh. "Refusing to take him from you is merely a crime of omission. Stealing him back from my tsar's sister borders on treason."

"Then you do not love me," Arabella said in a voice that broke his heart. "You never intended to marry me, did you?"

"I do love you, Arabella, and I did intend to marry you."

"Did," she repeated dully. "Past tense."

Konstantin took a deep breath and forced his voice to remain steady.

"It is . . . difficult now. The grand duchess is displeased with me for not bringing Raphael to her. It would be wise to wait for a little while before I tell her that we intend to marry. She ordered me to stay away from you."

"I see," Arabella said coldly. "And of course you will obey her."

"Just for now," Konstantin said, seizing her hands. "Please, Arabella. You must trust me for a little while. Catherine Pavlovna does not forget a grievance easily, and she will have me dismissed from the tsar's service if I try her patience too far. I do not care for myself, but my father and mother would be disgraced. The men of our line have served in the tsar's army for generations. And my young sister is a lady-in-waiting to the tsarina at court. It would break her heart to be sent back to the country because of something *I* had done."

Arabella turned her face away from him.

"My love, please understand," he said, gently cupping her face in his hands and forcing her to look at him.

"I understand perfectly," she said with a shaky, unnatural laugh. "All I have to do is wait. For how long, Konstantin? A year? Two years? Three, perhaps? You forget that I have been down this path before. Cedric swore he could not live without me, but he wanted to be established in his diplomatic career before we married. I waited for him, only to be jilted when he returned."

"Arabella, the cases are not the same! I *love* you!"

"So did he, until my father produced a male heir to inherit his lands and fortune," she said bitterly. "Then duty to his name compelled him to go back on his word."

"Only until I make some arrangement . . ."

"*No*, Konstantin," Arabella said, her voice dangerously calm. "I have learned my lesson at last. Kindly lend me your assistance back to my window."

He really had no choice. He gave her a boost up to the window and took her cold feet in his hands to help her the rest of the way when she managed to grasp the windowsill.

As he stood willing her to whisper his name or give some sign that all hope was not lost, his uniform coat dropped to the ground beside him, and he heard the window close with a snap of finality that made his heart plummet into his boots.

SEVEN

Arabella claimed she had a headache the next day so she could avoid going on afternoon calls with Mrs. Peabody. Her eyes filled with tears every time she looked at the cushioned little box Raphael had slept in, but she could not bear to have it removed. It was her last link with him. And with Konstantin. Once it was gone, it would be as if neither of them had existed.

She gave her ecstatic maid the rest of the day off because she wanted to be alone, and she knew Mary would fuss over her in a misguided attempt to lift her spirits.

Mary had been horrified when Arabella told her to burn the sea green gauze gown. With a little mending, the maid insisted, it would be almost as good as new. It would be a pity to destroy such a beautiful and expensive garment.

When Arabella told Mary that she could keep the gown on the condition she took it away and Arabella never had to see it again, the maid was incoherent with gratitude. She had been walking out with a young man for a fortnight, and she would dazzle him with her ravishing secondhand finery.

Arabella wished the girl joy of it. And of the young

man. She hoped for Mary's sake he would not prove
to be as faithless as Arabella's suitors had been.

To her credit, Mary tried very hard to contain her
pleasure in deference to Arabella's state of mind. Arabella had to grit her teeth until Mary stopped fussing
over her and left, obviously conscience-stricken at
leaving her mistress alone in her gloom.

Arabella decided she would leave for the country
as soon as she could arrange to do so. Her taste in
men was so defective that it was positively dangerous
for her to remain in London a minute longer!

Besides, she had behaved like a brazen hussy last
night with Konstantin, and her godmother was
right—a proposal of marriage had better follow such
scandalous public behavior or Arabella would, once
again, be eaten alive by the gossips. They probably
were salivating already.

Poor Arabella Comstock, they would say, pretending
to pity her. *Jilted by two men within the space of a year.
My dear, her gown was positively in tatters when she returned from the gardens with that Russian prince. . . .*

Her only choice was to thank Aunt Augusta for her
hospitality and leave London.

Again.

Arabella sighed as she thought of her six months
in the country after Cedric's rejection.

Once again she would be all alone. Arabella told
herself that it was for the best, but she could not seem
to stop these vexatious tears from clouding her vision
as she walked about the room, putting the things she
wished to take to the country into a little pile for
Mary to pack.

She hesitated over Raphael's makeshift bed and after a moment put it beside the things to take along.
It was foolish, but she could not quite give up hope

that he would return to her someday. Cats, she knew, had an uncanny sense of direction and sometimes turned up at their true homes after being lost.

When her fingers brushed the pillow that still bore a few of his short blue-gray hairs, she heard the crinkle of paper. Curious, she lifted the crumpled note out of the cushioned folds. Raphael, she thought with a pang, probably had found it and made a toy of it.

Arabella carefully pressed out the wrinkles and read it.

It was Emily's invitation to Gilly's birthday celebration on Sunday next—tomorrow.

Gilly. Named Giles after his father.

Her father.

All of a sudden, pride was not important anymore as Arabella looked into the future and saw another miserable six months in the country, alone except for servants, while her father and the little boy she hardly knew became more and more distant strangers.

She had denounced her father for marrying a young woman straight from the schoolroom and putting an end to all of Arabella's hopes. But was he so wrong? He had been devastated when Arabella's mother died. She still remembered how he had roamed the house late at night like a ghost in those first horrible months, unable to sleep. She had interpreted his remarriage a decade later as an insidious plot to make Arabella an outsider in her own home, but Arabella had achieved that dubious distinction all by herself.

Like Cedric—and like the grand duchess—Arabella had placed herself squarely at the center of the universe. Was her father to be denied his happiness in order to please a grown daughter who, in the usual course of things, could be expected to abandon him to start a household of her own? Arabella had gleefully chosen her trousseau and furnishings for her new home without the least regard for her father's probable loneliness when she went on to her new life.

Would Arabella have been happy married to Cedric if he had kept his word but spent the rest of their life together blaming her in his heart for not bringing him the wealth that was his true objective in offering for her? Certainly not! She should *thank* her father for unintentionally causing Cedric to jilt her.

Then there was Konstantin—the man Arabella had rejected when he begged her to trust him.

Arabella gave a long shaky sigh and sat down on the bed with her head in her hands. She could not let herself think about Konstantin now. That pain was too new. Of course he could not ruin his family to marry a woman who had incurred the wrath of the grand duchess. She had no right to expect it of him.

There was nothing she could do about Konstantin and Raphael. They were lost to her.

But she could mend the breach with her father, and to Perdition with her foolish pride!

It was seven o'clock in the morning when Arabella alighted from Mrs. Peabody's coach in front of her father's town house with her portmanteau in her hand.

Mrs. Peabody had offered to accompany her, but this was something she must do alone.

The house had not quite roused from slumber. The butler who opened the door was a stranger and looked surprised when Arabella told him her name.

He would have shown her into the parlor, but she insisted upon waiting in the hall.

She would not intrude further into her father's house until he invited her to do so.

"Arabella!" Mr. Comstock said excitedly when he came into the hall. He was still in his shirtsleeves, as if he had been interrupted in the act of dressing. His hair was all askew. Arabella noticed with a pang that it was thinner than it had been before. "Is it really you?"

Before she could answer, he quite drove the air out of her lungs by grasping her tightly in his arms.

"Yes, Papa," she said humbly when she could speak. "May I come in?"

"Of course, my darling," he said. His pale blue eyes sparkled with tears. He took her portmanteau in one hand and her arm in the other as he escorted her inside the house.

"Giles, what is it?" called Emily over the banister in a frightened voice as Arabella and her father approached the foot of the curved staircase. Emily's eyes were round as saucers, and her hair was still wound in curl papers.

"Emily!" Her husband threw back his head and gave a joyful laugh. "Our daughter has come home at last!"

"This must stop," Konstantin said through his teeth when Raphael lifted his head and gave a wan meow in his direction. The grand duchess's attendant was filled with despair and had finally consulted Konstantin because she knew he had a kindness for the stubborn little beast.

Since his forced separation from Arabella, Raphael

had grown listless and droopy. He ate nothing. He sat in the silk-lined bed the grand duchess had brought for him from St. Petersburg and cried pathetically. In the night the tiny creature had roamed the grand duchess's apartments and scratched at the windows, as if trying to find a way to get out.

Konstantin knew exactly how Raphael felt, for he missed Arabella, too.

The only time Raphael showed a ghost of his old liveliness was when the grand duchess deigned to have him admitted into her presence. On those occasions the droopy little kitten was suddenly transformed into a tiger.

"C'est impossible!" the grand duchess said, throwing up her hands when the kitten raised its back and hissed at her. "Take him from my sight!" When Konstantin suggested that she have the kitten conveyed to Miss Comstock, the grand duchess flew into such a rage that her attendants begged him not to mention the subject again.

On Sunday afternoon, upon being summoned by the desperate servant, Konstantin realized drastic means would be required to save the kitten's life. He pilfered some of the grand duchess's best caviar from her private stock and tried to tempt Raphael to eat it.

Raphael merely raised his head and looked at it with dull-eyed indifference before he sank back into the cushions.

"Enough!" Konstantin exclaimed. "Come along, Raphael. I am going to take you home."

"Prince Obolensky," the grand duchess's attendant cried in alarm. "What are you doing? Her imperial highness will have me thrown out into the street!"

"No, Daria. You have only to say that I overpowered you. *I* am the one who will be thrown out into the street."

His father would never forgive him for bringing disgrace upon his family, but he could not stand aside and watch the little creature die.

EIGHT

Arabella patted Gilly's baby-blond curls and laughed at Emily's shocked dismay when the child buried his grinning, cake-crumb-smeared face in her white muslin skirt.

"Never mind, Emily. He is only a baby," Arabella said, shifting to place the laughing toddler on her lap. "And such a sweet little one, are you not, my precious?"

The thought of Konstantin was a constant ache in her heart, but it would grow duller with time, Arabella told herself. She still missed Raphael and hoped, for the kitten's sake, it would adapt to the grand duchess's household.

But now there was this darling child for her to love. How could she have turned her back on her half-brother all those months ago in sheer spite over Cedric Wyndham, of all the lost causes?

"Have another tea cake, Arabella," said Emily. Her stepmother's eagerness to please quite covered Arabella with shame. And her father looked at her as if he could not bear to let her out of his sight.

The warmth of their welcome went a long way to soothing the ache in her heart. For now, it would be enough.

She cuddled little Gilly and strained to hear the comment Mrs. Peabody had addressed to her. The pleasant room was filled with well-wishers, and it was hard not to be cheered by their presence. Mercifully, no one mentioned the dashing Russian prince with whom she had made a spectacle of herself so recently.

"Mr. Comstock! Mr. Comstock!" shrieked a housemaid. "There is a gentleman here to see Miss Arabella, and he seems quite wild!"

"Get out of my way!" bellowed Konstantin. The butler and housemaid trying to block his impetuous entrance automatically fell back at his command.

"Prince Obolensky!" demanded Mr. Comstock, placing himself between Konstantin and Arabella. "What is the meaning of this intrusion?"

Konstantin was not his usual well-groomed self. His dark, lustrous hair looked as if he had been dragging his fingers through it. His uniform coat was unbuttoned. He looked distraught.

"Arabella!" he exclaimed, when she abruptly stood up and handed Gilly to Emily. Emily, true to form, had started having hysterics. The frightened child, sensing his mother's alarm, added his wails to the confusion.

"Konstantin, what are you doing here?" Arabella asked in bewilderment.

"Sir, we are entertaining guests," Mr. Comstock interjected, trying to impose order on what was promising to become a most extraordinary scene. "You cannot barge in here and—"

"It was absolutely necessary, I assure you, sir," Konstantin said, as he pushed by him. He grasped Arabella's arm, and Emily gave a faint scream. "Arabella, I do not have much time. I think the grand duchess and the rest of her guards are in pursuit."

To Arabella's astonishment, he reached inside his coat and brought out Raphael. The cat saw Arabella and sprang at her. She caught him in her arms with a little cry of happiness.

"Konstantin!" she cried, her eyes going wide. "You *stole* Raphael from the grand duchess?"

"It is no more than you did yourself," he said, sounding defensive.

"I did not imply it as a criticism," she said, unable to control the smile that broke across her face. "I thank you from the bottom of my heart."

The sound of a loud knocking on the front door sounded throughout the house, and Arabella grasped Konstantin's sleeve.

"It is the grand duchess," she cried out. "We must hide you!"

Konstantin detached her clutching fingers and gave her hand a bracing squeeze.

"No, Arabella. A man of honor does not hide," he said, drawing himself up to his full height. "She can do her worst."

"Do not talk in that silly, melodramatic way, Konstantin," Arabella scolded. "Have you forgotten that she threatened to *ruin* you?"

"No, I have not forgotten," he said, looking straight into her eyes.

Arabella's lips parted, but before she could say anything, the grand duchess herself burst into the room with Cedric Wyndham and several Russian soldiers at her heels.

Some of the ladies screamed when the soldiers pushed past them; one of them upset a tea cart.

"There they are!" the grand duchess cried out in French, pointing an accusing finger at Konstantin,

Arabella, and Raphael. "Seize them! The kitten, too!"

"Now see here, madame!" said Mr. Comstock, rising superbly to the occasion in defense of his daughter. "I have had quite enough of these unseemly intrusions into my home."

"Konstantin! Tell this upstart who I am!" she cried out imperiously in French.

"He knows who you are, your imperial highness," Konstantin replied. "He is Mr. Comstock, the father of Miss Comstock."

"Give me my cat, you dreadful girl!" the grand duchess screeched at Arabella, brushing past her father. Raphael promptly put up his back and hissed at her.

"Arabella!" shouted Cedric at the same time. "This has gone far enough. Are you willing to embarrass your family and your country over a *cat?* If you want a cat, I will buy you one. Any cat you wish."

"You!" shouted Mr. Comstock, grabbing Cedric by the collar. "How dare you come into my home and badger my Arabella after what you have done?"

"It is all *her* fault for taking the cat to spite me in the first place!"

Arabella handed Raphael to Konstantin and stepped forward to confront Cedric.

"For the last time, you self-centered oaf!" she shouted. "I did not take Raphael to spite *you!* I took Raphael to save him from that dreadful woman!"

Cedric made the grave error of laying rough hands on Arabella. Both Mr. Comstock and Konstantin gave cries of rage and leapt for his throat, but Mr. Comstock was closer.

"Get out of my house!" Mr. Comstock growled,

shaking Cedric furiously. "Get out of my house, and never come near my daughter again!"

He gave Cedric a shove and cast a sweeping look of disgust over the whole of the grand duchess's party.

"I do not care *who* you are! Get out of my house!" he commanded. "And you may stop yelling that foreign gibble-gabble at me, woman, because I do not understand a word of it!"

Apparently his meaning came through clearly enough, because the grand duchess flew into a rage.

"Teach that ill-mannered little man respect for his betters!" she cried to the guards, pointing at Mr. Comstock. "And do not bother to be gentle."

Emily screamed and clutched her terrified child to her bosom when the guards advanced on her husband. Konstantin leapt protectively in front of him.

"Do not lay a hand on him!" he shouted to the guards. "Try to remember that you are soldiers in the tsar's service and not a lot of spineless footmen! You are under *my* command until the tsar himself relieves me from duty!"

Arabella and Emily both flew to Mr. Comstock's side and glared at the Russian soldiers.

"Konstantin Mikhailovich, you forget yourself!" the grand duchess snarled.

"See here," Mr. Comstock remonstrated as his wife tried valiantly to shush him. "I will not have this bobbery going on in my house."

Most of the invited guests had inched toward the door and fled the house. Gilly was still wailing at the top of his lungs, and Raphael had joined in with an indignant yowling as eloquent as words.

"I am a British citizen," Mr. Comstock shouted at the grand duchess. "You do not have the power to arrest me!"

The grand duchess looked impatiently at Konstantin, who rolled his eyes and translated.

"He is correct," she said, smiling unpleasantly, "but *you* are not a British citizen, Konstantin Mikhailovich! Take the colonel away," she added to the guards.

One of them tentatively touched Konstantin's shoulder as if to escort him from the house and received a clout on the shoulder from Arabella for his pains. The man bore it stoically and exchanged a look of commiseration with Konstantin.

Then a half-dozen British soldiers forced themselves into the room and squared off with the Russian soldiers. Pandemonium broke loose when everyone started shouting.

The grand duchess threw her hands up in the air and by sheer force of will managed to be heard and understood when she commanded everyone to be silent.

"Konstantin! I wash my hands of all of you!" she cried in French. "You may tell them so." She paused while he translated.

"And the kitten?" he hazarded.

"The girl may keep him with my compliments," she said sarcastically. "She deserves the stubborn creature—and you!"

She turned to Cedric.

"As for *you*, Mr. Wyndham," she said, frowning at him, "you may be sure I will tell Sir Gregory that he must have you recalled at once from my service and send a replacement without delay."

Then, with magnificent contempt, she swept out of the room. At a nod from Konstantin, the Russian soldiers scurried out in the grand duchess's wake.

The officer in command of the British soldiers explained to Mr. Comstock that one of the guests had been under the impression that all of Mr. Comstock's family was about to be murdered by foreign cut-throats and had summoned help. Mr. Comstock thanked him for coming to the rescue, and the British soldiers departed.

Mr. Comstock then turned to Konstantin.

"I suppose you expect me to thank you for bringing this pandemonium into my house just because you defended me at the end," he said with a forbidding glare.

"No," Konstantin said humbly. "I expect nothing." His eyes met Arabella's. "Nothing at all."

"Papa—" said Arabella. "Konstantin—"

"You are not on Christian name terms with this man," said Mr. Comstock, all disapproving.

"Who cares if she is on Christian name terms with that fellow!" cried Cedric. "I am ruined. Ruined!"

Mr. Comstock looked down his nose at Cedric.

"My career is in shreds. I hope you are satisfied," Cedric said in a whiny voice to Arabella. "This was your aim from the beginning."

He gave a yelp when Mr. Comstock grasped him by the collar and hauled him to his feet. The two gentlemen squared off and proceeded to shout at each other with all the pent-up rage of the past year.

Arabella rolled her eyes and looked at Emily, who was calmer now that she knew no one was going to arrest her husband. Gilly had quite worn himself out with crying and fell into a fitful sleep. Arabella affectionately touched the child's damp curls in passing as Emily carried him out of the room.

Then Arabella saw Konstantin, and her heart turned over. He was down on one bended knee with Raphael in his arms, comforting the kitten much the

way Emily had been soothing Gilly. His strong hands
were so tender. And his beautiful dark eyes were vulnerable.

Arabella sat down on the floor beside him and
reached for Raphael. Her skin tingled where Konstantin's hand touched hers as he placed the kitten
in her arms.

"Miss Comstock," Konstantin said with a little
catch in his voice, "I will understand completely if
you never want to see me again."

"Oh," she said as a hysterical little bubble of laughter started in her throat. "So, you think *you* are going
to jilt me, too, do you?"

He looked up at that.

"You still want to marry me? After all this?" Konstantin's eyes lit with hope for a moment. Then it
faded. "No, I cannot compromise you that way. I may
not have anything to offer you, Arabella, if the tsar
dismisses me from his service and my father disinher-
its me."

"Possibly not. But *I* have a dowry of sixty thousand
pounds, and I have been a spinster long enough!"

"Arabella, I could not accept—"

But Arabella was not listening.

"Papa!" she said impatiently. "Stop exchanging in-
sults with Cedric and have someone show him the
door."

Mr. Comstock looked up in surprise as Cedric gave
Arabella a searing look and fled the room.

"What are you saying to my daughter, young man?"
Mr. Comstock demanded as his eyes took in the familiar way Arabella was leaning against Konstantin's
shoulder.

"Never mind my precious reputation, Papa," Arabella said impatiently. "Do I, or do I not, have a dowry of sixty thousand pounds?"

"You do, *if* your suitor meets with my approval!" He favored Konstantin with a cold stare. "And I take leave to tell you, Prince Whoever-you-are, that I do not hold with having some foreigner making a laughingstock of my only daughter."

Arabella deliberately kept a grip on Konstantin when he would have stepped forward to face her father man-to-man.

"I will have Konstantin and no other," she said calmly. "How soon can your solicitor have the settlements drawn up?"

"Arabella!" her father said, scandalized.

"Papa, I am three-and-twenty now, and I know my own mind," she said, giving him a look of entreaty. "My happiness depends on this."

"Young man," Mr. Comstock said to Konstantin, "I will want to know your expectations before I agree to let you marry my daughter."

"I have none at the moment, Mr. Comstock," Konstantin said humbly. "My family has a castle and extensive lands in the Volga River Valley, but by offending the grand duchess, I may well find myself disinherited by my father."

"Arabella, I can hardly permit you to marry a man with no expectations!" Mr. Comstock exclaimed. "Be reasonable, my dear."

"But he *had* expectations until he risked everything for me and for Raphael," she said. "Papa, if you will not let me marry Konstantin, I will never speak to you again."

This seemed to bring her father up short.

"No!" Mr. Comstock said, throwing up his hands. "I will not endure another six months of being estranged from my only daughter. Go ahead, girl. Marry him. Marry the bloody *cat* for all I care!"

"Thank you, Papa. And the dowry?"

"Arabella!" objected Konstantin. "The dowry does not matter. Do you think I am like that villain Cedric Wyndham, caring only for your money? Having you as a wife is treasure enough for any man."

Arabella gave him a look of pure delight.

"Very pretty, Konstantin, upon my word." She gave his shoulder a little pat of approval and turned back to her father. "Papa?"

"Yes, my dear. You may have the dowry."

"Splendid!" Arabella crowed.

Her father gave a snort of annoyance and began to leave the room.

"Prince Obolensky, I must go upstairs to reassure my wife that all is well," he said over his shoulder, "so I depend upon you to behave yourself with Arabella in my absence."

"Yes, sir," Konstantin said, looking dazed at his good fortune.

"There, now," Arabella said, snuggling up against him when they were alone again. Raphael was sniffing around the floor at the wreckage of the tea cart pastries. "We have a fortune of sixty thousand pounds, which should make us comfortable enough even if your father *does* disinherit you."

"The money is not important, my darling," Konstantin said reprovingly.

"Of course it is!" she exclaimed, kissing him on the cheek. "*We* can live on love alone in perfect comfort, but thanks to you, our darling Raphael has developed a taste for caviar."

EPILOGUE

October, 1814
Russia

"Damned cold country," huffed Mr. Comstock, who was still pretending to be disgruntled because his daughter insisted upon being married in Russia near the fairy-tale palace that had been in Konstantin's family for centuries. The Volga River Valley was a breathtaking vision arrayed in russet and yellow with the silver ribbon of the river itself winding gracefully through the land. There was a delicious crispness in the morning air that made Mr. Comstock wish he had brought along his wool greatcoat.

His wife shushed him and lovingly pointed out that his displeasure upon being obliged to travel to a foreign land to see his only daughter married did not stop him from proudly dropping the phrase "my daughter, the future Princess Obolensky" into his every conversation from the time the engagement was official.

Konstantin had not been disinherited by his family for marrying a woman of his own choosing, nor had the grand duchess used her influence with the tsar to have him dismissed from his service. Catherine

Pavlovna was far too busy laying determined siege to
the man she intended to make her second husband,
the crown prince of Wurttemberg, to bother trying
to ruin Konstantin.

So it was with all the prerogatives of wealth and
royalty that Prince Obolensky's bride was driven to
the ornate jewel of a centuries-old church in a light-
bodied, ornate carriage by two prancing horses.

Mr. Comstock felt tears start in his eyes.

There was his little girl dressed from head to foot
in gold brocade and ermine with an antique tiara of
diamonds, emeralds and rubies crowning her magnificent unbound hair. Her late mother's emeralds
glittered from her throat and earlobes and wrists.
The prince's betrothal gift, a huge blood-red ruby,
was on her finger. This turn-out, Mr. Comstock reflected with secret satisfaction, made all the fashion-
able London weddings at St. Paul's look like paltry
affairs.

Damned if the prince did not do well by Arabella
after all!

Konstantin, dressed in a long, flowing, gorgeously
patterned silk tunic of gold and green and cobalt
blue belted with a gold brocade sash over full Cos-
sack-style trousers, looked like Byron's *Corsair* come
to life. He rode beside his bride's carriage on a spirited black horse that had been brushed until it was
sleek as ebony. He could not take his eyes off Arabella, and her cheeks were poppy red as much from
his regard, Mr. Comstock suspected, as from the
crisp, cool air.

"How beautiful she looks," sighed Emily, when
Arabella smiled and waved at the cheering people
gathered in front of the church. The prince's labor-
ers had all turned out to greet his bride.

Mr. Comstock's heart swelled when Konstantin tenderly helped his little girl down from the carriage and came to stand in front of him. Konstantin kissed Arabella's hand as she stepped between Mr. Comstock and his wife. Then he strode to where his parents were already waiting at the entrance of the church. His mother's jewels made Emily's look like children's baubles, Mr. Comstock observed with a frown; he resolved to buy his wife some more impressive gewgaws as soon as they returned to London.

One had to keep up appearances when one was hobnobbing with royalty, he thought complacently.

Arabella felt her father's hand squeeze hers convulsively.

The inside of the cavernous church was illuminated by thousands of thick white candles in ornate iron holders, and the jewellike brilliance of the stained-glass windows teased at the edge of Arabella's vision. At the altar waited a bishop whose beard reached almost to his waist. He was dressed in richly embroidered vestments encrusted with jewels for this important ceremony.

On his way to the altar, Konstantin bent over little Gilly, where he waited in one of the pews with his nurse.

Arabella's heart swelled. How like Konstantin to greet her little brother. The little boy had taken a liking to the prince, and yesterday morning at breakfast Konstantin, Gilly, and his nurse had sat whispering secrets.

Konstantin and his parents had reached the bishop and turned to face Arabella as she approached with her parents when Konstantin grinned at Arabella and, like a conjurer, withdrew something from the voluminous folds of his clothing and placed it on the floor.

A bubble of laughter escaped from Arabella's lips as a blur of silver-blue fur launched itself down the aisle directly toward her and pounced on the skirt of her gown. So *this* was the conspiracy Konstantin and Gilly had been hatching!

Arabella picked up the cat—now a handsome adolescent—and carried him to the front of the church with her. Raphael perked up his ears and bowed his head left and right, as if he thought the procession was for him.

In a way it was, Arabella thought fondly as she luxuriated in the cat's warm, soft fur and contented purring. Raphael had brought her and Konstantin together.

Last night while they were dining informally by the fire in Arabella's suite, Konstantin had stroked Raphael's ears and told Arabella that in ancient tradition the name of the Archangel Raphael meant "God hath healed." In truth, the archangel's namesake had brought healing to Arabella's troubled heart.

She could not be certain in the flickering candlelight, but she thought she saw the flash of a gentle smile flicker across the bishop's lips when she and Raphael arrived in front of him.

Arabella took a deep breath, put her hand in Konstantin's, and knelt before the bishop to repeat the Russian words she had memorized so carefully.

Many miles away, where she, her brother, and all the rest of the crowned heads of Europe and their counselors had gathered for the Congress of Vienna, the Grand Duchess Catherine opened a small, ornately wrapped box that a messenger had delivered into the hands of the majordomo at her hotel with strict orders to present it to the grand duchess precisely at ten o'clock in the morning.

"Perhaps you have sent this, Alexei?" she asked her brother, the tsar, who had just come in to breakfast.

"Not I, *cherie,*" he said, frowning a bit jealously. "Is there a card?"

"No, but none is necessary," she said with a little crow of delighted laughter as she lifted the lid and recalled that Konstantin Mikhailovich was to be married this morning.

There, on a tiny velvet pillow, rested an exquisite brooch in the shape of a kitten wrought in silver-blue enamel over gold with a pair of sparkling emeralds for eyes.

THE NAUGHTY KITTEN

by

Debbie Raleigh

ONE

There were few establishments in all of London that could rival the town house of Lord Rumford. Situated near the park, it boasted a magnificent marble staircase and well-appointed rooms elegantly furnished in solid oak. It also boasted a rare collection of Ruben paintings.

On this fine spring day Hugo Langmead, Fifth Earl of Rumford, was seated in the crimson and gold salon admiring his latest acquisition with a critical eye. Perhaps not Rubens's most compelling work, Hugo conceded, studying the painting hung above the heavy mantel, but a priceless masterpiece nonetheless.

Engrossed in his survey, Hugo felt a flare of irritation as the door to the salon was thrust open to reveal his secretary, Charles Pierce. As always, the slender young man appeared decidedly harassed, as if the effort of keeping Hugo's affairs in order was more than any one man should have to bear.

"Oh, my lord . . ." Pierce stumbled to a halt in the center of the room, clenching a thick sheet of parchment in one hand. "Terrible news."

Accustomed to the man's delight in the melodramatic, Hugo remained comfortably sprawled in an ebony chair inlaid with brass.

"Has Napoleon landed at long last?" he drawled, stretching out his long legs encased in buff pantaloons and champagne-polished Hessians.

Never overly burdened with a sense of amusement, the secretary gave a sharp shake of his head.

"No, sir. This is a letter from your grandmother."

"Even worse, eh, Pierce?" Hugo grimaced, realizing that he had once more managed to displease his elderly relative. It was, after all, the only occasion on which she bothered to correspond. "What have I done this time to incur the wrath of the Dragon of Devonshire?"

"Lady Rumford writes that she has discovered your entry in the Four-In-Hand Club."

"Ah . . . that would explain it. I suppose she has convinced herself that I will break my fool neck before providing her with the next Earl of Rumford?"

A hint of color bathed the youthful features. "Yes, she does mention her . . . concern. . . ."

"You needn't hedge with me, Pierce, I am far too accustomed to my grandmother's blunt tongue to be offended. She is no doubt insulting to both my intelligence as well as my skills with a whip." Hugo shrugged in a casual manner. "Does she demand I withdraw my membership at once?"

Surprisingly, the young man gave a distressed shake of his head.

"Oh no, sir, it is worse, much worse, than that."

Hugo arched a golden brow that perfectly matched his thick mane of hair.

"Indeed?"

"She says . . ." The secretary stammered to a halt before nervously clearing his throat and beginning again. "She says that since you are determined to risk your life upon every occasion, then she will ensure that you perform your duty and provide an heir as swiftly as possible."

"Egad. I am almost frightened to inquire how the devil she proposes to do that."

"She says that if you do not wed by the end of the Season, she will cut you out of her will."

Caught off guard, Hugo gave a sharp laugh. Good God. He had realized that his grandmother would not be pleased with his decision to enter the exclusive club but had never suspected that it would inspire such a fierce punishment.

"Cut me out of her will, eh? Well, well, that cunning old minx." He narrowed his gaze. "Does she happen to mention who is to benefit from my lamentable misfortune?"

Pierce shifted his feet in an uneasy manner.

"Mr. Scowell, my lord."

"Mr. Scowell? Has she gone daft?" Hugo drawled in protest. Mr. Eddie Scowell was the disgrace of the Rumford family. An overdressed, overpainted fop, he had earned the reputation of consorting with a most unsavory crowd. But even worse, he never failed to presume upon his distant relationship with Hugo to force his way into society. A habit that had made Hugo long to lodge a bullet in his arse on more than one occasion. "Who the devil would leave an indecent fortune, not to mention the finest estate in Devonshire, to that buffoon? Why, he's an insult to the Rumford family."

"Indeed, sir, but he does possess a legitimate heir," Pierce pointed out.

"Legitimate?" Hugo gave another humorless laugh. "If that milk-faced brat is legitimate then I am Napoleon Bonaparte."

Clearly aware of the rumors surrounding Mrs.

Scowell and her numerous indiscretions, the young man gave an embarrassed laugh.

"Ah . . . yes, I suppose so, sir. But Mr. Scowell does claim him as his son."

"This is absurd." A growing frown marred Hugo's wide brow. "Clearly the old puss is attempting to bluff me into the parson's trap."

"Oh no, sir. It appears she has already contracted her man of business to draw up the papers."

"Has she?" With a sudden motion, Hugo rose to his feet and abruptly moved to stand in front of the large bay window. A tall man with a solid frame, he was imposingly elegant in his Weston-fitted coat and pale yellow waistcoat. However, it would be a mistake to presume him for yet another Bond Street beau. There was an unrelenting strength chiseled in the aquiline features and a keen intelligence in the deep green eyes.

At the moment those fabulous eyes simmered with frustration. His relationship with his irascible grandmother had never been smooth. They were both too willful, too fond of having their own way for the two not to occasionally be at sixes and sevens. And since his elder brother's sudden death in a hunting accident four years before, their relationship had become even more prickly.

She seemed to consider it her sole preoccupation to remind Hugo of his position as the head of the Rumford family. At every opportunity he was lectured to put aside his frivolous lifestyle and become a somber, stiffly proper earl. Most importantly he was told to fill the nursery of Langhorn Manor with all possible haste.

Unfortunately Hugo had no interest in the earldom or becoming a pattern card in propriety. And he certainly possessed no interest in saddling himself with a dewy-eyed chit to produce a string of Rumfords. He had never wanted to become earl and he resented having the burdens thrust onto his unwilling shoulders.

The contrary situation was bound to create difficulties, but Hugo had never suspected that Lady Rumford would go to these lengths. To blatantly blackmail him with the threat of leaving her inheritance to Scowell . . . it was beyond the pale.

"What will you do, sir?" Pierce questioned in worried tones.

With an effort Hugo smothered his brief irritation. It was hardly his secretary's fault that Lady Rumford was driving him batty. Turning about, he gave a nonchalant shrug.

"What choice do I have, Pierce?" he demanded. "I shall wish my fribble of a cousin happy. He is a fortunate man to be the heir apparent to such an illustrious estate."

The young man could not have been more shocked if Hugo had announced that he was emigrating to the colonies.

"What? Give up your inheritance?"

"My grandmother has meddled in my life once too often." Hugo's countenance hardened with stubborn determination. It was an expression that made his young secretary's heart sink. "On this occasion she has overplayed her hand. If she wishes to saddle herself with Scowell and his pack of in-laws, so be it."

Pierce tugged at his modest cravat as if it had suddenly grown too tight.

"But, my lord, surely you jest?"

"Not at all. If I do marry—which, I might add, is as unlikely as my enlisting in the French army—it will not be from threats of being disinherited. No, Pierce, I fear I shall have to muddle by with my ten thousand pounds a year." A wry smile curved Hugo's mouth as he crossed to pour himself a healthy measure of brandy. "In fact, I believe I shall travel to Devonshire and inform her ladyship myself," he decided with his usual impetuous manner. "I shall also insist that she invite the entire Scowell family to Langhorn as soon as possible to become better acquainted with her new heir." The green eyes shimmered as he raised his glass in a mock salute. "That is a reunion I would not miss for all the fortunes in England."

"Wellington . . ." Miss Abigail Stadford moved down the wide hall, occasionally pausing to peer beneath a satinwood table or Queen Anne chair. Experience had taught her that the inquisitive kitten could hide in the most unexpected locations. "Wellington, come out at once." Abby stuck her head behind an ornate chest, indifferent to the hidden dust that clung to her dark honey curls and marred her simple violet gown. Her soft brown eyes narrowed in irritation. Where the devil could that cat have gone? "Wellington . . ."

Without warning, the heavy oak door to the library was thrust open to reveal a small, silver-haired man with a petulant expression.

"Egad, what is that infernal racket?" he snapped, frowning at the rather mussed young maiden.

Accustomed to Lord Walter Stadford's gruff manner, Abby smiled with sweet patience.

"Oh, Grandfather, have you seen Wellington?"

A fierce scowl marred the thin face. "If you are referring to that wretched beast who had the audacity to pounce on my foot, I had him removed from the house."

"Removed?" Abby lifted a hand to her heart. Despite the fact that the tiny white feline was notoriously ill-mannered, Abby had grown fond of the kitten. "But his paw has not healed."

"Fah." Walter banged his ebony cane on the oak floor. "It was healed enough to leap halfway across the library. Besides, I have allowed you to fill the stables with every stray that happens by, against my better judgment I might add; I will not have my own home invaded."

With an effort, Abby conjured a consoling smile. "It was very bad of Wellington to pounce on your foot, Grandfather," she soothed, "but he is not healed enough to be out."

Walter gave a snort. "Ridiculous. That demon is perfectly healthy. He belongs out with the rest of the beasts."

Abby was all too familiar with the stubborn jut of her grandfather's chin. Clearly Wellington had roused the old man's ire and it was going to take more than an apology to get him out of the bumble bath.

A new tactic was called for.

"Perhaps you are right, Grandfather," Abby murmured, her expression one of thorough innocence. "Wellington does tend to become restless when he remains in the house. He will quite enjoy exploring the gardens and grounds." She gave a strategic pause. "And Talvert will no doubt ensure that a few of your quail eggs remain undisturbed."

Pale brown eyes widened in horror. If Lord Stadford possessed a soft spot, it was for the poached quail eggs that his chef prepared each morning as a special treat. The mere thought of the troublesome cat invading his private stash was enough to make him thoroughly forget his mistreated foot.

"Good God, Abby. I won't have it," he bellowed as his cane once again rapped against the floor. "Do something with that infernal pest before I have it shot."

"At once, Grandfather," Abby soothed. "Why don't you return to your nap and I will find Wellington?"

Grumbling at the devious nature of animals in general, and one small white kitten in particular, Lord Stadford stomped back into the library and shut the heavy door with a snap. Left on her own, Abby heaved a rueful sigh. It was always a delicate task to prevent her temperamental grandfather from putting a firm end to her collection of strays. He barely tolerated the presence of his fellow humans, let alone animals. Still, it was worth all his growling to care for her small friends.

With a brisk step Abby moved down the hall and through a narrow door that led to a formal garden. As with the rest of the estate, there was an immaculate perfection to the trimmed hedges that lined the marble fountains. Lord Stadford insisted that the massive sixteenth-century structure be kept in pristine condition. From the lofty attics to the cellars, there was not a defect to be found.

This morning the grounds appeared even finer than usual. After a week of rain the spring sunlight bathed the scythed lawns and distant lake in a welcome warmth.

Breathing in the sweetly scented air, Abby threaded her way along the flagstone path, peering into the budding roses and behind the Grecian statues.

"Wellington . . . here kitty, kitty," she called softly, cutting through a small gate to the grounds beyond. "Wellington?"

At her appearance a young undergardener tending the hedge abruptly rose to his feet and offered her a respectful bow.

"Good morning, Miss Stadford."

"Good morning, Thomas."

"May I be of help?"

Abby smiled with wry humor. "Perhaps. Grandfather has once again banned Wellington from the house. I have come to grant him a reprieve."

"Ah." Thomas gave a nod. "I thought I caught a glimpse of white slipping through the hedge."

"He's here?"

"Naw, it be farther down." Thomas pointed toward the front of the estate. "Next to the lane."

Abby widened her eyes in dismay. Although Rosehill was remote from the major thoroughfares, there was enough traffic from the village and nearby estates to create a danger. Especially for a small kitten with a penchant for trouble.

"Thomas, please go back through the garden and I will go around the house. Perhaps we can halt him before he goes too far."

"Yes, Miss Stadford."

Although not particularly fond of the numerous animals that invaded his garden, Thomas was as devoted as the rest of the staff to Miss Abby. Her generous nature and kind heart had made her a favorite throughout the neighborhood. With a brief nod he hurried into the garden.

Putting aside proper decorum, Abby lifted her gown and trotted along the hedge and down the long drive. What did she care if a hint of silk stocking

could be glimpsed as she rushed past the ancient
oaks? Wellington was far more important than modesty.

She had just reached the end of the drive when
she spied a flash of white darting through the long
grass beside the narrow lane.

"There you are, you naughty kitten," she breathed.

Hiking her skirt even higher, Abby prepared to
make a grab for the cat. Unfortunately the kitten
seemed to sense her purpose and with his usual con-
trariness abruptly leapt onto the muddy lane. Abby
muttered an inelegant curse, and reluctantly acknowledged that she had little choice but to sacrifice
her slippers to the thick mud. It was that or wait for
the kitten to tire of his game and return to the house.

Preparing to wade her way forward, she was suddenly halted by the unmistakable sound of hoofbeats
echoing through the air.

"No. Oh no."

An odd sense of unreality gripped Abby as she
turned to watch the massive black stallion round the
sharp curve. Wellington had crouched in the middle
of the lane, too far for her to reach in time. She could
do nothing but watch in horror as the tall stranger
galloped closer.

Abby pressed a hand to her frozen heart, praying
for a miracle. There seemed nothing that could save
the tiny kitten. Then, without warning, Wellington
made a sudden dash toward the safety of the far
ditch.

The sudden movement had a startling effect. With
a loud curse the gentleman abruptly tugged the reins
of his mount, attempting to slow the huge beast. At
the same moment the stallion sidestepped into the
treacherously deep mud that lined the lane. The

combination was disastrous as the horse slipped to his knees, throwing the rider directly into a towering oak.

Abby cried out as the gentleman crumpled into the thick grass, lying lifeless on the ground.

Wellington had been saved . . . but at what cost?

TWO

A decidedly distraught Abby paced outside the closed door of the bedchamber. It had been well over an hour since the doctor had arrived and taken charge of the golden-haired stranger. Until that moment Abby had been far too occupied with ensuring that the gentleman was carried to the house and the doctor fetched to worry. Now she had nothing to do but wait.

If only she had some means of helping, she acknowledged as she came to a distracted halt. At least then she wouldn't be simply brooding on the knowledge that the entire incident was her fault. But what could she do? Tending her various animals had hardly prepared her for a gravely wounded gentleman.

Her dark thoughts were scattered when the door to the bedchamber opened and the plump, rather shabbily attired doctor stepped into the hall. Abby hurried forward, her fingers nervously twisting together.

"Well?"

Mr. Flack gave a somber shake of his balding head. "I fear I possess ill tidings."

Abby felt her heart slam to a halt. "He isn't . . ."

"No, no, my dear," the doctor hastily reassured. "He will survive."

"Thank God," Abby breathed.

"Unfortunately the blow to his head was quite severe," the doctor cautioned. "It seems to have left him disoriented."

Filled with relief that the wounds were not grievous, it took Abby a moment to absorb the warning.

"Disoriented?" she at last demanded.

The doctor glanced toward the door to ensure that it was closed before continuing.

"He cannot recall anything of his past, not even his own name."

Her eyes widened in disbelief. Not remember his own name? It seemed absurd.

"How is that possible?"

"I have heard of such cases, of course," the doctor mused, seemingly more fascinated than concerned. "The human mind can be quite unpredictable. Most intriguing."

Intriguing was not the word Abby would have used. At least not when the man without a name or memory was lying in her guest chamber.

"What can you do?"

The doctor shrugged. "Nothing for the moment."

"What?"

"Only time can heal his wounds." Spying the overcoat that he had absently draped on a small table, Mr. Flack calmly moved to slip it on. "Hopefully it will also return his memories."

With a flare of panic Abby realized that the doctor was preparing to leave without his patient.

"What is to be done with him?" she demanded, her tone unconsciously sharp.

A shaggy pair of gray brows pulled together. "For

now I must insist that he remain here, Miss Stadford." He eyed her in a stern manner. "He is far too
ill to move."

The rebuke brought a guilty flush to Abby's cheeks.
It was entirely her fault that the gentleman had been
injured in the first place. The least she could do was
aid in his recovery.

Feeling shabby indeed, Abby gave a meek nod of
her head.

"Of course, Doctor."

For a long moment the older man regarded her in
a stern manner, then clearly satisfied that she wasn't
about to toss his patient out the door the moment
his back was turned, he reached out to pat her hand.

"Do not fear. I will begin making inquiries this evening. In no time we will discover where this gentleman belongs. Now, I must be off."

That strange sense of panic once again flared
through Abby.

"Oh, but . . . what shall I do?"

"Just keep him in bed and see that he has plenty
of hot broth and tea," the doctor briskly ordered,
firmly heading down the hall. "I will return in a day
or two."

Not giving Abby the opportunity to argue further,
the doctor disappeared down the wide staircase. Left
alone, Abby nervously bit her soft lower lip.

It was one thing to acknowledge her duty to care
for the stranger; it was quite another to be left virtu-
ally alone with the responsibility.

What did one do with an injured stranger without
a memory?

The sound of a low groan echoing through the
door abruptly made her decision.

The stranger was obviously in distress, she told herself sternly. And while she might be more accustomed to animals than gentlemen, she could not turn her back on anyone who might require her care. This was more than mere duty.

Squaring her shoulders, Abby pushed open the door and firmly stepped into the chamber. She paid scant regard to the impropriety of her presence in the vast room; instead she concentrated on the unconscious form lying in the canopy bed.

On his arrival the doctor had ordered a fire be built to ward off the lingering chill in the spring air. As Abby moved across the wooden floor she noted how the warm glow spilled over the dark male countenance and shimmered in the golden hair.

Why, he was splendid, she acknowledged with a small twitch of her heart. His brow was wide and noble, his skin gleaming with the rich bronze of a sporting man. And his features might easily have been the inspiration for the Grecian artists. A man who would turn the head of even the most particular of women.

Of course, she did not include herself in that category, she hastily reassured herself.

Years ago she had turned her back on such gentlemen. A brief engagement followed by several other hopeful suitors had taught her a hard-earned lesson in the fickleness of the male species. However they might claim to be enchanted by a young lady, it was the young lady's dowry that was the true inducement to marriage. Her grandfather had only to threaten to disinherit her to have her supposed swains fleeing in terror.

Now she firmly stifled the hint of pleasure that tingled down her spine at the finely chiseled countenance. She was no foolish miss to be swayed by such trivial matters. Indeed, she was a hardhearted spin-

ster with no interest in gentlemen, splendidly handsome or otherwise.

Unaware that she had bent forward during her intent survey, Abby gave a small start as the stranger
abruptly lifted his lids to reveal dark green eyes. She
was close enough to detect the faint flecks of gold in
the jade depths and to smell the clean scent of his
skin. Her heart gave another of those odd twitches.

The fine lines beside those fascinating eyes deepened as the gentleman conjured a weak smile.

"A vast improvement on my previous visitor, I must
admit," he whispered in a husky voice.

"Oh." The warmth of his sweet breath brushed her
cheek and Abby hastily straightened. For goodness
sakes, one would think she had never seen a man
before. "I did not realize you had awakened."

"I am not certain I am awake. I feel as if this were
all a dream." His golden brows furrowed in pained
bewilderment. "Where am I?"

"Rosehill Manor."

"Rosehill?"

She cursed herself for her stupidity. "In Devonshire."

"Ah." There was a pause, then his lips twisted with
a wry amusement. "I do not suppose you happen to
know who I might be?"

"No."

"I suppose it was too much to hope."

Biting her lower lip, Abby eyed him in concern.
"How do you feel?"

He grimaced. "As if a blacksmith had set up shop
in my head."

A flare of guilt swept through her. "I am so sorry."

"It is hardly your fault," he murmured. "The doctor tells me that I fell from my mount."

There was a hint of disgust in his expression, as if he found the knowledge hard to accept, despite his lack of memory.

Her innate sense of honesty forced Abby to confess the truth.

"Yes, but you only fell because Wellington was in the road."

"Wellington?" He blinked in startled surprise. "In Devonshire? How odd."

"Oh, not that Wellington. My kitten, Wellington."

"You possess a kitten named Wellington?"

"Yes, you see I discovered him fighting off a dog almost twice his size, and he reminded me of . . ." Her words stammered to a halt as Abby realized that the gentleman was battling to remain conscious. It was unforgivable that she should be rattling away when he was in dire need of rest. "Perhaps we should delay this discussion until later."

"I believe you are right." With a rather rueful sigh the golden lashes fanned downward. "I feel remarkably weary."

Resisting the urge to straighten the heavy quilt that covered his large body, Abby slowly backed toward the door.

She would go to the kitchen and ensure there was an ample supply of broth and tea on hand, she decided.

Tiptoeing from the room, Abby was on the point of closing the door when the sound of a cane banging through the hallway made her turn about to discover her grandfather making his way to the bed chamber.

"Abby, this is intolerable," he announced in a querulous tone, narrowly regarding Abby as she hastily closed the door.

"Grandfather," she protested in soft tones, "what is the matter?"

"First it was dogs and then cats and now this." His cane was stabbed toward the bedchamber.

Abby frowned in confusion. "What?"

"I may have indulged you with those mangy beasts," he growled, "but I absolutely draw the line at collecting stray men."

Abby rolled her eyes heavenward.

What next?

It was with a decided effort that Hugo lifted his heavy lids. For a moment he allowed his blurry gaze to clear; then he glanced about the shadowed room. His heart sank at the unfamiliar paneling and vaulted ceiling.

It hadn't been some horrible nightmare. He was indeed in this strange place without the least notion of his name or past.

A flare of frustration rushed through his weak form.

It was ludicrous.

There was so much he could recall. Hyde Park on a sunny afternoon. The smothering heat of Carlton House. The exquisite scent of jasmine on a beautiful actress. But the faces and names of those who were most intimate with him remained stubbornly elusive.

At least the stabbing pain had dulled to a bearable ache. With a great deal of caution he carefully inched himself to a semireclined position, surprised at the amount of effort such a simple task demanded.

Damn. Had a man ever had such ghastly luck?

Bad enough that he had lost his memory. Did it

have to be in the depths of Devonshire, where no one seemingly had the faintest clue as to his identity?

Brooding on his ill fortune, it was a welcome interruption when the door to his chamber was slowly pushed open. His gaze narrowed as a tiny woman with a mass of honey curls and warm brown eyes entered, bearing a small tray.

So, the sweet-faced angel wasn't just a figment of his fevered dreams. Somehow the knowledge lifted his bout of self-pity.

"Good, you are awake." The woman smiled, if somewhat warily. "I brought you some broth."

Hugo watched as the woman crossed the room and carefully placed the tray on a nearby table.

"Thank you, Miss . . ."

"Stadford. Miss Abigail Stadford. How do you feel?"

"The room has halted its spinning." His own smile was an effort. "Unfortunately my thoughts remain as muddled as ever."

The brown eyes instantly softened. "The doctor is quite confident that your memory will soon return."

"I wish I could share his confidence," Hugo murmured.

"Mr. Flack can be a bit eccentric, but he is rarely wrong." Her hands plucked at her violet gown, as if she was not as coolly composed as she would like to appear. "Now, would you like some broth?"

So that was the reason for her unease, he acknowledged with a flicker of amusement. She had overcome her reluctance to be alone with a strange man, no doubt convincing herself that duty outweighed propriety, but she was clearly reluctant to perform the more intimate task of feeding him.

A gentleman would firmly insist that he could manage on his own. After all, he had little interest in the broth, and he could always call later for a servant to lend him aid if his appetite sharpened. But a devilish imp thrust aside such a sensible resolution.

There was something quite enticing about the tiny face and velvet brown eyes. He would be a fool to deny himself the pleasure of having her close.

"I fear I must depend upon your kindness, Miss Stadford." He cast her a sorrowful glance. "I feel as weak as a newborn foal."

Just for a moment she hesitated, as if she sensed the amusement simmering just below his display of weakness. Then, gathering her courage, she forced herself to collect the bowl of broth and the spoon before cautiously perching on the edge of the bed.

Hugo hastily swallowed a smile at her stiffly held form. She looked for all the world as if she feared he might suddenly rise up and bite her. Ridiculous, of course. Granted, he wouldn't mind a nuzzle or two, but he was quite certain he was no seducer of innocent young maidens.

Covertly moving back so that she would be forced to lean over his large chest, Hugo meekly opened his mouth to accept the spoonful of broth.

"Mmm . . . delicious," Hugo murmured, referring as much to the feel of her warm body pressed against his own as to the rich broth.

An enchanting color bloomed beneath her pale skin, but with an obvious effort she maintained her stoic composure.

"I shall inform Mrs. Greene of your approval."

"Mrs. Greene?"

"Our cook."

Hugo suppressed a smile, quite enjoying the unconventional encounter.

"In truth I cannot be certain if it is the broth I am enjoying or the company." His tone was deliberately suggestive.

Abruptly moving back, she rewarded him with a stern frown of disapproval. "Sir."

With a glint in his green eyes, he tilted his head to one side. "Tell me about yourself, Miss Stadford."

"There is very little to tell," she hedged in repressive tones.

Undaunted, Hugo gave a small shrug. "Do you live here with your parents? Do you have brothers or sisters?"

"I live with my grandfather, Lord Stadford."

Hardly forthcoming, Hugo acknowledged wryly, "And of course the naughty Wellington."

"Yes."

"It must be very quiet for you, buried in the depths of the country."

"I prefer to live quietly."

Hugo carefully studied her set features. What was going on behind that pretense of cool indifference?

"But surely you intend to travel to London for the Season?" he protested. "It would be a shocking disservice to hide such beauty in this rural isolation."

Predictably her eyes narrowed at his frivolous flattery. "I have no interest in London."

His golden brows arched. "Then you are a rare maiden indeed, Miss Stadford. Unless, of course, your attentions are already fixed upon some local gentleman?"

"My attentions, sir, are fixed upon running my grandfather's household and caring for my animals, nothing more," she informed him in icy tones.

Hugo simply could not resist temptation. "Nonsense. There must be some handsome young farmer to distract you from such tedious duties."

"I assure you that I find my duties far from tedious. Indeed, it is the young farmers and supposed gentlemen whom I find tedious."

The green eyes flashed. "Perhaps that is because you have not encountered a gentleman worthy of capturing your interest."

"No doubt."

"And when you do?"

"I have no fear of that unlikely event ever occurring, sir."

"Ah . . . you tempt a man to prove you wrong, Miss Stadford."

Something in his teasing tone made her shy away, and with a sharply drawn breath, Abby surged to her feet.

"I fear you will have to excuse me. I must return to my duties downstairs. I will have one of the footmen return to finish helping you with your broth."

Hugo felt a swift stab of remorse. He had not intended to drive his prickly angel from his side. Indeed, he wished for nothing more than to continue their intriguing conversation.

"Wait, Miss Stadford," he pleaded softly. "I did not mean to tease you. I am very grateful for all you have done."

She eyed him in open suspicion. "I am only doing my duty, sir."

He conjured his most pathetic expression. "Does your duty include keeping me company through a tedious afternoon?"

"I do not . . ."

"Please, Miss Stadford," Hugo interrupted. "Have pity on a poor invalid. I may not recall my past, but

I am quite certain that I detest being forced to remain inactive with no one to talk with and nothing to occupy my mind."

Clearly torn between propriety and the guilty feeling that she was somehow responsible for his injuries, Abby hesitated. Then, allowing her gaze to rest on the enormous bruise that marred his temple, she reluctantly conceded to his demands.

"Very well. I shall return later," she said, then, as his smile became one of satisfaction, she added, "but only for a short visit."

"That is all I ask, Miss Stadford." Hugo settled more comfortably on the pillows, well pleased with himself. "I shall count the moments until your return."

Just for a moment he feared he had overplayed his hand. Miss Stadford was clearly no giddy young girl to be impressed by the teasing flirtations of an older man. Instead, she appeared to prefer the role of a staid old maid with nothing to interest her but a pack of animals.

"I would think you would be better served to try and sleep, sir. You have taken a grave injury to your head." Her glance was pointed. "It has obviously rattled your wits."

With her insult delivered, Abby smoothly turned about to sweep from the room. Hugo watched her exit with a smile. So there was a bit of spirit beneath that very proper composure. It would be intriguing to discover just what else was hidden beneath it.

THREE

Carrying the warm bowl of broth up the curved staircase and down the hall, Abby determinedly ignored the two maids who watched her progress with raised brows.

Really, it was absurd.

One would think that the servants had nothing better to do than count the number of occasions that she had visited the golden haired stranger, she thought with a flare of annoyance.

Why should they care if she had made a habit of passing a large part of each afternoon and evening with her patient? After all, the past four days had not been easy for the poor man. Forced to remain in bed with no memory of his past, he was in sore need of diversion.

And besides, she would be less than honest not to acknowledge that she had come to enjoy conversing with her unexpected guest. His keen intelligence and charming wit was a welcome change from her grandfather's abrupt manner.

It was all perfectly harmless, and there was no reason whatsoever to regard her as if she had grown a second head.

Halting before the open door, Abby smoothed her

features to a pleasing expression. There was no need to concern her guest with the ridiculous gossip of the servants, she told herself sternly. She was doing her duty, nothing more.

Unconsciously tilting her chin to a firm angle Abby swept into the bedchamber, only to come to an abrupt halt at the sight of her grandfather standing beside the bed.

Abby felt a flare of misgiving sweep through her body at the older man's grim expression. Although she had managed to convince Lord Stadford that it was impossible to move the intruder from the estate, he had remained adamantly opposed to his presence at Rosehill. Now she could only fear what he might have been saying to the poor gentleman.

"Grandfather," she murmured weakly.

Both men turned to regard her with unreadable expressions.

"There you are, Abby," Lord Stadford unnecessarily announced.

Oddly conscious of the unusual fuss she had taken in choosing her most flattering gown in a soft rose and the elegant arrangement of her curls, Abby shifted in an uneasy manner.

"I did not realize you were in here."

Lord Stadford straightened his thin shoulders. "I thought it was time that I became acquainted with our guest."

Better acquainted? Abby felt her heart sink another notch.

"I see. Perhaps I should come back later?"

"Not at all. I have said everything that I wished. And now that we have had an opportunity to understand one another, I shall return to the library." He deliberately cast a stern glance toward the gentleman propped in the center of the bed. "We do understand one another I presume?"

The younger man took care to appear suitably subdued. "Certainly, my lord. We understand one another perfectly."

Clearly satisfied that he had cowed the impertinent intruder, Lord Stadford gave a small smirk before noisily stomping across the room. Abby was not so easily fooled. She had not missed the roguish glint in the green eyes, nor the tiny twitch of the finely molded lips.

Her grandfather paused as he reached the doorway, regarding her with a stern frown.

"Abby, I will expect you to join me in the library."

"The library?"

"Yes, I wish you to read me the paper."

Abby frowned at the demand. Her grandfather never wished her to read him the paper. In fact, he rarely wished for her company at all. Now she could only suppose he was attempting to lure her away from the golden-haired stranger.

"I will be down presently, Grandfather," she hedged.

"Not presently; at once, young lady."

The older man regarded her with a warning glare before limping from the room.

Once alone, Abby regarded the gentleman lying in the center of the bed with a wary expression. What could her grandfather have been saying behind her back? He most certainly had not come for the innocent social call that he had indicated. Lord Stadford was not the social type.

It was only when the heat from the broth became uncomfortable that she reluctantly moved to perch on the edge of the bed.

"I hope my grandfather did not tire you?" she murmured, covertly watching him beneath lowered lids.

The dark countenance, which had only become more disturbingly handsome as the gentleman had slowly regained his strength, twitched with obvious amusement.

"Not at all. Indeed, I find Lord Stadford to be quite refreshing."

Her wariness only deepened. "*Refreshing* is not a description generally attributed to my grandfather."

He shrugged. "I suppose there would be those offended by his blunt manner of speaking his mind. He is certainly a man willing to share his opinions with others," the gentleman conceded, his smile widening, "I, however, found it quite diverting."

Abby clenched the hot bowl of broth. Whatever her grandfather had been saying, she was quite certain she wasn't going to like it.

"Really? And what precisely did he speak his mind about?"

"Actually it was about you."

Abby caught her breath as he confirmed her worse fears.

"Me?"

"Yes."

"What did he say?"

For a moment he paused, his eyes glinting with mischievous humor.

"Oh, we spoke on this and that."

She ground her teeth. "Such as?"

"Let me think . . . ah, yes, he told me how he had taken you in after your parents died and pointed out the fact that he was now your legal guardian."

"And that's all?"

"Oh no, he also told me that a few years ago another gentleman came into the neighborhood. A gentleman by the name of . . . Thomure."

Abby winced at the memory of the hateful name. Why couldn't her grandfather hold his tongue?

"How ridiculous for him to even mention Mr. Thomure. That was a very long time ago."

Hugo regarded her closely. "Your grandfather said that you were engaged to this man."

"Oh? Yes, I believe I was." She attempted to sound off-hand, only to fail miserably. "As I said, that was a very long time ago."

"But he claimed that once he stepped in and threatened to have you disinherited, your fiancée fled back to London."

She longed to sink beneath the floorboards.

"I can not imagine why Grandfather would bore you with such a dismal tale," Abby gritted in embarrassment.

The aquiline features revealed his obvious amusement. "I believe that the moral of the story was that any hope I might have of seducing you into marriage and stealing your fortune was doomed to failure."

Abby felt a painful heat crawl beneath her skin. "Oh lord."

"Lord Stadford obviously fears that I deliberately landed myself on your doorstep so I might take advantage of your kindness. His next line of reasoning was that I would manage to sway you into marriage and then set about fribbling away your fortune on women and horses. Or something to that effect."

She battled the urge to flee in humiliation. How could her grandfather be so absurd? This man was no fortune hunter. For goodness sakes, he had hardly wished to be an invalid at Rosehill. Indeed, the entire accident had been her fault.

And certainly he had never behaved in anything but the most circumspect manner. The unfortunate man must wonder if he had landed himself in Bedlam.

"I am sorry," she apologized in low tones. "My grandfather can be remarkably ill mannered when he chooses."

"Do not apologize. I prefer a man who speaks what is troubling him. Better to clear the air, I say."

"Oh yes, my grandfather is a great believer in clearing the air. You always know precisely where you stand."

"My only concern is you, Miss Stadford."

She gave a blink of surprise. "Me?"

The golden head tilted to one side. "Do you believe I have created this ruse to gain your fortune?"

"Certainly not," she denied, meeting his gaze squarely.

"Good." Quite deliberately he lifted himself off the pillow. At the unexpected motion the blanket abruptly fell downward to reveal the width of his chest beneath the white lawn shirt. Abby felt her breath catch in her throat as he halted mere inches from her tense body. He was splendid, indeed, she acknowledged with an odd tingle of excitement. "I assure you that if I desire to steal from you, it would not be your fortune, but rather this . . ."

Before Abby could discern his purpose, he had claimed her lips in a softly seeking kiss. She felt herself freeze in shock. Although Mr. Thomure had on occasion pressed his mouth to her own, it had been nothing like this.

His lips were warm, demanding a response, and for

a crazed moment, Abby gave in to the enticing sensations racing through her body. A heat as searing as the Egyptian sun blazed through her shivering form, darting to the center of her body with a blaze of pleasure.

Dear lord, who could have known that a mere kiss could create such a confusion of sweet emotions?

She swayed forward, thoroughly bewitched by the tiny flutters of excitement stirring to life. Then, as his hands rose to gently cup her upturned face, she abruptly stiffened in horror.

What was she doing? Did she possess no shame?

With a gasp, Abby struggled to her feet. She was not certain what demon had prompted her to behave as a common trollop, but she did know she wanted to be far from the man who was the cause of her disturbance.

"Abby, wait . . ."

"No, I must go."

"Please, Abby . . . I did not mean to frighten you," he pleaded in husky tones.

She kept her gaze firmly on the floorboards. "I really must go."

"When will you return?"

"I don't know."

"Why do you not sit down? I have not finished my lunch."

She could not think of lunch or anything else at the moment. All she could do was tremble from the heat still flowing through her veins.

She had to get away before he realized just how susceptible she was to his touch. Before he could sense that she wished she had never had to end that tantalizing kiss.

With a strangled moan Abby shoved the broth onto

the small table beside the bed and gathering her skirts she bolted from the room as if fleeing the Netherworld itself.

FOUR

Seated on a cushioned seat in the private garden, Hugo absently stroked the fur of the kitten that he had lured onto his lap. It was the first occasion that he had been allowed to escape the confines of the bedchamber and he struggled to combat the weariness that threatened to overtake him.

After seven days in bed he was determined to clear his head with a bit of fresh air. And just as importantly, he was determined to discover the whereabouts of Miss Stadford.

Since his impetuous kiss, the wary maiden had adamantly avoided any contact with him. A young footman had suddenly taken her place, bringing his meals and offering to play at cards to pass the day. Hugo discovered that he sorely missed the presence of his brown-eyed angel.

He missed her swift intelligence, her ready humor and lack of artifice. She had managed to keep him thoroughly entertained and his thoughts from dwelling on his annoying lack of memories. Indeed, his thoughts had far too often brooded on the delicate body beneath the muslin gowns and the tempting softness of her mouth, rather than the inconvenience of his accident.

Which was precisely what had led to his current state of disgrace.

At least the doctor had arrived this morning and managed to convince the stubborn footman that Hugo could survive a brief span of time in the spring sunlight. He had also brought an unexpected surprise. A fine linen handkerchief embroidered with the name *Hugo* that had been found in the grass where he had fallen.

"Hugo." He tested the name, wondering why it stirred no emotions. "Hardly a grand name, eh, Wellington? Still, I suppose it is better than nothing."

The kitten gave an indifferent yawn, before returning his attention to cleaning his paw. Hugo gave a wry smile. He might now have a name, but he was no closer to recalling his identity than he had been seven days before.

Allowing his restless gaze to wander over the well-tended roses, Hugo settled the kitten more comfortably on his lap. The doctor promised that he was making inquiries throughout the area and even as far as London, but there was no certainty that he would be successful. It left him in a decidedly awkward position.

The unpleasant thought was swiftly thrust aside as Hugo heard the unmistakable sound of approaching footsteps. His smile returned. So, his patience was about to be rewarded, he acknowledged with a strange flare of anticipation.

"Wellington," a soft female voice called.

Hugo gave the cat a rewarding pat on the head. "Ah, as I suspected, you have proved to be the perfect bait to lure your elusive mistress to my side. Such a good kitty."

He turned to watch as the young maiden rounded

the corner. As always she appeared quite fetching in a jonquil gown with sable ribbons and her honey curls framing her tiny face in charming disarray.

"Wellington . . . oh." Spotting Hugo seated on the garden bench, Miss Stadford came to a startled halt.

Hugo regarded her with open amusement. "Good morning, Miss Stadford."

"I did not realize you were here," she confessed before she could halt the revealing words.

"As delightful as the accommodations might be, I found I could not endure another day alone in my bedchamber."

An uncomfortable blush crawled beneath her skin at his subtle reproach.

"How do you feel?"

"Much improved, thank you."

"Good." She shifted uncomfortably, clearly preparing to flee. "Now I must . . ."

"Miss Stadford." Hugo deliberately halted her flight by hoisting the small kitten into view. "I believe you were searching for this?"

She blinked in surprise as the kitten growled at being disturbed from his comfortable perch.

"Yes. I am sorry if he has been making a pest of himself."

"Not at all." Hugo returned the feline to his lap, grimacing as Wellington promptly repaid his indignity by digging his claws through the fawn pantaloons. "I was glad for the company. He appears to be the only member of the household who is not attempting to avoid my presence."

"Nonsense," Abby hastily denied, her expression giving the lie to her words. "I have simply been occupied."

"Of course." His tone was laced with disbelief.

"Is there something you require?"

"The pleasure of your company," he promptly demanded. "Surely you can spare a few moments from your hectic schedule?"

Her lips parted to deny his request, but catching the blazing challenge in his gaze, her chin slowly tilted to a defiant angle. He had known quite well that she could not bear to appear a coward.

"Very well." Moving forward, she stiffly perched on the edge of a matching bench. A long silence descended during which he pleasurably studied the delicate lines of her profile. Odd how each beautiful line had haunted his thoughts. At last, thoroughly unnerved by his survey, she abandoned her dignified pose. "The weather is quite fine, do you not think?"

His lips quivered. "Exceptionally fine."

"Very warm for April."

"Yes, indeed."

"Perhaps it is a sign that we shall have a prosperous harvest."

"Perhaps." Hugo stretched out his legs and smiled with lazy humor. "Tell me, Miss Stadford, was I the first gentleman to kiss you?"

Her gasp echoed through the vast garden. "Really, sir, you have no right to ask such a question."

"No?" His head tilted to one side. "I find it far more fascinating than the weather."

"Well, I do not," she desperately denied, her cheeks hot with embarrassment.

Hugo gave a soft chuckle. "It was merely a kiss, my dear, and not the last, I hope."

An undeniable emotion rippled over her expressive features before she managed a stern frown.

"You are impertinent."

Hugo chuckled. "Yes, I daresay I am, but I fail to

comprehend why I should not admit that I thoroughly enjoyed kissing you."

"I will not discuss this further. If you cannot conduct a sensible conversation, I shall leave you to the company of Wellington."

There was a stubborn edge to her tone that warned Hugo that she was quite prepared to abandon him to the sleeping kitten.

"Please, Miss Stadford, I apologize for teasing you," he relented with a cajoling smile. "As you said, I am impertinent and in thorough need of your pert reprimand. May we be friends again?"

She hesitated. "Only if you can behave as a proper gentleman."

"Oh, I shall be excessively proper."

She glared at him for a long moment before a reluctant hint of humor softened her frown.

"I believe you must be odiously spoiled, sir."

"You are no doubt correct." He felt his heart stir in the oddest fashion. "I have missed our time together. The days have become quite flat without your presence."

The color returned to her cheeks. "Has Jonah not tended to your needs?"

Hugo shrugged. "He kept me fed and suitably clean. Unfortunately his conversation is severely limited to horseflesh and the charm of a local barmaid."

"If you prefer, I can have another servant take Jonah's place."

He slowly leaned forward, his expression intent. "What I prefer is for you to take Jonah's place."

"I am not certain that is entirely proper."

"Oh, the devil with what is proper," he growled, barely resisting the urge to reach out and pull her into his arms. Damn, no woman had any right to possess such tempting lips. "It did not concern you when I first arrived."

Her slender fingers plucked restlessly at the soft muslin gown.

"I was merely concerned for your health. Now that I am confident you will recover, I have realized that I behaved in a decidedly reckless manner."

"Fustian. You vanished because I kissed you," he retorted in blunt tones. "Now that I have promised to behave myself you have no reason not to return."

She abruptly rose to her feet, clearly disturbed by his insistence.

"I do not think that would be advisable. . . ."

"Miss Stadford." Fearing that she was about to flee once again, Hugo half rose to his feet, momentarily forgetting the kitten napping on his lap. With a furious hiss the cat lodged its claws deep into his leg. Hugo yelped in pain as he obediently sank back onto the cushion.

Intent on removing the dastardly claws, Hugo was unaware that Wellington's antics had gone unobserved by the young maiden, until she had thrown herself onto the bench beside him. Wrapping her arms about his shoulders, she regarded him with a worried gaze.

"Sir . . . Hugo . . . are you in pain? How can I help?"

For a moment Hugo battled the tiny voice in the back of his mind that urged him to confess the truth of his discomfort. Surely only a cad would take advantage of her sympathetic nature? Then, without further ado, temptation won the day. Laying his head on the softness of her bosom, he smiled in a wicked manner.

"Promise you will not leave me, Miss Stadford," he murmured in weak tones.

She briefly stiffened as her heart raced beneath his ear.

"Very well," she at last conceded. "You have my promise."

His smile widened. "Bless you, Miss Stadford."

FIVE

Although the long salon had not been renovated for several years, it possessed a charmingly elegant style, with classical furnishings and a fine collection of Renaissance paintings. It also boasted a magnificent view of the sweeping parkland.

Seated at a lion-clawed table, Abby leaned forward to move an ivory carved chess piece into a strategic position. Then, with a triumphant smile, she lifted her head to meet the glittering male gaze.

"Checkmate."

Hugo settled back in the gold and crimson seat with a rueful smile.

"You could at least make the pretense that I am not thoroughly outgunned, Miss Stadford."

"You do not properly concentrate," Abby chided.

The disturbing gaze made a slow, utterly shameless survey of her pale features, lingering on the tender curve of her mouth.

"There are far too many delightful distractions."

Abby struggled to combat the ready flush that rose to her cheeks. After being in the company of Hugo for a fortnight, she had discovered that he thoroughly enjoyed bringing her to the blush. But while she might chide herself for so easily allowing herself to be teased, she seemed unable to maintain her normal composure.

Thankfully the plump housekeeper chose that moment to enter the salon, carrying a heavy tray that she placed on a low table.

"Tea, Miss Stadford," she announced, a satisfied hint to her expression as she viewed her mistress and the handsome stranger so comfortably situated.

"Thank you, Mrs. Snow."

Abby gratefully rose to her feet and crossed toward the tray. For some reason she preferred to have something to occupy herself when in the company of Hugo. It helped to ease the odd tingles of excitement that ran rampant through her body.

"Your tea, sir." Abby swiftly poured the steaming brew with just the proper dollop of cream that her guest preferred. Then, choosing the hot scones she had ordered baked that morning, she arranged a large plate that she placed beside the delicate tea cup.

Ignoring the countless chairs placed throughout the vast room, Hugo moved to place himself on the sofa next to her. Abby was instantly conscious of the heat from his large form and the exotic scent of sandalwood that drifted through the air.

"Ah . . . my favorite scones." He attacked the pastries with relish, unaware that she was observing his pleasure with a sense of satisfaction. "Delectable. You must give my compliments to your cook."

Abby refrained from mentioning that she had personally overseen the preparation of the scones. Or that she had also supervised the evening menu that included his favorite roasted duck in apricots and stuffed mushrooms in cream sauce.

"Yes, I will," she murmured.

Leaning back, Hugo sipped at his tea and glanced across the room to the handsome painting that claimed an enviable position above the marble fireplace.

"Are those your parents?"

Abby turned her own attention to the happy couple pictured seated in the rose garden.

"Yes. That was painted shortly after their marriage."

"What happened to them?"

Abby felt a familiar pang of loss. Even after ten years, she still missed the loving sense of family her parents had provided.

"They were killed in a fire at my father's hunting lodge."

Clearly hearing the edge of pain in her voice, Hugo turned to regard her with an expression of sympathy.

"I am sorry."

"So am I," she softly agreed.

"How old were you?"

"I had just turned twelve."

The golden head tilted in a familiar manner. "Then you came to live with your grandfather?"

"Yes."

"It must have been very lonely for you."

It had been devastating. For a young girl who had been accustomed to dozens of friends and relatives surrounding her, the seclusion of Rosehill had been like a mausoleum. Day after empty day she had roamed through the vast corridors with nothing to occupy her mind but the memories of her loss.

"At times," she confessed. "Although I have always had my animals."

She hoped to make light of her painful past, unwilling to burden her guest with grim details of her childhood. But surprisingly the aquiline features tightened in disapproval.

"It is no wonder you were vulnerable to the charms of a fortune hunter," he growled, as if the thought offended him. "Did your grandfather never consider your need for companionship?"

"My grandfather prefers to live quietly." She perversely found herself defending her elderly relative.

Hugo was unimpressed. "At the very least he could have provided you with a proper London Season."

"I have no desire for a London Season." Abby leaned forward to set aside her plate and effectively hide her expressive face at the same moment. This man was stirring emotions to life that were better left undisturbed. "I am quite content with my life here."

"And what of a husband and family of your own?"

It was a question that she had not allowed to enter her thoughts for a very long time. She had few opportunities to meet eligible men, and those she had encountered had proven to be unworthy of her trust. She had at last convinced herself to put aside such fanciful notions. Now she shrugged uneasily.

"I have said that I am content," she insisted in low tones. "Would you care for more tea?"

"No, thank you." He dismissed her polite attempts to redirect the conversation to less troublesome waters. "Miss Stadford . . . Abby . . ."

"Please, I prefer not to discuss this."

With a firm movement he turned to face her, a slender hand reaching out to cup her chin and raise her reluctant gaze to meet his piercing survey.

"You are far too beautiful to bury yourself in the country," he insisted, a strange huskiness entering his voice. "So very, very beautiful."

Abby felt her growingly unpredictable heart give a

sudden lurch. She vividly recalled the sweet magic of his kiss and the delicious sensations that had flowed through her heated blood. The memory had haunted her far more than she cared to admit. Now she barely resisted the urge to press her lips to his for another taste of paradise.

The green eyes darkened, as if he read her treacherous thoughts, but even as her lips parted and his head dipped downward, the door to the salon was once again pushed inward to reveal the rotund form of Mrs. Snow.

"Miss Stadford, Lord Stadford would like you to join him in the library," the housekeeper announced in tones that revealed her annoyance with the elderly man's interference.

Abruptly jolted out of her momentary enchantment, Abby hastily scrambled to her feet. What was she thinking? Or not thinking?

She knew nothing of this man. Not his name. Not his position in society. Not even if he were already wed.

All she did know was that he had created emotions that she had never felt before. Dangerous emotions that threatened to tumble out of control.

"Thank you, Mrs. Snow," she muttered, frantically smoothing the silk of her skirt. "Tell him I will be there directly."

"Of course, Miss Stadford."

"Abby." Hugo rose to his feet, obviously intent on halting her escape.

"I fear I must go."

"Wait, please." His hand reached out to grasp her nervous fingers. "Will you return?"

She should decline. Over the past two weeks she had become more and more fascinated by this man.

She looked forward to each day in his company. She had begun choosing her dresses in the hope that he would find her attractive. And most telling of all, she had begun to order the entire household to suit his every whim.

The only sensible thing to do was once again place him into the care of her servants and return to her secluded life. At least then she could be certain that there would be no disillusionment, no pain.

Unfortunately she had no desire to be sensible, and before she knew what she was doing she discovered herself nodding her head in agreement.

"Yes," she whispered. "I will return."

She felt him gently squeeze her fingers before she was pulling free and crossing toward the door.

She was behaving as a reckless fool, but for once she did not care. Soon this man would be recovered and leaving Rosehill. When that day came she would have all the time in the world to behave in a sensible manner.

SIX

Hugo watched Abby depart with a great deal of reluctance. Just for a moment he had managed to sweep past her barriers to the vulnerable woman beneath. He had seen her lips tremble and her eyes darken with awareness of the attraction that lay between them.

Now she would have time to scurry behind her facade of respectable composure.

Of course, he thought with a flare of rueful humor, perhaps it would be best for both of them. He had come perilously close to abandoning his pledge not to repeat his kiss. It was a pledge that was becoming increasingly more difficult to keep when Miss Abigail Stadford was near. A pledge he had no true wish to keep, if the truth be known.

There was just something irresistible in her sweet innocence.

With a restless movement, Hugo crossed the polished floor, toward the decanters of brandy on the sideboard. He was beginning to devote far too much time to thoughts of Miss Stadford. Thoughts that went beyond simple appreciation for her beauty, to the realization that his entire day was brightened when she entered the room.

She had only to smile, to glance at him with those soft brown eyes, and he felt as if the whole world was a better place in which to live.

Oddly disturbed by the knowledge, Hugo poured himself a healthy measure of brandy. Then, lifting the crystal glass to his lips, he was abruptly halted as his gaze caught sight of the painting hanging above the table.

As paintings went it was hardly remarkable. There was nothing in particular to distinguish the pastoral scene. It was certainly not a masterpiece. Not even a collector's item. But there was something in the bold brushstrokes that fluttered on the edges of his memories.

Barely aware of his movements, Hugo set aside the brandy and reached out a hand to touch the painting. What was it? The vague image of a painting. And an elegant town house. And a man telling him . . . telling him . . .

"Oh my God." Staggering backward, Hugo gave a sharp shake of his head.

Like a curtain rising on a well-known play, the barrier that had so stubbornly hidden his memories lifted to reveal the past with startling clarity.

He remembered everything.

He recalled the threatening letter from his grandmother. His uncomfortable trip to Devonshire. His impetuous decision to ride ahead when his carriage had lost a wheel. And the fateful turn that had led him to the seclusion of Rosehill rather than the main road to his grandmother's estate.

It seemed extraordinarily difficult to believe he could have forgotten for a moment. How could a mere blow to the head have stolen his very identity?

Unless he hadn't wished to remember.

Ludicrous. He instantly dismissed the foolish notion. Why shouldn't he wish to remember? He had everything a man could possibly want. Position. Title. Fortune.

And the same aching loneliness that he had glimpsed in Abby's eyes?

Hugo pressed a hand to his throbbing temple.

It was true he had been lonely since his brother's death. A loneliness that had only been intensified by the demands that he fill his brother's position. And perhaps he had attempted to flee his loss by living a life of extravagance that allowed no room for his duties as earl.

But still, he could not accept that he would be so weak-willed as to hide from his troubles in such a cowardly fashion.

Besides, his concern should not be on what had caused his loss of memory, but rather on what he intended to do now.

Hugo glanced across the elegant room. Certainly the only sensible thing to do was to tell Miss Stadford that his memory had returned. He should politely thank her for her hospitality and then carry on to his grandmother's. After all, the elderly woman must be frantic with concern at his strange disappearance.

And certainly Lord Stadford would be delighted to have him far away from the estate.

And yet, Hugo found himself hesitating.

For reasons he found impossible to explain, he was in no hurry to change his situation at Rosehill. He needed time, he told himself, to adjust to the sudden recovery of his identity.

And what possible difference could a few days make?

He was still wrestling with his conscience when the

sound of a soft gasp warned him that he was no longer alone.

"Hugo, what is it?" Abby cried as she hurried to grasp his arm in a concerned manner. "Are you ill?"

Realizing the shock must have left him pale and unsteady, Hugo made a decided attempt to collect his scattered thoughts.

"No, my dear." He patted her fingers with a reassuring smile. "I am quite well."

Her expression remained unconvinced. "You are pale. Perhaps you should return to your bed."

Just for the moment he gazed down at her wide eyes. There was a beguiling innocence in those eyes that warned him that he was toying with danger. This was precisely the type of woman he had taken painful care to avoid in the past.

But like a child who has not yet discovered that playing with fire can be a dangerous pastime, Hugo tucked her arm firmly through his own.

"I would far prefer a turn in the garden," he announced as his gaze lingered on the tempting softness of her lips. "Shall we go?"

With an unconscious frown Abby paced restlessly across the length of the salon. She would rather have her tongue removed than admit she was impatiently awaiting a glimpse of Hugo. Even to herself.

But while she sternly assured herself that she was merely reviewing the menu for dinner, her gaze spent precious few moments on the list in her hand and instead strayed with annoying regularity to the double doors.

Where could he be?

A hint of anxiety darkened Abby's eyes. Over the

past two days she had noticed a subtle change in Hugo's manner. Certainly he had been as gracious and charming as ever. Indeed, if she wasn't such a sensible young lady, she would no doubt have tumbled desperately in love with him long ago. But there was no denying there had been a growing sense of restraint between them. It was as if he was deliberately holding a part of himself aloof from her.

Of course, there was nothing aloof in the simmering heat she occasionally detected in his lingering gaze.

She suppressed a pleasurable shiver as the door was abruptly thrust open. Expecting Hugo, she felt a sharp stab of disappointment as her grandfather entered the room, his cane banging sharply against the wooden floor.

"There you are, girl."

With an effort Abby smoothed the disappointment from her features.

"Good morning, Grandfather."

The older man glanced about in a suspicious manner. "Where is that interloper?"

Abby sighed. "His name is Hugo and he is not an interloper."

"Ha." Lord Stadford banged his way forward. "A born scoundrel if I ever saw one."

"Grandfather, you imagine every man you encounter is a scoundrel."

The bushy brows lowered. "And more often than not I am correct."

Abby deliberately dismissed the handful of gentlemen she had encountered who had indeed proved to be rapscallions.

"Not on this occasion." Her chin tilted to a stubborn angle. "Hugo is a kind and gracious man. I trust him utterly."

Lord Stadford gave a scornful grunt. "I see that he has you properly gulled. I would have hoped you were old enough not to make a goose of yourself over every stranger who happens by." He raised a gnarled finger. "Mark my words, that man will prove to be a loose screw of the worst sort."

A flood of unexpected anger rushed through Abby's stiff form.

"I will not hear another word against him, Grandfather," she snapped.

"So that is the way the wind blows." Lord Stadford gave a disgusted shake of his head. "You are determined to fribble your fortune away on a common . . ."

"I have determined nothing," Abby interrupted, unwilling to discuss the confusion of emotions that Hugo inspired. "Please excuse me, Grandfather, I must speak with Cook."

Clearly noting the dangerous glint in her eyes, Lord Stadford made no attempt to halt her retreat as she swept past him and out the still open door. Intent on her escape, Abby failed to note the large form standing in the hallway until she had nearly bolted into it. Coming to an abrupt halt, she lifted her head to meet Hugo's guarded gaze.

"Oh."

"Good morning, Miss Stadford."

Abby felt an embarrassed heat flood her cheeks as she realized that the gentleman could not help but have overheard the sharp exchange of words between her and her grandfather.

"Good morning."

"I was hoping to persuade you to join me in the garden."

After waiting the entire morning for this moment, Abby found herself too flustered to accept.

"I fear I am quite busy this morning."

"Please, Abby." His tone was unusually firm. "This will take only a moment."

She wavered; then, meeting his persuasive gaze, she felt herself melt in compliance.

"Very well."

With a familiarity that made her heart skip a beat, Hugo pulled her arm through his own and steered her to the door leading into the rose garden. As always, the nearness of his decidedly male frame made her breath oddly elusive.

Strolling between the neatly trimmed hedges he glanced down at her pale countenance.

"I will not pretend I did not hear your grandfather's warnings," he at last confessed.

"I am sorry."

"Please do not apologize. He is merely concerned for your welfare."

"Yes."

"He needn't be." Coming to a halt, Hugo gently clasped her hands and turned to face her. "Abby, I wish you to know that I would never do anything to hurt you."

For a moment their gazes locked, and Abby felt as if the world had slowed to a halt. She was quite certain that she could stand gazing into those beautiful eyes for an eternity.

"I believe you," she found herself whispering.

"Abby . . ." His hands tightened, pulling her willing body toward his wide chest.

Quite certain he was about to put her out of her misery and crush her lips with a kiss she had dreamed of for countless nights, Abby was abruptly distracted by the sound of a woman's querulous voice coming from the far side of the garden.

"Out of my way. Out, I say," the voice demanded.

Hastily stepping backward Abby unconsciously smoothed her honey curls.

"It seems we have visitors," she stammered, her cheeks burning.

Hugo frowned. "Yes."

Uncertain who could possibly be calling at such an early hour, Abby turned to regard the tall matron with silver hair and elegant silk gown rounding the corner of the house. She felt a flicker of surprise as she realized the woman was a complete stranger.

Catching sight of Abby and her companion, the strange woman lifted her lorgnette to study them in obvious irritation.

"So . . . it is you, Hugo," she snapped. "Well, all I can say is that you had better have an extraordinary explanation for your behavior, young man."

"Good God," Hugo breathed. "Grandmother."

"Grandmother?" Slowly turning, Abby regarded Hugo's tense countenance with a bewildered wariness.

"Yes, this is my grandmother. Clara Langmead, Dowager Countess of Rumford."

"You know," she accused in disbelief. "You remember."

SEVEN

"Remember? I should hope he remembers his own grandmother," the elder woman exclaimed. "Now, I demand to know what you are doing here, Hugo."

Feeling the burning gazes of both women, Hugo smothered a distinct desire to bolt for safety. For a man who had vowed never to become entangled with the fairer sex, he had managed to make a bloody mess of things.

If only he could get Abby alone to explain, he acknowledged with a burst of frustration. But first he had to rid himself of his grandmother. A task that would be as simple as teaching his horse to fly.

"Could we discuss this later, Grandmother?"

"Certainly not," Lady Rumford predictably refused. "A fortnight ago I was awakened by your groom, who claimed to have lost you on your way to my estate. Since that moment I have had my entire staff scouring the countryside. Now that I have at last managed to locate you, I demand an explanation for your peculiar behavior."

Hugo bit back an oath of exasperation.

"There was an accident. Thankfully Miss Stadford and her grandfather were kind enough to bring me into their home."

"An accident?" Lady Rumford eyed him with reproach. "I knew it was only a matter of time. Are you harmed?"

Hugo shrugged. "A blow to the head and a few bruises. Nothing that will not heal."

"And you could not send me a missive so that I would not worry myself into an early grave?"

"I could not recall who I was nor why I was in Devonshire."

"Could not recall?"

"I lost my memory."

The older woman frowned in disbelief. "But that is absurd."

"Perhaps, but true nevertheless."

A silence descended as Lady Rumford considered his strange explanation. Then a sly expression descended on her still handsome features.

"Ah . . . I believe I begin to comprehend." Her gaze shifted in a meaningful manner to the silent Abby.

Hugo gritted his teeth. "No, I sincerely doubt that you do."

Abby abruptly attempted to wrest her hands from his tight grasp.

"What?"

Lady Rumford gave a low chuckle. "A beautiful maiden of obvious means, a wounded gentleman in need of care." She batted Hugo's arm with her fan. "Quite a clever means of meeting a respectable young lady and of securing your inheritance."

Hugo felt his heart plummet to the bottom of his Hessians even as Abby struggled more vehemently.

"Securing your inheritance? What does she mean?"

"Grandmother, we will discuss this later," he insisted.

The older woman turned to smile smugly at Abby.

"As you will no doubt come to realize, my dear, I was forced to induce my rogue of a grandson into marriage by threatening to have him cut out of my will," Lady Rumford obligingly confessed. "Men, I have discovered, have little stomach for settling down even with a proper woman and must occasionally be convinced of what is in their best interests."

"Oh my God . . ." Abby breathed.

"Grandmother, please." Hugo flashed the older woman a stern frown.

"Of course, but I must say that I approve your choice." Lady Rumford returned her attention to the exasperated Hugo. "She will make a wonderful countess. Far preferable to those shallow chits in London. And no doubt she brings an excellent dowry with her. Yes. Quite an excellent match."

At the moment Hugo could have cheerfully strangled his grandmother. With every word she was driving Abby farther away. Turning to assure the young lady that he could explain everything, he was knocked off balance as she furiously pulled her hands free.

"I fear you will have to excuse me," she muttered before turning on her heel and rushing out of the garden. Hugo watched her flee, astonished at the flare of pain that stabbed through his heart.

He wanted to rush after her. To draw her into his arms and assure her that everything was going to be fine. But before he could take a step his grandmother gave a loud sniff.

"Well, I could wish for better manners," she complained. "Does she always dash about in that unfortunate manner?"

"Please go inside and wait for me there," Hugo

commanded, for once unconcerned by Lady Rumford's steely glare. "I will return momentarily."

"Really, Hugo, I insist that you . . ."

The elder woman's demands fell on deaf ears as
Hugo turned and sprinted down the narrow path.

He had to find Abby. The moment he had seen
Lady Rumford step into the rose garden he had realized why he hadn't confessed that his memory had
returned. It wasn't because of the injury. Or any need
to slowly accept his identity.

It was because he couldn't bear to leave Abby.

He wanted to be near her. To hold her. To care for
her.

To . . . love her.

Yes, he acknowledged in disbelieving surprise. As
difficult as it might be for him to accept, he loved
her.

He loved her delightful humor, her caring nature,
and her spirited sense of adventure.

He even loved her refusal to bow to the dictates of
a mere man.

But he possessed a horrifying fear that he had bun-
gled the entire affair.

How the devil was he to make it right?

Kneeling in a stack of hay in the corner of the stables, Abby absently stroked the head of the white kitten.

"Oh, Wellington, what a ridiculous ninny I have
been."

How had she been so easily swayed? she silently
chastised herself. After all, she had discovered long
ago that her enormous fortune made her the target

of fortune hunters. She had also discovered that they could be the most devious of gentlemen.

And her grandfather had certainly warned her to beware. He had not been fooled for a moment by the convenient accident that had placed the wounded gentleman in her own home.

So why hadn't she heeded the warning signs that were now so obvious?

There had simply been something so utterly trust-worthy about Hugo, she at last conceded. Something that had stirred her emotions and touched her soul . . .

No. Abby screwed her eyes shut at the painful re-alization. The gentleman she had thought she knew was a dream. A mere figment of her gullible imagi-nation.

Lord Hugo Rumford was a man intent on lining his coffers with her inheritance.

"Abby."

The sound of Hugo's voice had Abby scrambling to her feet in an awkward motion. It had never oc-curred to her that he might follow her to the stables. She clutched the tiny kitten to her pounding heart as his tall frame stepped out of the shadows. Abby instinctively backed away.

"Abby, please wait," Hugo commanded.

A dull throb of loss clutched at her heart as she gazed at the finely carved features that had grown so dear.

"Why, my lord? So that you can delight me with more of your Banbury Tales?" she demanded, her voice not quite steady. "What a fool you must think me. An innocent fool."

He managed a credible wince of pain, his eyes dark-ening.

"I think you a beautiful, extraordinary woman. And I never meant to mislead you."

"No?"

"Please, Abby, let me explain."

How did he manage to appear so utterly sincere? she wondered as she forced herself to turn away from his persuasive tenderness.

"I will have to agree with Lady Rumford on one point," she said in stiff tones. "You were indeed clever to invent such a hoax. I refused to believe for a moment that you had not genuinely lost your memory. Clearly I should have heeded my grandfather's warnings."

She felt the heat of his body as he stepped close behind her.

"Do you truly believe I would risk my neck just to hoax you?"

She suppressed the renegade shiver. Her mind might consider him a cad of the first order, but her body still reacted with the same fierce excitement.

"You cannot imagine the lengths some men will go to, my lord."

"Actually, I can imagine all too easily," he argued in dry tones, "but I assure you that I am far too fond of my neck for such a witless act. Not to mention in possession of enough fortune not to need a wealthy bride."

For an absurd moment she almost wanted to believe his off-hand explanation. After all, even she had heard of Lord Rumford. His exploits in London were often the gossip of the neighborhood, as well as the rumors that the streets of the city were lined with the broken hearts of women who had tossed themselves at his feet. An absurd tale that was far too easy to believe after meeting the dashing earl. He could presumably have any woman he might choose, so why go to such an effort for her?

Then the memory of his grandmother's words brought her back to painful reality. Clearly he had been ordered to marry a woman of fortune or risk losing his own. Why not choose a gullible country chit whom he could easily dupe, rather than a more sophisticated woman who might make demands on his carefree life?

"A fortune you were obviously about to lose," she pointed out in icy tones.

"This is ludicrous," he sighed in frustration. "I fell from my horse and unfortunately lost my memory. There were no devious intentions, no desire to harm you in any way."

"Luckily I wasn't harmed," she forced herself to lie, slowly turning to face him with admirable composure. "And since you have obviously healed from your supposed injuries I am certain that you will be ready to leave with your grandmother. If I don't see you again, I wish you the best. Good-bye, Lord Rumford."

"Abby . . ." He reached out to grasp her arm, but Abby was too swift.

With a sharp move to the side she managed to avoid his outstretched hand and hurried to the side door that would lead back to the grounds.

She had to get away. She had to find the privacy of her room.

It was that or reveal to the entire world that her heart had just been effectively broken in two.

EIGHT

It was with a great deal of reluctance that Abby forced herself to leave the sanctuary of her room for a reluctant appearance at lunch. She had no desire to encounter Lord Rumford or his grandmother. Indeed, nothing would please her more than the knowledge she would never have to be in the company of either again.

But worse than the thought of coming face to face with the Earl of Rumford was the fear of appearing wounded by his deception. She would go to any lengths before allowing Lord Rumford to realize just how deeply her disappointment ran.

So changing into a gown in a soft peach with satin ivory roses embroidered on the hem, she stiffly made her way down the staircase and to the formal dining room, where she had ordered lunch to be served. She had devoted long moments to standing before the dressing room mirror and ensuring herself that her pale features revealed nothing of her inner turmoil. Now she managed to force a stiff smile to her lips as she stepped into the dining room.

Her gaze searched through the long room, with its heavy oak table and sideboard. She had personally overseen the red damask draperies that matched the chair coverings, and the elegantly painted panels that contrasted nicely with the black marble chimney piece. It was a room designed to impress. Thankfully, she possessed no desire to consider why she had chosen to have lunch served in such formal surroundings.

With a frown she realized that she was alone; then the door opened to reveal Lord Rumford imposingly attired in a coat of pale blue with a pristine white waistcoat and blue pantaloons. His Hessians had been polished to a blinding gloss and his golden hair carefully styled by his personal valet. Abby felt a renegade flare of pleasure at his arrival that she was swift to stifle.

Did she possess no sense at all?

"Lord Rumford." She dipped in a rigid welcome.

His bow was equally stiff. "Miss Stadford."

"My grandfather is not with you?"

"I believe he is meeting in town with his solicitor."

Abby swallowed a desire to curse. Of all the rotten luck. Her grandfather never left the estate. It was a source of pride with him that he refused all inducements to enjoy the numerous entertainments the neighborhood offered. His one exception, however, was his quarterly meeting with Mr. Smith to discuss his numerous investments. Naturally it had to be today of all days.

"I see. I presume Lady Rumford will be joining us?"

With a nonchalance that made Abby grit her teeth, Hugo strolled to stand at her side.

"The journey has proven to be quite tiresome for Lady Rumford. She has requested a tray in her room."

Abby stiffened in horror. She was to be alone with this man? No. It was too much to bear.

"How unfortunate," she murmured, her mind frantically searching for some reasonable excuse to flee to her own room.

Any hope of retreat, however, was effectively destroyed as Mrs. Snow entered the room. With a pang of guilt Abby realized that the staff had no doubt gone to a great deal of effort to prepare a special meal for her guests. She could not disappoint them now.

With a sense of resignation she watched as Hugo moved to hold out her chair with a challenging glance.

"Allow me, Miss Stadford."

"Thank you." With as much grace as she could muster she moved to settle herself in the seat. "You may serve now, Mrs. Snow."

"Very good."

The housekeeper left as Hugo took his own seat. Abby determinedly studied the gold pattern on her china plate as a uniformed servant entered to pour the wine. Her gaze never wavered as Mrs. Snow returned with an army of servants to place the turtle soup, roasted fowl, and endless assortment of side dishes onto the table. It was only when a silence descended and she abruptly realized that the staff had inexplicably disappeared that she lifted her head to discover Hugo regarding her with wry amusement.

"Is it your intention to ignore me throughout the entire meal?" he demanded.

"We have nothing to say to one another, my lord," she said in frosty tones.

"I fear I must disagree, Miss Stadford. We have a great deal to say to one another."

She arched a honey brow. "Such as?"

"Such as my reason for coming to Devonshire."

She didn't attempt to hide the distaste that rippled over her features.

"I believe we both know the answer to that."

The green eyes narrowed as he abruptly leaned forward.

"I came to assure my grandmother that she was welcome to hand her entire fortune to my twit of a cousin. Regardless of what you think of my character—or rather my lack of character—I would never allow myself to be so blatantly blackmailed."

She attempted to ignore the persuasive intensity of his voice.

"That is easy enough to claim."

"It happens to be true." He thrust aside his plate, no longer even making the pretense of eating. "I have devoted a considerable amount of effort to avoiding the Parson's Trap. No amount of money could induce me to enter it. Now or ever."

She met his gaze squarely, her expression one of disbelief.

"Then you have no intention of ever marrying?"

There was a short pause as his mouth twisted. "Actually that is a rather awkward question at the moment."

Yes, she could imagine, she acknowledged with a sharp sniff.

"Indeed?"

His gaze swept over her delicate features, lingering on the mulish jut of her chin. It was only with an effort that Abby managed to maintain her icy composure beneath the unnerving scrutiny.

"Abby, perhaps this would be simpler to explain if you realized that I was not born to be an earl."

His low words were so unexpected, she couldn't prevent her frown of bewilderment.

"What?"

"I was the younger son," he explained, his countenance unusually somber. "My brother was the one groomed to inherit the title. Unfortunately he was killed in a carriage accident four years ago."

Regardless of her current ill feelings for Hugo, there was no denying the sharp edge of pain in his voice.

"I am sorry."

"Yes, so am I." His eyes darkened with remembered emotions. "Not only did I lose my closest companion and dearest friend, but I was suddenly thrust into a position I was ill prepared to fill."

Abby shifted in a nervous manner. She was furious with this man. He had deceived her, manipulated her, and taken advantage of her in a shameless fashion. She did not want to feel sympathy for his loss.

"I am not certain . . ."

"I possessed no desire to become a respectable member of Society." He overrode her attempts to divert the conversation to a less intimate discussion. "Indeed, I wished for nothing more than to continue my life of revelry with my cohorts. My grandmother, however, sternly disagreed." His grimace revealed far more than his words. "She was quite insistent that I give up my frivolous pleasures and perform my proper duties. The most important being to grace the nursery with my heirs."

Abby blushed even as she silently conceded that Lady Rumford was no doubt a woman accustomed to having her way. The few moments she had been in her presence had been enough to reveal that she was a powerful force of nature.

Still, Hugo was hardly without his own share of arrogance, she told herself sternly. They clearly deserved one another.

"Hardly an unusual expectation," she pointed out.

"Perhaps not." He shrugged, his gaze never wavering. "Certainly she could not comprehend my reluctance. In truth, I am not certain that I understood my reluctance until these past few days. But having lost my memory and viewing the world—and especially you—without the burden of responsibilities has allowed me to realize how I have been hiding from the truth."

Abby caught her breath. Once again she experienced the potent tug of his persuasive will.

"I . . . I think you would be better served to discuss this with your grandmother."

"No, Abby," he said in soft tones, "this is between you and I."

With an abrupt movement Abby pushed back her seat and strode to the window overlooking the distant chapel. How did he manage to unsettle her so?

"I do not wish to hear anymore, Lord Rumford."

Predictably Hugo ignored her plea, following to stand closely behind her.

"The reason I refused to give in to my grandmother's demands was because to do so was to admit that my brother was indeed lost forever." His hands reached out to lightly grasp her shoulders. His touch sent a blaze of heat through her body. "That was something I was not prepared to do. I did not want to be alone, Abby."

Alone . . .

He knew precisely where to strike where she was the most vulnerable. She knew how it felt to be alone. And how difficult it was to accept the loss of loved

ones. Hadn't she herself refused to unpack the tiny
bag of her personal belongings when she arrived at
Rosehill? Even as a child she had realized that to
place her most precious belongings in her room
meant that she was never going home again.

It had been years before that suitcase had disappeared from beneath her bed.

But while her heart might long to turn in his arms
and assure him that she understood his feelings perfectly, a more practical voice in her mind demanded
caution.

His arrival at Rosehill just when he was in need of
a respectable bride was far too coincidental to be
brushed aside.

"Please do not do this, Hugo," she pleaded in a
choked voice.

His hands only tightened on her shoulders. "Abby,
after meeting you I realized that I do not have to be
alone. That there could be someone who could help
me become the type of earl who would make my
brother proud."

Abby quivered as his husky words brushed against
her cheek.

She wanted to believe him, to trust that he was sincere. But it was happening too swiftly. She needed
time to think. To ration through the tangled emotions that battled within her heart.

"Hugo, I must . . ." With an agitated movement
she pulled from his disturbing touch and turned to
meet his heated gaze. It was a mistake. How easily
she could become lost in those compelling eyes. With
a low moan she stumbled away from his large form
and toward the door. "I must see to my animals."

"Abby." His commanding voice halted her in the
doorway, although she refused to turn about. "I will

not leave here without you. I need you in my life. In my heart."

Her hand lifted to press against her trembling stomach. How easy it would be to stay. To simply thrust aside her suspicions and allow her emotions to gain control. But years of fierce determination never to trust again refused to be so easily dismissed.

"I must go."

Abby never looked back as she hurried down the hall and through the tiny door to the gardens.

Oh Hugo, she thought with a pang of dismay, *how dearly I wish to believe you.*

NINE

Hugo barely prevented himself from chasing after the distressed young woman. He desperately wished to pull her into his arms and assure her that everything would be fine. That she need only open her heart to him to discover happiness.

But even as the longing swept through him, a more rational part of his mind assured him that he would only drive Abby farther away.

She needed time. Time to accept the truth of his words. To sort through the confusion of emotions he had seen in the depths of her lovely eyes.

He couldn't force her to believe in him. He would simply have to wait. Not an easy task for a gentleman who had never had to wait for anything in his entire life, he acknowledged.

With a rueful grimace he wandered back toward the window. He was lost in dark thoughts when he was interrupted by the sound of someone imperiously clearing her throat. He turned, caught off guard by the sudden appearance of his grandmother. As always she was elegantly attired in a dark rose gown, with her hair stiffly pulled from her thin face. Entering the room she cast him a stern glare.

"Really, Hugo, I do hope you dissuade Miss Stadford from rushing about in that ill-mannered fashion," she instantly chided, clearly having witnessed Abby's impetuous flight. "It is hardly fitting for a countess."

Crossing his arms over the width of his chest, Hugo leaned against the windowsill.

"If Miss Stadford will agree to be my countess, then she may rush about as much as she cares to," he admitted in blunt tones.

"Indeed?" Lady Rumford arched startled brows, regarding Hugo as if he had grown another head. "What has come over you, Hugo? For a man who has been so reluctant to acquire a wife, you seem to be going to a great deal of effort to capture Miss Stadford."

Hugo shrugged, unconcerned that he was being so unfashionable as to reveal his feelings for Abby.

"Why shouldn't I? She is the most remarkable of women."

"I'll grant that she comes from a respectable family and her countenance is not ill favored," his grandmother conceded.

"She is the most charming, exquisite creature in all of England."

With a sharp movement Lady Rumford crossed toward Hugo, the heavy silk of her gown rustling loudly. Despite her frail body and silver hair, no general could have appeared more commanding.

"Are you quite certain that the blow to your head did not rattle your wits?" she demanded.

Hugo could not prevent a small chuckle. "If it did, then I hope they remain rattled."

The older woman regarded him for a long moment before giving a small shrug.

"As long as she fills the Rumford nurseries, I shall be content with her."

"Nothing would please me more." Hugo smiled in a self-derisive manner. "Unfortunately, Miss Stadford is far from convinced that she wishes to become my countess."

Lady Rumford's eyes widened in shock. "Is the girl daft? Why wouldn't she wish to become a countess?"

Hugo was not surprised by his grandmother's re-action. To her narrow mind there were two classes of people in the world—those with titles and those with-out.

"Because she fears my only interest is in her for-tune."

"Fah." The older woman waved a heavily jeweled hand. "Of course you are interested in her fortune. What man worth his position would not be?"

"Me," Hugo retorted without apology. "I would not care if she did not possess a farthing."

"Nonsense. It is the duty of every gentleman to improve the standing of his family. To marry beneath one's station is sheer indulgence."

Hugo might have agreed with the ridiculous words a fortnight ago. After all, before arriving at Rosehill and meeting Abigail Stadford, marriage was simply another burden that was being thrust on him. Now the mere notion of sharing his life with another sent a thrill of pleasurable excitement through his veins.

He smiled with wicked amusement. "Perhaps. But what is the purpose of being an earl if I am unable to indulge myself ?"

A stern frown marred her thin face. "I see that this young lady has not managed to curb your flippant manner. There is nothing amusing about family duty."

His flare of humor swiftly faded.

"On that I must agree with you," he said in soft tones. "Duty at times can be a heavy burden. But I assure you, if I do wed Miss Stadford, it will have nothing to do with duty. I will marry for love."

"Love." The older woman gave a dismissive shrug. "An absurd notion. In my day we understood our obligations and did not bother to fill our heads with such foolishness. How is society to function if everyone goes about marrying whomever they please?"

Hugo arched a mocking brow. "A quandary, indeed."

His grandmother rewarded him with a smack with her fan. "Annoying boy."

Intent on their argument, neither noticed the door to the dining room open, or the appearance of the slender, silver-haired gentleman. It was not until the familiar sound of a cane tapping on the floor echoed through the room that Hugo turned his head to discover that they were no longer alone.

"What the devil is going on here?" Lord Stadford demanded with his usual lack of manners, his temper clearly not improved by his brief visit to town.

Hugo felt a flicker of alarm at the sight of the elderly gentleman glaring at him with obvious irritation. The combination of Lady Rumford and Lord Stadford might very well be the clash of the Titans, he acknowledged as he made a bow toward his host.

"Good afternoon, Lord Stadford."

"Did you hear me?" Lord Stadford demanded, not even making an appearance of goodwill. "I demand to know what is happening."

Hugo suppressed a smile. "May I introduce you to my grandmother, Lady Rumford? Grandmother, Lord Stadford."

On the point of acknowledging Lord Stadford, his grandmother was halted when the older man gave a sharp bang with his cane.

"Egad, more of you?" he demanded. "Now that you have conveniently regained your memory, do you intend to move your entire family into my home, sir?"

Lady Rumford drew herself up in a regal fashion. Accustomed to being surrounded by toadeaters, Lord Stadford's gruff indifference to her superior position was a decided shock.

"I beg your pardon?"

"Are you deaf?" he accused. "I wish to know precisely how many Rumfords are plotting to land themselves on my doorstep."

Lady Rumford's expression froze in fury. "Do you realize who I am, sir?"

"I would have to be a sapskull not to. We were just introduced a moment ago. Much against my will, I might add."

"Really, sir."

Thankful that there were no weapons present in the room, Hugo attempted to soothe the brewing tempest.

"Forgive us for intruding, Lord Stadford, but my grandmother was concerned when I did not arrive at her home. She came to assure herself that I am well."

Lord Stadford gave a loud snort as he moved farther into the room. He was clearly unimpressed with Hugo's gracious apology.

"She has obviously assured herself. Now you can both leave."

Never one to avoid a battle, Lady Rumford thrust Hugo aside as she stepped forward. With an inward shrug Hugo moved out of the fray. He had no intention of being singed in the crossfire.

"Lord Stadford, I have never encountered a more ill-mannered gentleman in my entire life. Indeed, you are not fit to be called a gentleman. I have a good mind to put a halt to this marriage."

There was an awful silence as Lord Stadford's gaze narrowed to dangerous slits.

"What marriage?"

"The marriage between my grandson and your granddaughter."

"Ha." Lord Stadford pointed his cane toward the silent Hugo. "I will be in my grave before I allow that sly boots to marry my granddaughter."

Knowing from first-hand experience just how intimidating his grandmother could be, Hugo couldn't help but be somewhat impressed by Lord Stadford's courage. After all, there were less than a handful in all of England who would dare to stand up to the formidable old woman. Not that he particularly cared for being labeled a sly boots, he acknowledged wryly. Especially since he had every intention of marrying Lord Stadford's granddaughter, with or without his approval.

"Clearly, sir, you have taken leave of what few senses you possess," Lady Rumford snapped in frustration. "This marriage would be a great honor to your family. I assure you, there is not a young lady among the *ton* who has not yearned to capture the attention of my grandson."

"Bunch of fools, the lot of them," Lord Stadford growled. "My Abby has more sense than to toss herself away on a fribble."

"A fribble?" the older woman demanded, her voice progressively working its way up to a screech.

"That is right. A fribble with his eye on Abby's fortune," Lord Stadford retorted in scathing tones. "Mark my words, if he tries to marry her, I shall have her cut from my will."

About to protest at the continued disparagement of his character, Hugo abruptly bit his tongue. A sudden, wholly wonderful notion just entered his head.

Unaware of her grandson's slow smile, Lady Rumford clenched her hands in annoyance.

"Oh you . . ."

"Now what do you think of this marriage?" the older man taunted.

"I think if Hugo ever speaks the name of Miss Abigail Stadford again, I shall have him disinherited."

"Delightful." With a sudden laugh Hugo stepped forward. "Consider us both disinherited. Oh, and thank you. You have just given me the perfect means to prove to Abby that I do, indeed, love her."

"What?" They both turned to regard him in horror.

"Oh . . . and you might wish to call a ceasefire. At least until after the wedding."

TEN

Ignoring the suspicious glares from Lord Stadford and his grandmother, Hugo marched from the dining room. He no longer cared if the two argued until they dropped in exhaustion. For the moment his only concern was locating Abby as swiftly as possible. He at last possessed all the evidence that he needed to prove his love was sincere.

Without pause he headed toward the side door and into the garden. He knew his beloved well enough to realize that she made a habit of retreating to her stable of animals whenever she was troubled.

No doubt if he did manage to convince her to become his bride, he would discover his town house overrun with every stray that wandered past. Of course, it would be a small price to pay for a life with Miss Abigail Stadford, he acknowledged as he cut directly through the garden toward the stables. She could fill every room with strays if she wished, just as long as she would agree to become his wife.

Passing through the rose garden, Hugo paused as he recognized the servant busily pruning the fading blooms.

"Oh, Thomas, have you seen Miss Stadford?"

Rising to his feet, the young man gave a revealing grimace.

"She went looking for that devil of a cat."

"Wellington," Hugo breathed, the name sounding more a curse.

"Aye. Out toward the woods." The servant jerked his head toward a thick line of trees. "Told her not to go. Smells like rain to me."

Hugo glanced toward the threatening sky with an inward sigh. Typical.

"All the more reason for her to tromp across the countryside, no doubt. She would never admit that that cat is far more capable of taking care of himself than she is."

"Aye," the man agreed with a chuckle.

"Thank you, Thomas."

Quite certain he would end up with muddy boots and an uncomfortable drenching from the impending spring storm, Hugo angled through the hedges and to the narrow path that led to the woods. He never considered simply waiting for Abby to return to the house. He had waited a lifetime to find such a woman. He wasn't wasting a moment more to claim her as his own.

Entering the shadows of the woods, Hugo wound his way past the ancient trees, occasionally pausing to peer into the thick brush. A vague unease began to gnaw at his stomach as he traveled farther and farther into the copse.

Where the devil had that cat led her? Surely she wouldn't have come much farther without realizing that someone was bound to become concerned by her absence.

On the point of retracing his steps, Hugo was startled by a sudden flash of white that caught the corner of his eye.

"What the devil?" His brow furrowed as he plunged off the path and into the underbrush. Within a few steps he once more caught sight of the cat leaping behind a large bush. "Where is that absurd mistress of yours?" he demanded, brushing aside a branch that was caught in his hair. "Abby . . . Abby . . . ?"

His voice echoed eerily through the trees. Then, a faint cry in the distance brought his heart to his throat.

Abby.

With a burst of fear Hugo plunged his way through the tangled undergrowth. He barely even noticed the cat running beside him as he fought his way toward the sound of the voice. His every thought was focused on finding the woman he loved.

Together he and Wellington moved deeper into the woods until he came to an abrupt halt at the edge of a narrow pit.

"Abby?"

"Hugo, I am down here."

"Good God." Hugo fell to his knees as he attempted to peer into the dark depths. "Are you hurt?"

"I fear my ankle is twisted."

Hugo felt a flare of relief that it was not worse. The foolish child. She could easily have broken her neck.

"Do not move. I shall return in a moment."

"No." There was an edge of panic in her voice. "Please do not leave me."

"I must go for help, Abby," he explained gently, his heart twisting at her fear.

"No, please."

"Abby, listen to me." Leaning farther into the pit, he attempted to make his voice as reassuring as possible. He had to convince her that their only option was for him to find help as swiftly as possible. Unfortunately, he was so intent on Abby that he forgot his feline companion. It was therefore quite a nasty shock when the cat chose that moment to leap onto the center of his back. "Egad! Wellington . . . get off, you abominable cat."

Attempting to dislodge the hideous beast, Hugo twisted to the side. He could have no suspicion that the ground around the edge of the pit would be so precarious, or that it would cave beneath his awkward struggle, sending him crashing into the darkness with a cry of fury.

Standing at the bottom of the hole, Abby's heart clenched in horror as Hugo tumbled onto the rocky bottom.

She had been more annoyed than harmed when she had fallen into the hidden pit. After all, she had known it was only a matter of time before someone came in search of her. And a twisted ankle was no more than she deserved for wandering through the woods with her mind on her tumultuous emotions rather than her unpredictable surroundings.

Now, however, she experienced a fear that froze her very heart. Because of her stupidity Hugo might very well be seriously injured. He might even be dead. And she knew beyond a shadow of a doubt that if that was the case, that her life would no longer be worth living.

With a strangled moan, Abby scrambled to the

crumpled form, her shaky hands moving to stroke his face and soft hair.

Please, please let him be alive, she prayed.

She couldn't bear to lose him. Not when she loved him with a desperation that made her heart ache.

"Hugo . . . are you injured?" she cried softly.

The battered gentleman gave a low groan as he struggled to a seated position.

"I do not believe so, although it is no thanks to that demon you call a cat," he complained, rubbing a growing bruise on his forehead. "This is the second occasion that he has attempted to break my neck."

"I am certain he meant no harm."

"No indeed." Hugo sent a glare toward the kitten smugly perched at the edge of the pit. "That does not, however, alter the fact that he is up there and we are both trapped in this hole."

Abby felt a stab of guilt. Poor Hugo. Since arriving in Devonshire he had been tossed from his horse, insulted by her grandfather, branded a fortune hunter, and now tripped into a damp hole. It was a wonder he did not condemn them all to the Netherworld.

"I am sorry."

"No. I am the one who is sorry." His voice softened in that tender manner she found so disconcerting. "You must be chilled. Here."

With a swift motion Hugo slipped out of his coat and carefully placed it about her shoulders. Abby gave a violent shiver, but it had nothing to do with the cold. There was something quite delicious about the scented heat that enveloped her.

"But you will become cold," she weakly protested.

"With you next to me?" His gaze locked with her own in the dim light. "Impossible."

An entirely different heat rushed through her body, bringing a blush to her cheeks.

"Oh." She ducked her head in embarrassment.

"Abby. Abby, please look at me." Hugo gently cupped her chin to bring her face upward. "For the first time we are truly alone. I must tell you how I feel." His hand softly stroked her heated cheek. "Abby, I never believed I could care in this manner. When I was young I had no thoughts but for my own pleasure. Certainly I had no desire to acquire a wife. Then my brother died and I refused to even consider marriage. Now I find I cannot bear the thought of existing without you."

Abby's breath caught in her throat. How had she ever doubted this wonderful man?

"Hugo . . ."

"Please allow me to finish while I possess the courage." He unwittingly halted her confession of love. "I know you have no reason to trust me. Our relationship has been decidedly peculiar."

Gloriously peculiar, she thought with a smile.

"Yes."

"But I would never harm you, Abby. And now I can assure you beyond all doubt that my interest in you has nothing to do with your fortune."

Her desire to assure him that she loved him without question was halted as she regarded him in curiosity.

"What?"

"I managed to have us disinherited."

Abby gave a sudden gasp. Caught off guard, she was not certain whether to laugh or faint.

"You had us disinherited?"

He appeared remarkably proud of himself. "Actually, I cannot accept the full glory. I did little more than watch the battle from a distance."

She flashed him a bewildered frown. "I haven't the faintest notion what you mean."

His soft laugh echoed through the small confines of the hole.

"Your grandfather has just made the acquaintance of my grandmother."

Abby's eyes abruptly widened. She had been far too occupied with her own troubles to give any thought to her grandfather or his reaction to Lady Rumford. Now she could only wonder if Rosehill remained standing.

"Oh my."

"Oh my, indeed," Hugo agreed in wicked amusement.

"Was it very bad?"

"It was not for the faint of heart. I do not believe there has been a more impressive match since Brouhhton and Slack."

She attempted to regard him in a stern manner. After all, the fact that their grandparents detested one another on sight was hardly something to treat with such indifference.

"This is not amusing."

"Of course it is," Hugo argued, his lopsided smile making her heart flop in the queerest manner. "They were both so determined to outdo the other that they threatened to disinherit the both of us if we so much as mention one another's name."

Abby discovered herself searching his handsome features before she could halt the long-held habit.

"And that does not bother you?"

"Nothing could please me more." Hugo leaned forward, his voice husky. "You are now penniless, Miss Stadford. So the only reason I could possibly wish to wed you is because I am desperately in love with you."

Her entire body tingled with a growing heat. It was becoming strangely difficult to concentrate on anything beyond the nearness of his large form.

"Hugo, my grandfather is quite stubborn enough to hand his entire fortune to a stranger just to punish me," she warned.

Hugo met her gaze squarely, his expression one of determination.

"I shall personally insist that he does. I have fortune enough to keep us comfortable without either of our grandparents."

Without warning Abby felt her eyes fill with tears. She was not certain that she deserved such happiness, but she meant to grasp it with both hands.

"Oh Hugo . . . I do not know what to say."

With a smooth movement Hugo slipped his arms about her shoulders and pulled her against the width of his chest.

"Say that you love me," he whispered. "Say that you will be at my side forever."

Lifting her face in an enticing manner, Abby smiled. "Yes. Oh yes."

Unable to wait another moment, Hugo lowered his head to claim her lips in a searing kiss. Abby made no protest. Indeed, her arms crept upward to encircle his neck and pull herself even closer.

Thoroughly absorbed in one another, neither noticed the soft spring rain that began to fall. Or the white kitten that turned to slip away with a superior flick of his tail.

The wicked stray had at last found a home in the arms of the woman he loved.